World of Rage

ISBN-13: 978-1-7334044-2-6
ISBN-10: 1-7334044-2-2

First printing: June 2020

Edited by Angela K. Durden

Cover design by ThomasMax

Front cover photo from Pixabay.com

Published by:

tm

ThomasMax Publishing
P.O. Box 250054
Atlanta, GA 30325
www.thomasmax.com

World of Rage

A. Shane Etter

ThomasMax

Your Publisher
For The 21st Century

ACKNOWLEDGMENTS

First of all, I would like to thank Lee Clevenger and Robert Preston Ward of Thomas Max Publishing for believing in *World of Rage*. Thank you to my editor, Angela Durden, for your professionalism and genius. Jedwin Smith, my mentor, deserves all the credit for bringing me along for the eighth novel under your tutelage. To all the friends who have given me their support and encouragement during this literary journey, please forgive me for not mentioning you all by name. It would take more space than I have here. You all know how important you are to me. Thanks to my sister Amy Etter Mills, for your support and love.

Thank you to my good friend, Brit, Tony Wilson, for help with all things U.K. Readers, please forgive me for any mistakes I made. Tony is blameless.

And to Bonni Newberry, my primary and first reader, for everything.

All mistakes in settings or timing are completely my own and I take full responsibility for them.

For

My Legacy

As I have no sons or daughters to carry forth my DNA after I am gone, I hereby dedicate this book to the continuation of my family names,
Etter (paternal)
and Vaughn (maternal)

They are now as immortal as the printed word itself!

OTHER BOOKS
BY A. SHANE ETTER

Bottom Dwellers

Mind Dwellers

Trail Dwellers

A Brain in Third Person

A War in The Bronx

*A Brain in Third Person II
– The Return of The Bad Penny*

Devil's Sympathy

Cumming, Georgia: The Good Guys' HQ
Earthwalkers and One Dweller

Sawnee Mountain, Georgia: Evil Dwellers' HQ
Evil Dwellers (The Undead)

Z

Scotland and England Travelers: Destination — Stonehenge
Earthwalkers in Search of Answers

Σ

U.S. Eastern Coast Travelers: Destination — Georgia Guidestones
Earthwalkers in Search of Solutions

❯❯ Prologue

Sawnee Mountain, Georgia:
Evil Dwellers 'HQ

Old Timer One: *"So, when does the fun start?"*
Old Timer Two: *"You know what they say. There's no time like the present."*
Old Timer One: *"Agreed. But has She Who Must Be Feared approved it?"*
Old Timer Two: *"Approved it? Are you shittin' me? She ordered it."*
Old Timer One: *"And how many people do we think it will kill?"*
Old Timer Two: *"All of them. It's a global killer. Except for the less than one per cent of the world's population that have the natural antibody that protects them, of course."*

As members of the undead — those that had been people, animals, or even trees before they died but couldn't make it to the afterlife — the two old-timers thalked their conversation. A combination of the words think and talk, "thalking" was the word the Dwellers had coined for communicating telepathically. The two old-timers were Dwellers, from the sect known as Bottom Dwellers who usually lived at the bottom of Lake Lanier; they were recruited because they were big and dumb and sometimes muscle that wasn't overly bright was called for. These old-timers were huge and green but were now at the top of Sawnee Mountain in North Georgia.

They communicate with others similar to them on every continent just by thinking their words. Somehow when they mutated to what they'd become, their brains were able to translate whatever language they heard into their own almost immediately. It was not a modern-day Tower of Babel, the Biblical site where all the different languages of the world were created, but one where language was no longer a barrier. And since all Dwellers could do it, they're able to communicate seamlessly and instantly, even with non-mutants, living human beings, by reading their minds and then projecting their thoughts into the humans' brains. Because the amount of time they could spend out of water each day was limited, these two old-timers mostly spent their time hanging out in the elegant mansion's swimming pool until they were needed.

The mountain around them was beginning its annual late October change into vivid autumn colors. The dazzling oranges, brilliant yellows, and sunlit hues of red were still a week or more away from peak. The scent of the early winter was on the disembodied wind and evil with it comes. Today, heavy gray clouds crown the mountaintop and cloak the mansion and ensconce the colors from casual observation.

Ancestors to some that are now among the Dwellers' numbers, the trees listened — and understood.

Old Timer One: *"Wow. Remind me to do my best to stay on her good side. Ordering the deaths of so many innocents. What did anybody ever do to piss her off?"*

Old Timer Two: *"Don't know, but when our predecessors caused it the first time it was called the Black Plague...or Death, whichever you prefer. Anyway, the only reason it didn't kill the entire world back then was because people weren't as mobile as they are now."*

Old Timer One: *"The Mongols? I know you remember those assholes. Somehow Dwellers leaders at that time got them to do our dirty work by catapulting infected bodies over city walls to infect and spread it to others. Today, we calculate that with international travel commonplace, more than ninety-nine percent of the world's population will die in no more than ninety days."*

Old Timer Two: *"Three months! And the whole fucking planet belongs to us."*

Old Timer One: *"They had their chance. They've been screwing it up for over ten millennia. Now it belongs to us."*

Old Timer Two: *"It will be fun to see what we can do with it. But what about animals? Some of us are kin to animals and if they're not kin, we still need to eat."*

Old Timer One: *"That's one thing harder to predict. Some will die. Some won't. We know for certain some entire species will be wiped out, like scavengers — rats, coyotes, crows. But others, some in the species may die, others won't. One cow may be left standing in a field, one right next to it — bam, dead. She Who Must Be Feared said it was a calculated uncertain risk, but a risk worth taking. And the other part of the equation is as most of the people on earth, half of the animals and most plant life all perish, the ecosystem will be fucked and for years the entire planet will resemble a huge gray sarcophagus. Possibly forever."*

Old Timer Two: *"Wow. And how'd we end up here on this mountain, anyway?"*

Old Timer One: *"She Who Must be Feared acquired it under threat and promise. She told that old dude who owned it she was going to destroy the earth, but that he could stay here and she would save him, if he'd sign over the estate to her. How else do you get an extravagantly appointed sixteen thousand square foot mansion on a mountaintop with a spectacular million dollar view of the Atlanta skyline, for a song?"*

Old Timer Two: *"Of course when the skyscrapers collapse it won't be such a great view anymore. But by then the world will be ours for the taking."*

Old Timer One: *"What happens when the lights go out?"*

Old Timer Two: *"When the workers at the power plants die, we'll go to home improvement or hardware stores that have closed and get generators. The stores won't have employees either. They'll all be dead and we can just take whatever we need."*

Old Timer One: *"By the way, what is the real name of She Who Must Be Feared?"*

Old Timer Two: *"Queen Gertrude."*

Old Timer One: *"Queen Gertrude. Have you ever met her, by the way?"*

Old Timer Two: *"Are you kidding me? Those two bodyguards of hers won't let anybody near but her innermost circle, her brain trust. And they are some bad dudes, those two. I mean, we're all bad dudes, but those guys...shit."* He shook his head just thinking about them, *"The one calls himself Bad Penny. The other one they call Professor. He's the real badass, even badder than the first one — and his name is Bad. Rumor is the Professor's walking stick has a single-fire twenty-gauge shotgun in it, and he loves to use it. I wouldn't want to go cross with either one of them."* He shook his head again.

Old Timer One: *"And when we all come out we'll communicate with the others around the world like us?"*

Old Timer Two: *"Yes, when it's over we'll all come out together, as one. To rewild the world."*

As it turned out, it didn't take three months for most of the planet's population to die. It didn't even take three weeks. It was written in stone in three days. By then there was no doubt about what the outcome would be.

« Chapter One

Cumming, Georgia:
The Good Guys 'HQ

Recalling The Past

"Hi, Cuz."

"Duncan! Long time no hear," Patrick replied telepathically.

"You're gonna wish you weren't hearing from me now," Duncan said.

"Why? What's up?"

"Can you put on some classical music?"

"You're shitting me?" Patrick wondered what trouble was brewing.

"Wish I were."

Patrick's and Duncan's fathers were brothers. The federal government dammed up the Chattahoochee River in 1956 to create Lake Lanier in North Georgia. It became the largest manmade lake east of the Mississippi River. At that time, Duncan's father chose not to leave the lake. Consequently, Duncan had become one of the first green-skinned mutants. For many years nobody knew about the mutants. They called themselves Bottom Dwellers since they lived at the bottom of Lake Lanier.

On the other hand, Patrick's father had heeded the warnings and retreated, so Patrick was all human. Each grew up knowing nothing of the other's existence.

Duncan Dylan was a former member of the colony of Bottom Dwellers. Cousin Patrick had discovered Duncan's underwater civilization while scuba diving in Lake Lanier. After a while, they figured out that the Dwellers who lived on land, and were mostly evil, couldn't read their minds if they were listening to Bach, Beethoven, or any of the other great composers.

They seemed to be particularly annoyed by the two greatest, Bach and Beethoven, classical composers' music. From poking around in the brains of some of the evil Dwellers, Duncan found out that the worst, and his sworn enemies, were Caliph and Medinah. But they died completely, the first by the hand of an Earthwalker, the latter at the hands of fellow Bottom Dwellers, so it was unlikely that any others from the Bottom Dwellers had joined forces with the outcasts now led by Queen Gertrude.

"Then give me a sec, Duncan. Let me get some going. It'll take a minute. It's been awhile since we needed to do this." Patrick chose Beethoven's Fifth Symphony, cranked it up loud. *"So, what's up?"*

"Are you sitting down?"

"Dude, for God's sake, just tell me." Patrick was getting a little frustrated with the obliqueness.

"Alright, alright. The evil Dwellers, the expatriates, must have forgotten about me and that I have the same telepathic abilities as them."

"Okay, okay. I get it. Just tell me."

"They're planning something big. Remember, they talked about the 'Reckoning'?"

"Yeah, I remember. They were going to take over the world, or something like that." Patrick had been skeptical at the time.

"Well, before they do that they have to kill everybody on the planet." Duncan paused. *"Got your attention now?"*

That got his attention. *"Get the fuck out of here."*

Dwellers were often full of bluster and shit, but Patrick didn't discount their nastiness or their resolve. He could still recall how one of the tree people used a knife to carve his own small limbs down to razor-sharp points, inflicting excruciating pain to himself, all so he could slice Dwellers' icons into his wife's stomach. That ultimately killed Trudy, his beloved wife.

"How're they going to do it?"

Duncan filled him in. *"Remember how they claimed they were responsible for the Black Plague in the fourteenth century?"*

"Yeah, I always thought that was just more of their big talk."

"Well, think again. Apparently they have a new version, evolved and airborne, highly communicable, and resistant to every antibiotic on the

planet. They believe that it will wipe out the entire world in three months. And apparently they set it off this morning."

Patrick examined the elegant coffered ceiling of his study thoughtfully. Kill everyone on the planet in a season, he mused.

Duncan continued. *"But wait. That's not the worst of it."*

"Not the worst? What could be worse than that?"

"Are you still sitting down?" Duncan hesitated because he didn't want to say what he was about to because he knew it would change his cousin's life irreparably. *"Trudy's one of them."*

"What?"

"Actually, that's not entirely accurate. She's their leader."

Patrick took a deep breath and held it before letting it out slowly. He said not a word. Duncan thought maybe he'd passed out or fainted from the shock.

"Cuz? Paddy? You okay?"

Patrick felt like he'd been punched in the gut and had stood at the news. But to keep from collapsing he used his hands on the large rolled arms to lower himself back into his favorite leather chair.

"Hell no, I'm not okay. You just told me my wife is…is…alive."

"No!…No! She's not alive. She's like all the Dwellers. Half-alive, half-dead. I guess they're what Bram Stoker and other authors would call the undead."

"So, what do we do?"

"That's up to you. If we're going to go to war again, you're our leader, but I figure we'll need your friend Jeff Byrd and anybody else you can think of. From the scuttlebutt I pick up there are thousands, like the dwellers, all over the world. But hey, three or four of us against thousands seems unfair — they may need to get some help."

Although it pained Patrick to say so, he replied, *"But, if Trudy is the leader of this worldwide movement we need to strike them here, and although I can't believe I'm saying this, we need to cut off their head. Hit them at the top. And you're right. I need to call Jeff and my friend, Bill Crain, real quick-like before cell service is completely gone. You haven't met Bill. He's a retired army colonel and he could be a big help. He was in intelligence. Strategy and tactics. He helped me one time before."*

"Sounds like we could use him."

Z Chapter Two

**Edinburgh, Scotland:
Destination — Stonehenge**

The Decision

Monday: Day One of The Reckoning

"Three people didn't show up for work today," Jeanette King said. She'd been the Math Department admin for six years.

Dr. Aidan Walker, Department Head, was not happy. "What are you talking about? We cannot possibly function with three members missing."

Walker was short-tempered anyway. This certainly wouldn't help his demeanor. Due to how active he was in the womb, before he was even born his mother had given him the name Aidan, meaning ardent flame. However, that appeared to be the apex of his personality. He was a deliberate man of deep contemplation. His students thought him to be unpassionate about anything but The Maths. When younger he'd had dreams of becoming a Dean. He now knew those were nothing but pipe dreams going up in smoke.

"Don't shoot the messenger, sir." Jeannette understood Dr. Walker's concerns, of course, but they weren't hers.

He was a triathlete, forty-two years old, married to his job, and paid well to manage one of the larger departments at The University of Edinburgh. His naturally ruddy Scottish complexion, enhanced from being outdoors when he was racing, was more than offset by hours spent behind a compulsively tidy desk, never seeing the sun with no more than a lamp to illuminate his world. His anxious green eyes looked grey in desultory light. He considered being a triathlete his avocation. He'd taken up fencing as a hobby because he thought single women would think it was cool. Turned out, he just enjoyed the hell out of it.

Tuesday: Day Two of The Reckoning

What's going on? Five more sick today, Jeannette thought. Doctor Walker won't be happy about that.

She delivered the department head his usual coffee; white, one sugar. As a competitive athlete, the packet of raw sugar was one of the few indulgences he allowed himself. "Five more are out today," she said, sitting his cup down.

"Goddammit. How am I supposed to run this department with eight people missing in action? The school will send my arse packing if I can't control my unit." He tilted back in his chair and raked a hand frustratedly through the longish blonde hair. He had a somewhat more than passing resemblance to the popular American actor Owen Wilson; with the fairer sex he used it to his advantage.

"Call me if you need me," she said as she turned her back on him and exited his corner office on the third floor in the ancient stone building overlooking a quad that could have served as a setting in the Harry Potter films. Unfortunately for the great Scottish University, that setting had been at Oxford. Mostly due to the jealousy Edinburgh held for Oxford winning the informal but still all-too-real competition, at least in Edinburgh minds, for the Harry Potter film, no one at either school liked the other. Aidan looked down on his favorite bench where he liked to sit when he wanted to think. Like most Edinburghers, he thought the ancient city the center of the universe. Since virtually, if not literally every invention of the world had occurred in Edinburgh, the world wouldn't be the same without it. Or so they thought.

He coughed a reply to his assistant as she left.

She returned after lunch. "Three won't be back," she said, eyes wide.

"What are you talking about?"

"Jean, Thomas, and Louise. They died."

"Died? What the fook's going on?" His face turned pale with the quite unexpected news.

"I had the radio on. There seems to be a new strain of the flu that appears to be super deadly and highly contagious."

"What else are they saying?"

"Not much yet. Just that there's somethin' breaking out all over the U.K. It appears to be spreading rapidly and could affect all of Europe before it's run its course. Tens of thousands might die." Jeanette pulled out a handkerchief and coughed harshly into it.

"Well... shite." He wasn't as uncaring as it sounded, but what else was there to say?

Wednesday: Day Three of The Reckoning

Jeanette entered Aidan's office. "Oliver and James died overnight."

"Fook." He didn't look surprised, but the reality was unsettling.

"Yes, it looks bad."

"We need to do somethin' to protect ourselves. You know, I'm feeling very strongly about going to Stonehenge."

"You think that will help? I'm going to call Mally. See what he thinks."

Mally, Jeanette's husband, a steelworker in his early fifties, was strong and beefy and still able to outwork men twenty-five years his junior. They were polar opposites. Jeanette, university educated, and Mally, who struggled to finish high school. It wasn't that he wasn't clever, teachers just never knew how to motivate him. They were perfect examples of the old saw 'opposites attract'. Jeanette returned to her fanatically tidy desk to retrieve her cellphone in her pocketbook from where it resided in a deep drawer. She heard only half a ring before he clicked on.

"Hey, luv. What's up?" Even though Mally answered sweetly, she detected desperation in his voice.

"I've been talking to Aidan. You know how he's always believed Stonehenge is the answer to all thin's unexplained? Actually, more than that. He considers it his creed, the plexus of the universe, even."

"I remember you mentioning he believed that."

"Well, I think he's thinking about making a trip down there to meditate and pray before the stones. Maybe it could stop The Plague. And if he decides he's going, maybe we should go with him. With his brain and your brawn and street smarts, we could probably handle anythin' we might encounter along the way."

Mally was shaking his head. "You know how barmy that sounds?"

"Maybe, but what do we have to lose? People are dying all over Europe. If he's right — that the stones can help if we ask them to — I think we should. It might save our lives, and it's better than sitting around here waiting to die."

"Where did this side of my wife come from? I like it." Then his voice dropped to a sexy whisper. "And I think I'm getting turned on."

She laughed. "So, what else is new? You get turned on when the wind blows."

"No truer statement was ever said."

They both felt they were lucky to still have a satisfying physical relationship in their fifties, and after more than thirty years of mostly wedded bliss. And they still got on well. They'd met in a pub on Penny Lane in Liverpool, the street made famous by one of the most popular Beatles' songs of all time, and had been inseparable ever since. Neither could imagine life without the other.

Back in the day, Mally hadn't wanted her to work. He was old school and felt it was a real man's responsibility to take care of his wife. An outgrowth of his conservative Catholic upbringing and harsh discipline from the nuns. His Catholic school education had been important to his honest, hard-working parents, who were proud of their headstrong son, but he hadn't been an earnest student. Besides, Jeanette had been determined to work. She was intractable and wouldn't have stayed at home. And that was what he loved most about her. That she knew her own mind. They were a lot alike in that regard.

"Bye, luv. I'm going to talk to Aidan and see if he's made a decision."

"Let me know what he says."

Z Chapter Three

**Edinburgh, Scotland:
Destination — Stonehenge**

The Boulders Call

Jeannette knocked on Aidan's closed dark-stained wooden office door. It seemed to be more a metaphorical than a physical barrier to the ills of the outside world.

"Aidan. Sorry to bother you. Can we talk?"

"No bother. Of course. What's on your mind?"

"Well, I was wondering. Er, I mean, I talked to Mally, and I…I mean *we*, were wondering if you're serious about deracinating to Stonehenge."

"I'm still considering going. Why?"

"If you do, we want to go with you."

Aidan sat back in his chair. "That is splendid, but it might not be easy. Who knows what we might encounter if civilization is crumbling."

"That's why we want to go. We think you could use our help."

"You never know. Bad people. Could be gangs of people with dreadful intentions. Animals. Cold weather this time of year, too. Might encounter almost anythin'. I don't know if we'll be able to get petrol. We start out in a car and who knows, might end up on foot."

Jeannette smiled. "Sounds like an adventure."

"To put a nice spin on it."

"So, when do we start?"

"How about Saturday? I've been looking at a map. It's about six hundred-forty kilometers. If we get lucky, we could get down there, do our thin', and be back by nightfall on Sunday."

"What do you mean 'get lucky'?"

He put his feet up on the desk, hands behind his head, and pondered the quad below. Truth be told, he liked the idea of not being solivagant. He would enjoy the company.

"Assuming I can find some petrol before we leave, find more down there to get back, and we take first-aid supplies, snacks, anythin' else we can think of we might need, as long as the roads remain clear, and we don't run into any roaming gangs of killer zombies. You know, the everyday sort of thin' one encounters during Armageddon," he said, tongue firmly planted in his cheek and giving her a mischievous grin.

Jeanette didn't even react to his attempt to lighten the mood. Instead, she said, "I'll be thinking about anythin' else we could use. Mally has an old pistol. I think he calls it a Webley. His grandfather, his namesake, Sir Mally the Elder, brought it back from World War I. It's an ugly looking, worn out old thin', but I think it still shoots. I'll ask him to bring it if it does."

"Good, you never know if we might need it...and make sure to tell him to pack some silver bullets...for the zombies, you know."

"Of course," Jeanette said doing her best to match his apparent lightheartedness, even though her heart wasn't in it. "So, you want to meet here Saturday morning?"

"No. I'll pick you guys up. No need to leave your car here. I think I remember how to get there. And we should take my Range Rover, you know, for its size and if we have to go off-road. In the event any roads are blocked by, you know, cannibals."

Jeanette thought he was overdoing the post-apocalyptic references, but she didn't think he meant it. Humor was just his way of dealing with the seriousness of the situation. Aidan had bought the biggest Range Rover made with a powerful, five-hundred and fifty-seven horsepower V-8 engine. Except for that vehicle, he was not what one would call prodigal in his life. It was his pride and joy.

"Eight a.m. Our house?"

"Sounds good. Best to leave when it is light."

Σ Chapter Four
New York, New York:
Destination — Georgia Guidestones

Strange, Fleetwood, Lace, and Cody

"Strange, Strange, we've got to get out of here," the sound engineer yelled as he skidded to a stop in the station manager's office.

"Fleetwood" Smith was the only one who called the manager by his self-bestowed last name. He just thought it sounded cool calling his friend Strange. Levi Strange's name was a holdover from his time as a late night deejay; he encouraged people to use his stage name. Never one to mind getting a laugh at his own expense, even Fleetwood liked to joke about his own unusual handle because, after all, he was conceived in the backseat of a Cadillac. Nobody knew if it was true or not, but it was a good story and Fleet was sticking to it.

But today, Fleetwood was frantic. "People are dying. On sidewalks. In their cars in the streets."

"I know. I'm seeing reports online. Dammit! Nobody's listening to FM anymore. They won't even miss us when radio is gone. People get all their news from the Internet now. It will be the last to go down because of the government and military use it." Strange's voice still held evidence of the Tennessee drawl colored by Jack Daniels, the world's most popular whiskey. Even after fifteen years in the Big Apple. He was a clever deejay and knew when and how to use that drawl to his advantage.

"Then let's shut it down and get the hell out of here."

Levi Strange. Most of his New York friends didn't even know his real name; he himself had almost forgotten it. But it wouldn't matter anymore for him or Fleetwood Smith. They were both in their late thirties, grew up in FM Rock. Even before The Plague started, they knew FM Rock's days were numbered due to technologies like Spotify, Apple Music, Pandora, Deezer, and others like them fighting for market share.

But now —

Except for those who were jumping out of the top floors of Manhattan's tallest skyscrapers before the elevators could stop working, choosing a quick demise rather than the slow one of their guts rotting out unceremoniously, literally eating them to death from the inside — yes, now the future of FM Rock, if not all of radio was over, just as was mankind's.

Polar opposites, neither Strange nor Fleetwood had loved ones in the city. Strange, a Southern white man, when he was a young man in his twenties left his family behind in the Tennessee hills somewhere between Nashville, one of the South's more storied cities and the home of Country Music, and Lynchburg, the home of Jack Daniels, the renowned Tennessee sipping whiskey. He'd drunk more than his share of the charcoal-mellowed Old No.7 before moving to the Big Apple and switching to Irish whiskey.

His Southern twang helped make him a household name on late night New York radio. He loved the anonymous celebrity of being a deejay. No one ever saw his face. He was almost never recognized in public unless he wanted to be. Then he'd say his trademark, "Who's drinking with the deejay?" It worked pretty well for picking up women. He'd justified over-imbibing by saying the popular Southern whiskey gave him the artistically gravelly voice that had become his trademark, his *sine qua non*. That he drank only for the art, for benefit of his craft.

Strange withdrew from the Deep South right after high school and hadn't often been back, though he called regularly. However, since the start of The Plague, what with cellphone coverage spotty at best and nonexistent at times, he hadn't spoken with his parents and didn't even know if they were still alive. In their mid-sixties, they weren't exactly elderly but so exceedingly uncool they seemed a lot older than they were.

Fleetwood was African American. His family now lived in the New York of the South, otherwise known as Florida. If they were still alive, that is. Like many New Yorkers, they had retired to the southern part of the finger state to leave the desolate winters behind. His father had driven a city bus, like Ralph Kramden in *The Honeoners*. Mother had been a housekeeper. Fleetwood never had all he wanted but always had all he needed. Many had observed that there were more former New Yorkers in south Florida than native Floridians. And as many New York Jets fans as those of the Miami Dolphins in the home stadium once a year.

Neither Fleetwood nor Strange currently had a steady girlfriend.

But none of that mattered now.

Reports said the Empire State Building was having more visitors than it had had in years. But they weren't tourists. Thousands were jumping from its eighty-second floor open-air terrace each day since The Plague began. The building's management, those still alive, could have shut it down, but they felt like they were doing people a favor, showing them a kindness in this darkest of days. They'd even disabled the metal detector assuming no one would have a weapon if they were coming there to commit suicide by jumping. And why would someone want to shoot someone else who was going there to kill themselves anyway?

A traffic jam of jumpers rode the elevators…when they worked. Crowding the large open air terrace, waiting to take the deathly plunge. Many hand-in-hand or embracing, and sobbing. Lovers. Parents with children. A traffic jam in the air plummeting to their deaths. The rumor was going around that one could hear the sound of the people ripping through the air as the jumpers accelerated toward terminal velocity. If it weren't true, then it was *ben trovato*, an urban legend. It was true however, that when the first bodies began to slam into the sidewalk and street the sound of the impacts could be heard blocks away, though it abated as bodies piled deeper and deeper and the landing was softened. But the results were still as deadly.

At first when they slammed into the sidewalk, they sometimes killed pedestrians unlucky enough to be in their paths. The sidewalks and streets around the building got deeper with the bloody bodies and parts of the poor souls. Someone with a vivid imagination, someone like a fiction writer, might have imagined a Keith Haring graffiti-like art piece composed of all the bodies. After the first day of jumpers, City sanitation workers…those still alive…gave up trying to remove human debris or clean up the pavement. It was an endless and thankless task. And dangerous. The risk of death from a jumper crashing into them was very real.

Now the unauthorized and unappreciated clean up was left to the wharf rats, some as big as house cats, feeding on the remains. But even the animals were dying from The Plague, their fat black bodies mixing with human remains. At first, with their fanciest latest-model smart phones, people took pictures and videos of the carnage — both the dead and the jumpers. Of course it wouldn't be long before their batteries died, with no way to recharge them. But they couldn't know that. Some photographers reported hearing moaning among the bodies, but that was an unsubstantiated story already being dismissed as rumor and urban legend.

It was only a matter of time until the power went off for good. Even with a population of over ten million people, the largest city in the country by far doubling that of Los Angeles and tripling Chicago, the city was quickly being brought to its knees by The Plague. New Yorkers knew how lonely one could feel even in a city as large and anonymous as the Big Apple. With people dying all around them it began to feel even more derelict.

With reports of the deaths of millions coming in from all over the world, many were already calling this the end of the world. Armageddon, from scripture. It would appear to anyone observing, that the world itself had listened to, and heeded, Nietzsche's prophecy: "Man is something to be overcome."

Strange told Fleetwood, "See if Cody wants to go with us."

Cody Cahill hosted the midday show from ten until two. Just twenty-seven, she was old school. All about the music. Older than her age, her favorites were Led Zeppelin, Pink Floyd, and The Who. She was Native American and Caucasian with beautiful mahogany skin. Her parents were Rock fans, so she grew up listening to their faves. She drove other people crazy talking about the old music. Everyone, except Lace, her African-American girlfriend.

Sixties hippies, Cody's parents had met on a dude ranch in Wyoming and figured they'd name her for the place where she'd been conceived on the return trip. She considered herself lucky they didn't name her Triple R Ranch.

Fleetwood replied, "I'll ask her but she probably won't go without Lace." The two young women planned to get married, but who knew when, or even if, that would happen now.

"I wouldn't expect her to. Tell her Lace can come too."

"Where should I tell her we're going?"

Strange explained. "I have an idea, but, ummm…for now just say 'away from the city'. The experts are saying to avoid large crowds and to keep away from corpses to try and slow down the spread."

Fleetwood shrugged, "But she's doing show prep right now."

"Fuck the show prep. I'm pulling the plug right now." He pushed a button on the wall behind him that flashed red in the studio telling Cody to shut it down. "WAYN is off the air as of this moment." The original owners of the station had been fans of and influenced by the great novel

"Atlas Shrugged" by Ayn Rand, so they thought it would be clever to take the writer's given name as its call letters. They pronounced it W-Ayn. And in light of the current crisis, all of them thought it ironic, at best, or a harbinger of dark foreboding, at worst.

A few minutes later Fleetwood returned. "I talked to Cody."

"And?"

"She said they'll go. She said she could speak for Lace."

"Good."

"Actually, what she said was she'd kick her ass and drag her out of Manhattan by her dreads if she had to."

Strange thought it couldn't hurt to have Lace along. She was a trauma surgery resident at Lenox Hill Hospital. He hoped they wouldn't need her skills but it was better to be safe than sorry. "By the way, I think I know where we're gonna go."

"Do tell."

"You remember I've told you about the Georgia Guidestones?"

"Yeah."

"Well..." Strange paused before continuing. "Since this plague began I've been having dreams about the Guidestones — nightmares, to tell the truth. I think maybe they can give us some insight into what's happening. Who knows? Maybe if we meditate before them, we can stop this thing."

Fleetwood stared at Strange. "Do you know how strange that sounds? No pun intended."

Strange stared loosely at his WAYN coffee mug and said, "Yeah, actually I do. "

"So, when do we leave?"

"Tomorrow morning? Get an early start? Less traffic on Saturday."

"Sounds good. I'll tell Cody."

"I'm glad I kept my car." Strange had an aging but reliable Toyota 4Runner he was confident could make the trip without incident. He'd kept the oil changed and knew that that alone would keep a Toyota running forever. Most people in the city didn't have a vehicle. It just didn't make sense with the huge number of people and the traffic. Too expensive since a parking spot could cost as much as apartment rent. Besides, New York had the best transit system in the world. "Tell Cody to get to your place early and I'll pick you guys up at dawn's early light."

"When's that?"

"Seven."

"Oh. Okay. You got it. But how will we get gas?"

"We can probably make it down there with only one or two fill-ups on the way. We'll keep eyes open for a gas station. I have a hand pump attached to an empty propane tank that should work to top us off when we need it."

"Cool. Sounds like that will work.

But as Strange, Fleet, Cody, and Lace would soon find out: The best laid plans of Dwellers and Earthwalkers often go awry.

Z Chapter Five

Edinburgh, Scotland:
Destination — Stonehenge

On the Road

Friday night, Aidan packed his shiny black Range Rover. Non-perishable snacks. Bottled water. One plastic jug of gas. And two sleeping bags. His last girlfriend had enjoyed camping. He thought making love under the stars sounded simply splendid, but the relationship didn't last until summer. It would never have worked. Her, an uneducated lowly bar wench, and him, the distinguished and respected department head at Edinburgh. What would people think...or say? They would say they only had the one thing in common.

Aidan added a duffle bag containing three changes of warm clothes. Just in case. Late October in the Queen's Land could be a wee bit chilly. He wasn't exactly a bon vivant or even a fop; he only looked a wee bit stuffy, or mayhap a gentleman who cared a wee bit too much about his appearance or, as he preferred to think, quietly dignified. An odd sort; a natty dresser. He couldn't help the way he was since coming from landed aristocracy was his birthright and not his choice. The problems that caused him always found a way of arising. People expected him to act a certain way. But no matter, he didn't. When he was a kid, other kids expected him to have money and treat them. When he started dating there was always a willing female available to let him spend some of his assumptive pounds on her.

Aidan had the cool professor's requisite long fair hair, oftentimes tied back in a short ponytail. He'd worn contact lenses when he was in his twenties. He'd opted for glasses about the time he became a professor. Thought they gave him a professorial look. His current pair were round-lensed tortoise shell. He was dressed in designer dungarees, a khaki shirt with flap pockets on the chest, bottom, and sleeves, and a British tan corduroy jacket with tartan flannel lining of the type English gentlemen wore when quail hunting in the nineteenth century. Nikon Monarch 7 binoculars, the kind used for birding, were hanging around his neck. A handheld compass and what could only be described as a hunting knife, even though he couldn't imagine what he might need it for — he could never kill a man, or an animal, for that matter — sheathed in a scabbard, hung from a wide brown leather belt. Ecco lace-up brown leather hiking boots matched his belt. Completing the outfit were brown leather driving gloves, the type with cutouts over the knuckles that matched the expensive leather interior of his Rover.

His personal mantra was it was better to have it and not need it than to need it and not have it. Running had taught him that. He looked ready for a morning of birding rather than an adventure of indeterminable length to try and save mankind.

Yawning, and looking like he could have used more sleep, Aidan said, "Good morning to both of you. Mally, long time no see. I think it was the Christmas do at your house year before last?" He reached over the seatback to clench the man's meaty hand in a firm cordial grasp one would expect from two men who weren't exactly friends but liked each other.

He could see the white cloud of Jeanette's breath billow on the cold morning air as she climbed into the front passenger side. He matched her cloud with one of his own from his white-bowled meerschaum Calabash pipe similar to the one Sherlock Holmes puffed. If he'd been but bewhiskered, he could have passed for the less famous Holmes, his brother Mycroft.

Jeanette wore designer Polo dress jeans with a heather grey Oxford University crest sweatshirt and designer sneakers and hoped she wouldn't have to do much walking in them, since they were mostly meant to be cute. The only jewelry she wore was a diamond engagement ring with a marquise cut. Mally had secretly stashed money away for a year so he could surprise her with it. She'd been surprised and thrilled with the three-quarter carat ring. She was so proud of her man for picking it out by himself.

Mally, a burly hillock of a man, was dressed in a workingman's clothes; rugged heavyweight chinos stained but clean, khaki colored, with pleated front, and a denim work shirt he usually wore at the mill with his steel-toed work boots. His clothes had to be as rugged as he or they wouldn't have withstood the rigors of the job. A tobacco-colored waterproof oilskin jacket was worn for the warmth it provided.

Jeanette would never let him go to work, even at the mill, in unwashed clothes, but he couldn't help being blue collar or looking a wee bit unkempt. It was just his way. The only jewelry that adorned him was a thick gold chain around his neck and his gold wedding band he'd never removed since the first time he put it on. He considered the holy sacrament the best decision of his life and never regretted it for even a second. A flat grey tweed cap, known as a bunnet in the homeland and worn by all working class Scotsmen, warmed his head of thinning brown hair turning to grey. It was everything Mally was. Strong, solid, supportive.

His warm brown eyes stood in sharp contrast to his scarred, tattooed, workmen's hands, the backs of which were covered in obstinate dark hair as yet untouched by grey. The ink: A crucifix and Jesus' crown of thorns. His huge muscled workman's forearm had the image of a Phoenix emblazoned in vibrant colors from wrist to elbow. The other, a beautiful black script spelling out Jeanette. He thought she had raised him from the dead, like the famous mythical bird. So the two artworks in ink had to be considered together.

Warm, intelligent and curious eyes were gentle; no…more than that, soft. Still clear even after years of more Scotch whiskey than a lesser man could bear. His knuckles delighted in the hideously artistic scars, a result of breaking teeth and busting noses. His own as bent as Aidan's was straight, with a pale white scar that wouldn't tan, running from its bridge arcing underneath his left eye and down the same cheek. It was offset by the damaged cartilage on his right ear. It gave character to his otherwise unremarkable face.

His skin was unreddened by drink except for that memento from an encounter with a flying pint bottle in a bar fight from his younger days. He'd been proud that even though the serious gash had required over a hundred stitches — he couldn't recall exactly how many; either too many years or too many glasses of whisky since — it hadn't stopped him. Only pissed him off, which made the bloke who cast it at him rue the day that he did. If someone he met in a bar and wasn't a friend called him Mal trying to establish nascent familiarity, it would earn them a scowl at best, a swift rebuke at worst. He would have none to do with the insincere bonhomie. Named for his sainted grandfather meant he was proud of his heritage and thought the formal version of his given name sacred because of it. He recalled his beloved mother regaling him with stories of his namesake, always ending with weeping because, as she said, Mally the younger "was the spitting image of his grandfather he was," right down to his barrel chest and arms carved from pig iron.

A man of contradictions, yes. Although blessed with loving parents, a wee wild streak and too much time spent in its caress caused him to think of himself as raised by the street.

Mally and Jeannette had shoved overnight bags in ahead of them over the plush, buttery-soft leather seats; theirs older and well-worn, and not as expensive as Aidan's large handmade Gladstone brown leather one he carried for university work. In the rear floorboard Mally plopped a medium-sized plastic tank with a coil of black hose wrapped around the top. The huge SUV wreaked of Aidan's signature scent — Penhaglion's Blenheim Bouquet. Jeanette shouldn't have been surprised. She'd been smelling it every day for the past six years. She would have been surprised if he hadn't worn it even as they were faced with the possible end of the world.

Jeannette buckled her seatbelt. Mally said, "Good to see you, Professor."

"Hello, Jeannette. Mally, please call me Aidan. We've known each other far too long to stand on formality. And what's that you have there?" he asked, leaning over the seat and pointing at the plastic tank in the floor.

"Thanks, Aidan. I'll try. But you are Jeanette's boss." He patted the opaque plastic tank. "A pump in case the petrol stations are closed and we need fuel, we just run the hose into tanks and take what we need," he said.

Mally leaned forward to gently squeeze his wife's shoulder with his stout right hand from the rear seat. She sighed comfortingly as he did.

"Brilliant thinking," Aidan said, putting the vehicle in motion and pulling out onto the street. "But bye the bye, I would have thought by now you'd know Jeanette runs the place."

Before they reached the A68 that would take them south almost without a single turn and bypassing Liverpool and Oxford and straight on to Stonehenge, Aidan said, "Just to get a feel for the situation, to find out, more than anythin', I want to stop at a petrol station. After that we'll get back on the main highway just as quick as we can. I think it best if we stay away from the shunpikes."

Mally said, "I think that's a grand idea. It will most likely let us know what we can expect for the rest of the trip."

In the next block they stopped at a service area to get the lay of the land. Although there seemed to be no misbehaviour — Scots were too proper for such actions — at least a hundred cars were queued up for petrol. It appeared that the drivers of some of the vehicles were either dead or near death behind the wheel. That told them all they needed to know.

Aidan had topped off the huge tank two days before and unless everything went completely awry they would be fine. So, instead of getting in the long queue, he pulled into the cracked asphalt parking lot of the old connected convenience store. Built fifty years before, it wasn't much of an establishment. Decorating the windows were cardboard cutouts of smiling white-sheeted ghosts and orange snaggle-toothed jack-o-lanterns. Jeanette thought it sad that children would most likely not get to celebrate Halloween in a few days. She and Mally had already assumed a neighborhood costume do for the adults would be canceled.

"Let's see if there's anythin' we think we might need — that is if the shelves aren't stripped bare already."

With a toothache flaring up, Aidan hoped to find a tube of Orajel. They entered the store to the stares of a long line of customers. The old wood plank floors creaked with age. Except for hotdogs, a relatively new treat in England, cooking on a rolling spit, and buns steaming over a vat of red-stained hot water, the establishment smelt of the mustiness of old age. The shelves of the small store were near empty. They would buy an assortment of all the snacks they could imagine. And water. They would need as much as they were able to carry.

An orange plastic jack-o-lantern, more cheerful than scary, carefully situated for maximum exposure on the old dingy-white laminate counter held change to be donated for some unknown good cause; that would probably never receive another pence. Most who dropped in their change wouldn't know jack-o-lanterns were, in a roundabout way, named for British night watchmen who carried lanterns. The Brits called men whose names they did not know, Jack. So, Jack of the Lantern.

Flaunting British law with no second thoughts, the proprietor wore an unlicensed pistol holstered on his right hip.

Aidan's turn at the counter came. He'd been unable to find Orajel. When his gaze lingered on the ancient weapon a second too long, the man of Pakistani heritage shrugged and said, "I've already had two punch-ups break out this morning and been threatened myself. And the police are stretched too thin, if they are still on patrol at all." Then, "You look like an educated man, my friend. Why do you think this is happening? How long do you think it will go on?"

"Your guess is as good as mine. But I believe that it's an indication of bigger problems. Perhaps historical problems."

Aidan was not going to tell him what he really thought; that it was caused by some ancient minor deity that mankind pissed off and who was now raining down hell on earth. Nor would he tell him that they were on a mission to pay their respects to try and get that minor god to reconsider. Aidan hoped the man wouldn't need to use the old gun; it didn't appear to be well maintained. It looked like it would break apart in his hand if it were fired.

Mally and Jeanette joined Aidan to the glares of the customers they passed in line behind them and piled the necessities on the counter. They pooled their pounds and settled the bill.

The proprietor was happy to get the cash. "Thank you for the quid, my friends. The credit card reader has been offline since yesterday. Cash really will be king if things continue the way they're going."

When they returned to the Range Rover, a pair of men, both in their thirties, looking like they might be up to no good, hovered near the expensive SUV. Fortunately, Mally looked more like trouble than they. After all, Mally's muscles had muscles. And he wasn't a jovial fellow.

He didn't think these two misbegotten sons of wenches would be much of a problem. Mally, a sensitive, yet complicated man, strode purposefully toward the miscreants, his countenance grim. He heard the blood pump in his brain. The muscle in his jaw pulsed. At the end of his long arms — good for fighting — he drew his fingers into fists and his knuckles cracked. Even his walk was intimidating. Mally had an earnest manner in all things not Jeanette.

"Get away from the fookin' truck. And I shan't say it again," he said, calmly but firmly and without dignity, calling on the something innate in him that was imbedded deep inside his DNA. Saying it calmly was more frightening than if he'd said it menacingly. He hocked up a big one and spit on the ground, probably for show, before stifling a yawn with his hand, looking bored with the whole scene. No one could tell if he'd faked it or if it was real.

He could speak the proper king's English as well as the royals, but when the situation called for it, he could talk street with the worst of them. Then, always the chivalrous one, he glanced back at his wife, a wan look of apology in his adoring eyes for using the earthy language in front of her. What he didn't know was she'd heard worse from students after seeing their grades in the professor's tutorials.

One of the men, the one with the stupider look similar to that of an imbecilic donkey with his close-placed vacuous eyes, looked as if he wanted to push the issue; the other, obviously the brighter of the pair — which wouldn't have taken much — understood that discretion was the better part of valor. He shook his head almost imperceptibly at his mate. Way more than just a formidable opponent. Both backed up in the direction of a rusty railroad track that would most likely never be traveled again, all the time keeping their eyes trained on Mally, like one would a rabid dog. A good decision on their part or their bad day would be turning to worse.

Mally didn't even consider pulling the old gun he'd brought. He wouldn't have needed it to get the best of those two. Of course he wouldn't have minded having a blackthorn shillelagh, or in the land of golf's birth, one of his old niblicks. Probably a seven or eight iron. But all it took was an obvious desire to be truculent, a willingness to get shirty, and a look in his eyes that filled them with terror. He had the appearance of an explosive charge that had waited too long to relieve its pressure.

"That was bloody brilliant," said Aidan thankfully, shaking his head for the good fortune of Mally being along. The man's tough-guy visage belied his easy-going manner. Then Aidan turned to Jeanette and said, "He is an unruly sort, isn't he?"

"Hmmph," was all Mally said, followed by, "Haven't done that in a long time. That was nothin'. A fine set-to in the middle of the day always lifts me spirits."

That's what he said, but the look on his face was one of vexation. In dark contrast to the avuncular persona that he considered his true being. Of course that might have been only because he wanted to finish what they'd only thought they wanted to start.

"Bye the bye, what route are we taking to Stonehenge?" he added quickly in an attempt to change the subject.

"A68 South, all the way."

"Splendid. Just curious."

Σ Chapter Six

New York City:
Destination — Georgia Guidestones

Georgia On My Mind

Strange struck out from his apartment at five a.m. thinking he'd make it by seven with no problem at all. But he didn't expect the number of disabled cars and trucks in the middle of every roadway nor the corpses he had to inch around. Every day that passed had added to their numbers. He pulled up in front of Fleetwood's building at 7:15. All cellphone service was disrupted and, being unwilling to get out of the vehicle until he saw friendly faces, he honked the car's horn in a short staccato pattern. On a typical New York City morning the horn wouldn't even be noticed among the cacophony of sounds from traffic, people, and life. But in the deafening quiet of a dying city a moment later the door to Fleetwood's building opened cautiously and Strange recognized his friend peeking around it. Lace and Cody were behind him; all three had overnight packs and sleeping bags. Strange saw a bottle Fleetwood carried and recognized the label as being from Bushmills, his favorite Irish whiskey.

Strange jumped out of the truck and said, "Dude, I could kiss you. I was out. I figured we'd have to break in somewhere to try and get a bottle. And we'll need it to keep us warm in this chilly shit."

"Got your back, Strange."

"Fuck, it shouldn't be this cold in October." Strange shivered in the chill and pulled up the collar of the worn brown leather bomber jacket covering the back of his exposed neck just below the blue and red New York Giants cap jammed down on his head. It was unseasonably cold. A drizzle that might change to snow was just beginning. He wondered if The Plague was making the world a colder place or if it was his imagination. An October snow wasn't a rarity, but it wasn't normal either.

With everyone loaded up and their gear stowed, Strange began inching his way north on the West Side Highway through the soft luminescent gray dawn of morning to midtown, to exit the island through the Lincoln Tunnel. He picked his way slowly from lane to lane. The highway resembled a congested mall parking lot but with abandoned and torched cars. Normally there would be a substantial number of homeless milling about, but they too had been unable to escape The Plague. While driving slowly Strange cracked his window to let in some invigorating cool air, but it had a choking smell of ash.

"What are we going to do about that?" Fleetwood pointed at two cars that couldn't have blocked the road any better if they'd been placed there by the giant hand of God. It could've been placed by dangerous men up to no good.

"That's what four-wheel drive and sidewalks are made for."

Strange pulled up on the wide east sidewalk of the broad road. He drove through a blue NY Times vending machine, crashing it out of the way and scattering newspapers to the air. He crushed a bicycle chained to a No Parking sign. Pulling around the two derelict vehicles, he sped all the way up to twenty miles an hour until he passed the driving range where, with potential advertisers, he'd once sailed golf balls into the Hudson River. In a different time, he would have thought it a nice morning to hit a bucket. Next to the range was the Christopher Street Piers where luxury ocean liners docked in the first third of the twentieth century, after their trans-Atlantic voyages to the old country, alongside their less hedonistic brethren, cargo ships.

Lace became a trauma surgeon because she had a visceral need to help people. She saw the cars that someone had purposefully placed to block the major artery. She was shocked how something like The Plague could bring out the worst in mankind. Evil folks who wanted to benefit from a disaster. No, this was worse than a disaster; it was a catastrophe of biblical proportion.

Fleetwood looked over at the speedometer flirting with twenty-five mph and said, "Man, you better slow the hell down. You don't want to get a ticket."

"Funny, dude."

Of course, none of the four had ever experienced anything like what they were seeing. People processed things in different ways. Strange and Fleet cracked wise. In the backseat, Lace and Cody were speechless.

They reached the massive entrance to the Lincoln Tunnel where twelve lanes funneled into two going west to New Jersey and doing the same on the other side, going east. But now, hundreds of disabled cars clogged the concrete. Two NYPD mounted patrol lie dead among the disabled car carnage along with their horses still wearing their equine uniforms of blue blankets with bright gold trim and NYPD emblazoned in the same on their flanks. A leopard —a refugee of the Bronx Zoo or somebody's pet — with its terrifyingly long fangs, was eviscerating the exposed belly of one of the noble steeds.

"I think I'm going to be sick," said Lace, buzzing down her side window. These were the first words she'd spoken since getting in the vehicle,

"Just don't get it on my paint," said Strange, still trying to keep the mood soft in light of the dire situation. A worthy but, most likely, hopeless goal. Even so, it was unlikely it would have harmed the paint of the old vehicle.

When she turned back to the others in the car, she said, "I don't even know how many surgeries I've done so far and I've seen things no one would want to see, and I've never gotten sick. But that was the ugliest vision I've ever seen. And I don't think I'll ever be able to unsee it."

Entering the darkened tunnel, Strange turned on the aging sport utility vehicle's headlights and saw thousands of red taillights in the dark black ahead.

The party let out a collective gasp when they realized it wasn't the taillights of vehicles at all, but the reflected red in the eyes of wharf rats feeding on rotting corpses.

Though never what one would call bright, the ceiling of the tunnel was usually lighted, bequeathing enough illumination to make one's way. Those lights were now nonexistent. The city had completely lost its power grid.

Strange had to creep at a speed slower than a walk to dodge as much debris as possible. But after awhile in the tunnel, he began to recognize the familiar thump and crunch when he rolled over a corpse. The rancid smell of death in the enclosed tunnel was even worse than the crunching of the dead. To try and staunch the execrable fetid smell of death, Strange and Cody rolled up their windows.

Water poured down the curved sides of the tunnel from the pipes above, dislodged by an oversized truck that had crashed into the wall.

Thirty minutes into the urban crevasse, Lace screamed. "Out. Shit. Go! Go! Get us out of this goddamned tunnel."

"I'd love to, but as near as I can guess we're not quite halfway through yet," said Strange.

"Fuck. Fuck. Fuck!" she bellowed, pounding her fists on the car seat, "I can't stand it! I can't stand the sound or the feel of running over anymore bodies."

The crunch felt like a combination of having an ear pierced and a tooth pulled at the same time, multiplied by a thousand. Accompanied by the first bump of the front tires followed by the last bump of the rear.

"I'm sorry I can't do anything about it, but you probably should get used to it, because I suspect it's going to get worse before it gets better as we get closer to the exit."

In truth, Strange himself was beginning to feel sick. He fought to tamp down the bile rising in his chest. People had gotten sick as they drove in the end-to-end congestion of the channel, and rather than wait for their imminent deaths, had gotten out of their vehicles to continue on foot, dying in their tracks.

Strange had been right about more bodies as they neared the exit. He couldn't move ten feet without crunching over the remains of another lost soul. Especially difficult were the smaller bumps. Those were the bodies of children.

Three hours after entering the tunnel — usually a fifteen to thirty minute passage depending on traffic and the time of day — they were blinded by the last vestiges of the almost derelict sun after the dark of the underground channel, not so much exploding through the maw of the exit but secreting into their being. The parking lot of cadaverous vehicles at the exit was as bad as it had been at the entrance.

"Thank God," said Lace, not for herself, but she was worried about Cody.

A few minutes later, happy to be out of the death-ridden tunnel, when he turned south onto the New Jersey Turnpike, Strange said enthusiastically, "New Jersey has never looked so good."

Funny only because everyone in the SUV was aware of the fact he wasn't a fan of the Garden State.

"Doesn't smell any better, though," said Fleetwood. Nobody disputed that. He then observed, "The world looks like Depeche Mode sounds."

All had to admit that was a clever line since none of them, except for Cody, was huge fans of the British band's dark music. A highway sign indicated there was a Starbucks among the eateries in the next service area. And after a couple miles of driving south, Strange pulled into the Grover Cleveland Service Plaza. Not that they thought the

Starbucks or Popeyes would be open — the lights were out — but they had to check, mostly to try and use it as a gauge to determine how the world was doing. If it happened that the eateries were open, well, they certainly wouldn't mind having some spicy fried chicken.

Trying to avoid the now-unsurprising mishmash of cars and bodies as he pulled into the trash strewn service area, Strange said, "I don't think we'll be having any spicy fried chicken or lattés of any type."

"How can you even think of food after seeing all the death in the tunnel?" Cody asked sadly.

"It was just an idea. Besides, I'm sure nothing will be open."

"I haven't had my coffee this morning and it's almost noon. What am I going to do?" Lace whined.

Strange wanted to be kind but didn't have the energy. "Lace, none of us have had coffee, and just remember, this could be the end of the world as we know it and you may have already had your last cup. At least from Starbucks. When we stop for the night maybe we can brew our own. I did bring ground beans, just in case."

Lace said, "I sure could use a latte though, preferably a cinnamon dolce for fall. They're wonderful in the cooler fall temps."

"Tell the truth, I could use one, too," said Fleetwood. "Wait, there's a soda machine. Around that corner, Strange," he said, pointing left through the dirty windshield.

"Hey, Lace. Maybe we can have some caffeine, after all."

Strange jerked to a stop at the sidewalk directly in front of the machine. The curb was painted red, restricting it as a fire zone, but he had nothing to worry about. All climbed out of the SUV. Fleetwood and Strange rocked the clumsy vending machine back and forth on its short legs in an attempt to turn it over. Cody and Lace shouted encouragement. On the fourth shove it fell to the concrete cracking the glass front. Strange gave it a hard, shattering kick. Free Pepsi products for everybody although, with no electricity, the plastic bottled drinks wouldn't be cold. But with the chilly late October temperatures, the beverages would be cool.

"Alright. Diet Mountain Dew," said Fleetwood, collecting them all.

"Diet Pepsi for us," said Lace.

"Dr. Pepper for me," said Strange, sheepishly. Out of habit, he looked around to make sure there were no policemen to arrest them for vandalism and theft. He actually hoped there were, then they wouldn't feel so alone at the end of humanity.

They got back in the vehicle and examined their treasures. Strange pulled away slowly to avoid trashed cars and bodies. Out of habit, he checked his rear view mirror for the blue flashing lights of law enforcement vehicles.

Cody sniffled some more. "I didn't ask before. You said we were getting out of the city? Where are we going?"

"Georgia," Strange said.

"Georgia? What's in Georgia?"

"We're going to meditate before the Georgia Guidestones. I think if we do, it's possible we can stop this thing in its tracks."

"What are the Georgia Guidestones?"

"Some people call it America's Stonehenge. It was commissioned during the seventies, by a man in his seventies, so he's most likely long gone now, and he used a fake name, so he never could be identified."

Lace swallowed a sip of her drink and asked, "What's the purpose of them?"

"He put forth his rules for the world to follow. I don't have them all memorized, but they included 'Maintain a world population of five hundred million.'"

Fleetwood shook his head. "Kind of hard to do when it's more than seven billion now."

Strange said, "Without a worldwide pandemic, at least. Makes what's happening now even scarier, or prophetic, or if you believe in conspiracies maybe the result of the stones. Anyways, to continue, he said we should form a one-world government, a one-world religion, a single currency and a one-world language."

"Yeah, like everybody's going to accept any of those," Fleetwood interjected again.

"Well, my hope was that if we meditated before the stones, maybe the gods would intervene and stop this thing."

Cody rubbed spontaneous tears from her eyes and said, "I guess it's better than sitting in your apartment waiting to die, and besides, the Centers for Disease Control advised everyone to stay away from large numbers of people. Isn't that right, Lace?"

"That's what they were telling us at the hospital two days ago," she said. As the medical expert of the group, they trusted her on this. That was the last day she'd worked. It was staggering the sheer number of people walking in or being carried in with The Plague. It would be worse now, if the hospital were even still functioning, which was unlikely with power plants failing, fresh water supplies being exhausted and pharmaceutical delivery systems deteriorating. Not to mention dying doctors. Some succumbing while performing surgeries.

Z Chapter Seven

Scotland:
Destination — Stonehenge

Best Laid Plans

Through the sparsely populated and equally barren mountain wilderness in the western half of Scotland, Aidan began their trek south to Stonehenge.

"Would you like some music? I have the latest album by Radiohead and Snow Patrol's greatest hits on my iPad." At least the tablet didn't need an internet connection to play music. "Unless you like American music. I have the Allman Brothers Greatest Hits. Personally, I've always liked their big hit 'Melissa'."

Mally said, "We probably should listen to the radio. Find out what we can."

"If any are still broadcasting." Aidan was skeptical.

The Edinburgh station he listened to for the weather had gone off the air two days before. Mally nodded his head considering the likelihood. By Aidan's calculation, with luck they could make Stonehenge shortly after nightfall. Although he wasn't sure he wanted to be on the road after dark. They probably should try and find a secure place to shelter for the night before continuing the next morn.

Σ Chapter Eight — Six Days After Plague Begins
New Jersey:
Destination — Georgia Guidestones

The Garden State Drive

"I'm surprised how many people have died so quickly," said Fleetwood.

"Yeah, this is some serious shit," Strange said.

There weren't as many vehicles stopped on the freeway like in the Lincoln Tunnel, but it was still unnerving how many there were. The biggest challenge they encountered was when they neared a jackknifed tractor trailer blocking all southbound lanes, forcing Strange to drive off the roadway to pass. The huge eighteen wheeler's tires were flat. It looked like it had been there longer than it had. It had only been six days since The Plague started. It sure seemed like it had been longer. The driver of a vehicle in front of the big rig had probably died behind the wheel and the semi's driver had locked the breaks attempting to avoid a collision, then died when he was exposed, and thus The Plague claimed another soul. The New Jersey farmland, soggy from the previous summer's thunderstorms, meant the Toyota's four wheel drive came in handy when Strange had to edge off the road to get around the big rig.

Back on the highway and continuing south, Strange gazed over the rolling New Jersey farmland to the west. Cattle dead in the fields. Not one buzzard circled the carcasses. It seemed no living creature was immune to The Plague except for the V of geese flying high above determined to go south for the winter. A barn with a message scrawled on the old gray, weathered walls in four-foot tall desperate red letters 'Living Life is a Living Hell.' In smaller letters underneath someone else had written 'But Dying Is Even Worse.'

They saw no other vehicles moving on the broad ribbon of concrete. Extraordinary, since New Jersey was the only state in the country designated entirely urban because of the population density. Rain lightly spackled the windshield as they continued south. Making their way among the bramble of vehicles at less than twenty-five miles per hour, however, the slight shower wouldn't slow them down any worse.

» Chapter Nine

Sawnee Mountain, Georgia:
Evil Dwellers 'HQ

The Queen Commands

"Get Drummond and get up here. On the double." Queen Gertrude commanded.

"Will do, Your Majesty," Bad Penny replied. He couldn't even think anything negative about her or she'd know, and there would literally be hell to pay. He called Drummond, *"She Who Must Be Feared wants us."* Queen Gertrude liked the title they'd given her, thinking it showed respect.

"See you on the stairway."

"10-4."

In her mind as much a queen as that of England, Queen Gertrude's private quarters was on the highest level of the estate. The fourth. Her master suite was a bedroom boasting the biggest lace-covered canopy bed most people would have ever seen and a private marble bath. Doors led from the suite to an intimate outside terrace with sitting area featuring the finest view of the North Georgia mountains. Here she called last-minute private meetings. From the entirety of the suite of rooms she had a 360-degree view of the beautiful millennia-old mountains of North Georgia.

Once meeting on the third floor landing, Bad Penny and Drummond took the stairs two at a time. Must do their best not to keep the Queen waiting. One of the magnificent oak double doors to the suite was open. Bad Penny knocked. It drew her out of her deep contemplation where she sat on the small terrace. She gestured for them to enter.

"How are you assimilating?" Queen Gertrude asked of Drummond. As the newest one of her organization she wanted to know how, or even if, he was fitting in.

"Splendidly," was his less than candid reply.

"I knew you would," she thalked. *"You know I depend on you two more than any of the others."*

"*We know,*" said Bad Penny.

"*I just wanted you men to be on high alert. Since we began The Reckoning, I won't be surprised if we, or me particularly, are subject to attack. And since it could come from any quarters, be aware it is not possible to read the minds of all of our potential enemies.*"

"*If I may be so bold,*" said Drummond, "*you have nothin' to worry about.*" And he bowed.

"*I knew we made a good decision when we chose you.*"

"*And I'm delighted you did,*" he said, laying on the butter a wee bit thick.

"*Is there anything you need of me?*" Queen Gertrude asked.

"*I think not,*" Drummond assured her.

"*We're good,*" added Bad.

Z Chapter Ten

Scotland: Destination — Stonehenge

Sojourning South

Chasing Cars was the first hit on the Snow Patrol album. A popular song by the Irish band that was particularly good for a road trip of unknown duration and indefinite purpose. They drove west to pick up the highway that would take them south to England. Before that they had to go through the Cambrian Mountains.

At the end of the mountain range Aidan stopped at the elevated mouth of The Hardknott Pass. The landscape showed nothing but boulder and ash. They stepped out of the comfortably warm vehicle into the north wind that was crisp and fragrant with the aromatic scent of distant evergreens. Colder than it should be for October, even November. Snowcapped distant mountains. Heard not a sound. Not a car engine. Bird on the wing. Not the rustle of a leaf, even though the wind blew. Mally lit up a cigarette. He usually smoked only during breaks at the plant. Jeanette would have his hide if he attempted to smoke in the house. And he never wanted to get in a row with her; it would be an unwinnable pursuit.

Aidan squatted, removed one driving glove, and picked with his bare fingers at a piece of crumbling macadam on the side of the road. He emptied the ash from where it rested in the bowl of his Calabash by gently tapping the lip against the side sole of his boot. He withdrew his tortoise shell spectacles from an inside vest pocket, put them on, and gazed at the valley stretched out below. The upper part of the descent was barren. The lower elevation changed to scrub brush and short trees. Crumbling concrete slabs of a solitary life in a long-ago hamlet of the shire faced a lake where the range bottomed out. An ancient chimney rose from a one room shack, a silent sentinel watching over its concrete slab neighbors, all cloaked in low dense fog. Aidan lifted the binoculars from where they rested against his chest and put eye to glass and examined the melancholy scene. The loose stone chimney looked as if it could be toppled with one hand. A light wisp of white smoke curled from it.

"Looks like someone's in that cabin."

"We should probably avoid it, then," said Mally.

"Probably just fishermen trying to avoid The Plague."

"Or fisherwomen," said Jeanette.

"Or that," Aidan agreed. Mally just looked at her and shook his head behind her back.

Although the elevation was not quite four hundred meters at the top of the pass, it tended to get quite a bit of snow and ice in the dead of winter. Not on this day, shrouded as it was in ashen fog and light rain, but on clearer days Aidan had seen the Isle of Man in the Irish Sea to the west, even making out the dark profiles of the medieval castles along its rocky shore. It was too early in the cold season to make out iceblink but he knew it too was on its way. A few lonely seagulls sauntered above the horizon. It wouldn't be long before they joined the ranks of the dead. If not before, definitely once they began feasting on the bodies of the departed.

Normally, the long two lane road proceeding to the bottom might be closed to vehicle traffic due to the many hairpin turns occluded by brumal fog and snow.

The lonely howl of a dog sounded from the distance. At least they hoped it was a dog and not the fabled beastly hounds of winter.

Not dressed properly for the chilly temperature, Jeanette said, "I'm getting back in the car," and hurried back to the protection of the Range Rover. She got a jacket out of her bag to put on over her cute sweatshirt. Aidan turned up the collar of his jacket against the chill and returned to the warmth of the vehicle. Keeping it in low gear, they began the arduous drive down the thirty-degree mountain slope to the valley floor, made even more treacherous by the number of disabled vehicles they encountered, all containing the dead or gruesomely dying.

"Shouldn't we see if we can help anyone," asked Jeanette.

"They're beyond help," said Mally. "Forby we don't want to get it."

"Mally's right. We need to keep ourselves healthy above all."

After being in the cold for a few minutes, the big SUV's cabin was too warm for Aidan; he cracked his window to let in some fresh air. The original road through the pass had been built by the Romans beginning in 500 A.D. Fortunately the current one was in way better condition, even if it didn't seem like it at the moment with all the cars serving as coffins for the dead or dying. Once the snows came, still a month or more away, it would be their lasting necropolis. The valley's tribute to future generations, if there were to be anym but looking less likely by the day.

Mally wasn't educated like Aidan, but he was street smart. In fact he was quite canny, capable of figuring things out. He certainly hoped it would be warmer in the south, in the lowlands nearer to Stonehenge. Especially if it takes longer, and lasts longer, than Aidan believes, at least it should be warmer down there. The most important thing will be finding water and food.

They reached the valley floor, the crumbling remains of a village from a different age, and the house with the smoke coming from the chimney. They were in agreement that they would cautiously approach but knew the Range Rover's loud V-8 would ensure they didn't hooly up on anyone. Aidan pulled to a stop next to an ancient truck in a worn, brown dirt flat.

The rickety wooden door creaked open and a gaunt man of seventy with a week or more's worth of scraggly grey beard pointed an Italian-made shotgun that looked too expensive for his means. He stepped onto the rotten old wooden porch, too late for Aidan to do anything but turn off the engine and raise his hands. Mally withdrew his birthright pistol from the old bag.

The man motioned with the shotgun for them to get out of the most expensive SUV he'd ever seen. They obediently, but reluctantly, followed his direction. Three doors opened. Each exited without looking at their feet or their step from the vehicle since they were keeping their eyes on the man with the shotgun. Mally held the old revolver behind his leg. Although he did pocket the keys, Aidan couldn't see a reason for locking the doors remotely.

Ceramic wind chimes hanging above the porch pealed gently. The surprise visitors stepped carefully around the Range Rover trying to keep the massive steel engine between them and the armed man for as long as they were able.

A sudden massive blast and fire flew from the long barrel. Just to let them know it wasn't for show. It was worth wasting the one shell. He had a whole crate in the cabin. Overhead, a conspiracy of ravens scattered in a shower of black feathers. Rattled by the shockwave from the blast, the airy wind chimes pealed louder.

"Sir, sir. Please. That isn't necessary," Aidan said. Jeanette slowly collapsed. Now Mally was mad and, still concealing his weapon, knelt to his wife.

"Just making sure the wolf of winter stays away from the door. You aren't bringing it with ye, 'ere ye?" He spit onto the dirt in front of the rickety porch to emphasize his point.

"What's he mean?" whimpered Jeanette.

"The Plague," Aidan said to Jeanette. Turning back to the old man, he said, "No sir. That's why we left the city. To avoid getting it."

"Well, you don't look like you're ailin'."

"That's because we're not, sir. And we plan on keeping it that way."

"Then you're welcome to come on in and set a spell."

"We'll take you up on your kind offer, but only for a minute, though."

"Watch your step on those old boards," he said as they stepped on the well-worn porch. "I should've mended 'em last summer, but now I'm glad I didn't. Sort of the second layer of my early warning system, if you know what I'm talking about. In the event they're walking. Not driving. Even if I don't hear a car's engine, I'll hear 'em on these creaky old boards. Those damn Scottish wildcats are the only other thin' I have to keep a weather eye out for. And you wouldn't believe how loud their claws sound scratching on those old wood boards. Those damn cats aren't that big but they sure can have a nasty way about them, and I'd hate for one to catch me unawares. Excuse my manners. Percy, Percy Schofield."

"Think nothin' of it. Nice to meet you, Mr. Schofield. Aidan Walker. And this," he said extending his hand to Mally helping Jeanette get to her feet, "is Jeanette and Mally King."

"Nice to make your acquaintance."

"Likewise," said Mally, the stringent word lodging in his throat, still pissed off about the shotgun blast scaring Jeanette.

Entering the one-room cabin perfectly sited behind a rippling lake of azure turning to dying grey, they grouped in front of the fire warming the kitchen, proper sitting area, and bed in the corner. Considering the cold outside, it was surprisingly warm. It smelt of woodsmoke, comfortable leather, old lumber, and an aftershave Aidan couldn't place. He thought it smelt like one his Pops wore. A rod and reel hung above the cobblestone fireplace's massive mantle made from a timber far too heavy for one man to lift. A nearly foot-high stone hearth a person could sit on to warm one's back below. One room. Ramshackle but clean.

A four-foot-wide handmade unit with four shelves held aged hardbacks without dustjackets. Mostly novels written by British authors.

Mally studied the titles. He was a conscientious reader. He noticed a few of his favorites. *The Day of the Jackal* and *The Odessa File* by Frederick Forsyth. *Eye of The Needle* and *The Third Twin*, by Ken Follett, *A Clockwork Orange*, by Anthony Burgess.

"Nice collection," Mally said begrudgingly.

"Just somethin' to do when I get tired of fishing," Percy acknowledged. "A man can't fish all the time." He looked sheepishly at his guests when he said it like he wasn't even sure of that for himself. There was no electricity, so all assumed he read by firelight. Percy took off his worn barn jacket and hung it on a cedar coat tree.

"I guess not," said Mally, though thinking he'd like to try.

"Serry up to the fire," Percy said to his guests. "Two days ago a car full of people pulled up, coughin' and wheezin' and carryin' on. I had to run 'em off. That's why I held this scatter gun on you folks," he said, leaning it against the corner where the stone fireplace met the wooden wall. "Sorry about that now, but you can't be too careful these days. They're probably dead by now, un-hum." He nodded knowingly.

A greenish-brown round rug was centered in front of the fireplace. Two easy chairs at rest on the rug faced the blaze. Percy hitched up his baggy trousers and sat on the stone hearth to make room for the others. He spat into the fire where it sizzled. The trousers had probably fit at one time. His galluses looked as if they might be too loose to hold. It seemed everyone was losing weight since The Plague began, if they weren't dead. A handmade broom with long bristles leaned in the corner. Mally pulled up a hand-painted wooden rocker probably handed down from Percy's grandparents so Jeanette and Aidan could sit in the worn easy chairs.

Percy then stood and, saying it like he just thought of something important, said, "Don't have no tea. Sorry. But how about a cup of coffee? Just made it. Fresh."

They assured him coffee was fine and all three accepted.

"This was my great-grandparent's permanent residence over a hundred years ago. It was part of a small community then. It's just a rundown shack now and was handed down twice before I ended up with it. Once folks started dying I figured it would be the best place to be. So far it's working out pretty well."

Obviously pleased by the arrival of the unexpected company, he was talking a lot. His visitors poured the proper ceramic mugs he'd placed before them filled from the ancient pot where it roasted on the old iron stove. Mally drank his black, Jeanette and Aidan took theirs white with sugar.

"I have a cask of proper mead put down in the cellar. Just set to drink. Made from local honey and blood oranges. Don't suppose ye fancy a wee taste, would ye? Like they always say, it's five o'clock somewhere," he said with a youthful grin.

Percy shared the mead in tin cups, then set his coffee on the wood floor between his feet. The mug's heat clouded the spot on the plank where he sat it.

Aidan said, "None for me; thank you." He thought it best to keep his wits about him in the current climate.

"We didn't mean to intrude," said Mally, unable to escape the feeling they were being watched from afar. He was ready to get back on the road.

"Speaking of not intruding," said Aidan, "we probably best be on our way."

"Where ye going?" asked Percy.

"South," said Aidan, thinking it best not to explain what their plans were.

"Well, if you change your mind…"

"Thank you, my friend, for your hospitality. Maybe we'll see you on our return trip."

Percy didn't respond, contemplating their chances of survival. The new world seemed intent on chewing up those who weren't prepared. He was of a mind they might not make it. He saw them out and gave them a wave as Aidan backed up the large SUV to turn around. A mist shrouding the grey lake might as well have draped the continent, perhaps the planet. A deathly shroud of grey.

Everything grey. Dust, dirt, fog, and a sad rain.

Σ Chapter Eleven

New Jersey-Pennsylvania:
Destination — Georgia Guidestones

Brotherly Love

Approaching southern New Jersey, Strange decided to exit the turnpike, taking a chance of going through Philadelphia in hopes of stocking up on additional supplies.

What should have been only a two-hour trip even in New Jersey traffic had taken almost five hours. And seeing the downtown skyline appear to the west, Strange took the 38 West exit for the Benjamin Franklin Bridge to cross into the city. One of the side benefits of a decade and a half in radio was being possessed of a large amount of esoteric knowledge; some might call it trivial. Strange inched slowly around the unmanned toll booths to enter onto the monolithic steel girded structure that had once been the Delaware River Bridge.

Even through his pale green pallor, Fleetwood was proving his sick sense of humor was still intact. "That's one good thing about the arrival of an apocalypse."

"What's that?" asked Strange.

"No more paying tolls."

"Yeah, I have to agree. Even though I left Tennessee fifteen years ago, I've never gotten used to those," Strange said.

Cody just shook her head.

Strange hoped Philly truly would prove to be the City of Brotherly Love and not just a meaningless sobriquet. Of course, being a Giants fan, he couldn't stand the fuckin' Eagles or their asshole fans. He'd gotten in too many fights with them at their annual game at the Meadowlands to want to be in the same city with them. He didn't even like the popular Mark Wahlberg movie, *Invincible*, or the actor himself, since it was about the Eagles, or, as the locals called them, The Iggles.

If this is the end of the world as we know it, but he was left here, he was going to miss Giants football more than anything.

They passed through the New Jersey conurbation before reaching the bridge. It wasn't as congested a body dump as the Lincoln Tunnel had been; nevertheless the going was slow around many more stalled vehicles of death. Finally, the bridge emptied into Franklin Square two blocks north of where blue signs pointed out directions to the Liberty Bell where it was housed at Independence Hall.

"Hey, Strange, you ever been to the Liberty Bell?"

"Nah, man. I never wanted to come to Philadelphia. I'm a New Yorker."

"Yeah, right. You're Tennessee born and bred," said Fleet.

"You know what I mean. I'm a New Yorker at heart," Strange snapped.

Fleetwood held up a hand. "Yeah-yeah-yeah, man. I hear you. Sorry. But I've always wanted to see the bell. On my bucket list as they say. Just always something else going on I guess."

Strange took a deep breath. "Well...if we don't die, maybe I'll go see it with you sometime. Or we can stop and see it on the way back."

"You think people are going to care about things like that if the world's dying?"

"Yeah, probably not. Most people will just be trying to stay alive. We've never before seen the kind of future we're facing now."

Having had enough talk about the end of the world, Cody said, "You know, I sure wish we could have a Philly cheesesteak."

Lace said, "I'd love a Nathan's hotdog."

Strange said, "Yeah, that'd be good, but only if it's at the original restaurant at Coney Island. Especially on July 4th when they have the hotdog eating contest."

"Definitely," Lace agreed. "Eating while listening to the surf and smelling the salt air. One of life's great pleasures." She didn't catch the irony in her comment about life.

They creeped slowly along Market Street, memorable for being where Rocky ran through the street in training for his fight with Apollo Creed — him running and street stand vendors tossing him fruit and shouting Rocky! as he passed their produce marts. The local hero. Fleet hummed the theme from the movie. The others joined in...but not for long; Rocky could have passed them at a jog as slow as they had to go to make their way past the abandoned cars in the narrow lane.

While pulled alongside a parked yellow taxi, their thoughts were shattered by a terrible explosion, followed by a loud car alarm sounding, all amplified by the quiet of nothingness as battered and bloody bodies crashed into the hood. Sheetmetal crumpled and thousands of shards of shattered glass flew. Unable to cope with their horrid reality, a young mother, clutching her toddler, took what she saw as the only way out for her and child. A quick death — the easy way out, rather than dying slowly and painfully in her arms.

Lace screamed. Cody hugged her as she sobbed, "That poor baby."

Strange stared at the mother and child. "I'm afraid it's only the beginning."

>> Chapter Twelve

Sawnee Mountain, Georgia:
Evil Dwellers 'HQ

Success

Queen Gertrude convened a meeting of the High Council and without preamble began magisterially, a trait she had not possessed in her previous life. *"It appears that our plan is succeeding. Kudos to you all."*

Nods of agreement and acknowledgement but shifting in seats. Everyone was uncomfortable; no one wanted to incur the Queen's ire. It was well-known her mood could change on a dime — and what could happen once it did.

She continued, *"Even though they would be unable to interrupt our plan, I'm mildly concerned that we could be the target of those who might do us harm, so I need everyone to be on their toes."*

They nodded agreeably. She asked two to go out and acquire a pair of generators. Revealing a sense of humor she wasn't usually known for, she said, *"Be sure and get the extended warranty,"* and grinned at her own joke. She dismissed them and went on with her meeting.

The pair quickly made their way to the mansion's massive six-car garage and retrieved keys for an old Toyota pickup from a hook on the garage wall. They pulled nose out and began the steep drive down the mountain, past the First Baptist Church of the Last Day's Resurrection and a used car lot at the bottom. Not long after, they pulled into one of two home improvement stores in Cumming. Given they were in Georgia, they thought it apropos to go the nearest location of the large chain of the famously orange building supply stores headquartered in Atlanta. The parking lot was nearly full of abandoned cars and trucks, but they saw not a single person walking to or from their vehicles. Entering the darkened store the stench of rotting corpses was overpowering causing them to wretch. Having had the foresight to bring large flashlights, they snapped them on. Searching for portable generators, they stepped over and around the putrefying bodies of dead employees, easily identified because of their orange aprons, and customers with fists clinched around lists of materials they would never need.

They found what they came for in the rear of the store next to the lawnmowers and near the restrooms. They decided on two ten-thousand watt Duromax generators. Both gasoline- and propane-powered.

"It's a good thing that old dude installed that propane tank," said the younger of the two. *"I wonder what happened to him."*

The previous owner of the mountaintop mansion had installed large, silver gasoline and propane tanks behind it. Using uncommon common sense, the pair thought the propane unit would be best, saving gas for the vehicles. The generators had small rubber tires making it easy to get them to the pickup. They rolled them around dead bodies and right out the front door.

Nobody asked to see a receipt.

Z Chapter Thirteen

Unknown Shires of England:
Destination — Stonehenge

Comes the Queen's Land

"He was such a nice man," said Jeanette.

"Yes, he was, and he can probably stay in that old cabin undisturbed for as long as he chooses if only the world leaves him alone," said Aidan.

Aidan almost immediately noticed a vibration in the steering wheel. His desire was that it would prove to be nothing. The route would take them almost due south, in some places close enough to see the Irish Sea, before crossing the border into England and the expanded land mass toward Saint George's Channel which would course them inland just to the east of Liverpool.

Between Scotland and England they crossed the border with an abandoned guard shack and a raised crossing barrier standing as a silent sentinel and reminder of a time when the two countries weren't such close friends and allies.

It wasn't long before they passed near Hadrian's Wall, which had demarcated the northern limits of the Roman Empire and served the purpose of keeping out the unconquered Scottish. Its construction credited with being started by the great Emperor Hadrian and remaining unfinished upon his death, while his successor, his adopted son Emperor Antonius Pius, decided to build a second wall deep in Scotland. Without a blood son, Hadrian adopted the follower in much the same way he'd been claimed by his father's first cousin, Emperor Trajan, and had gone on to succeed who history described as one of the greatest Caesars.

The nearer they got to populated areas the slower going it was due to the congestion from vehicles, mostly small saloons, since SUVs weren't nearly as popular in the UK as in other parts of the world. Chockablock with bodies, all.

In the more populous area midway between Liverpool to the west and Manchester to the east, they encountered the first live group they'd seen since leaving the small store outside of Edinburg four hours before.

A two lane road with a petrol station, a small mom-and-pop market, and a diner had been a center of commerce for the small community.

Appearing lost, extreme in pallor, coughing; all were stooped, their dirty rags hanging on thin sickly bodies not yet emaciated. Tired, or worse, in a daze; like they couldn't comprehend what was occurring all around them.

"Mally, I think we should probably use that contraption of yours to try and get some petrol. I don't want to wait until we're desperate to have some."

"Brilliant." Mally was a man of few words. And he was old school. "This thin' doesn't need high test, does it?"

"Just regular no-lead petrol," Aidan said.

He pulled into the carpark of the service station. It's large front window was shattered; the metal frame of the glass door, off its hinges. With plastic canister and siphon in hand, Mally located a small steel lid that gave access to an underground tank where gas was stored until dispensed from the pumps. He flipped it open and smelt the pungent odor of fresh gasoline. Aidan stood watch over him while he worked, Mally's old revolver at the ready. Mally fed the black tubing into the mouth of the underground tank until he heard and felt it splash into the liquid below. Then, the tattooed muscle of his forearm flexed, working the small attached hand pump until a moment later orange liquid splashed into the ten liter container.

When full, he grabbed the handle with both scarred hands. Aidan keyed the remote, opening the rear; Mally swung it into the cargo area of the large vehicle.

"Now, let's see if we can find any salvageable food in the market," Aidan said.

They collected Jeanette from the Range Rover and walked to the small store attached to the service station. The diner next door had a big red neon sign topping the front reading "Good Food" that was dark and broken into angry shards. Hungry, angry people? They entered the market. The fading sunlight finding its way into the establishment's shattered windows gave them sight of the half dozen bodies that greeted them. Most of them had probably been regular loyal customers.

The stench from the bodies and rotting food was indistinguishable. Rotting bodies had attracted a pack of feral cats. The felines keeked at the three instead of looking at them full on, as if the humans were the ones intruding.

Passing the aisles, Aidan said, "Look for canned food. I'm sure we'll find more along the way. But let's take as much as we can carry. And let's do it fast."

Mally had been a non-com in the British Royal Army and was accustomed to giving orders but knew when to let the senior officer take command and this was Aidan's mission.

"Here's the canned food," said Jeanette from the next row over.

While they foraged in the dark rear of the store, a cold rain began to fall outside. The shelves were picked over but they found cans of butter beans, English peas — pre-mushy, yellow corn, asparagus.

Aidan heard large raindrops begin to ring on the tin roof and said, "Let's get on the road. We've got miles to go and the rain won't help."

Mally looked at the cans of beans and said, "You all usually have your fancy university bean-feasts, and now we're just going to be having beans."

"I've always disliked that term," said Jeanette with a frown.

"Me, too," agreed Aidan.

Mally found a box of large plastic garbage bags, ripped it open. He put their finds in a bag. Being the strongest one of the three, he swung it over his shoulder, looking like Saint Nicholas with his huge bag of presents.

"Humph," he grunted, "heavier than it looks. Or maybe I'm just older than I think I am."

"You certainly aren't getting any younger," said Jeanette, with an evil grin.

They rushed to the SUV to get out of the rain, coming down harder now. All except Mally, going slower laden as he was by the bag full of canned goods. The sudden rain had brought with it a winter-like chill to the air. All in, Aidan turned on the vehicle's wipers to swipe away the big raindrops like tears of their apocalypse.

"It certainly looks like the end of the world," said Jeanette. "So grey and dismal."

"Now don't you worry your pretty little head," said Mally comfortingly. "We'll be fine. And if we're not, at least we'll go together. I won't go without you, and I give you my oath I won't let you go without me."

He could barely say the phrase without his voice cracking. Jeanette was his life and he wanted to grow old with her. It had been his sensitivity and his toughness that made her love him and why she would love him for eternity no matter who went first.

Jeanette said, "I don't even care. Even if we survive, nothin' is ever going to be the same. I'd rather not live in the world we're bound to face, especially without you. How would I survive alone?" she lamented. A lonely tear trailed an unfamiliar path down her cheek. The saltiness surprised her when it kissed her trembling lips.

"You hush now," he said. "Everythin's going to be fine. We'll still have each other."

Aidan wondered if this was the end of the world, how long it would take them to forget things that once were. Things that now needed no effort to remember because they just were, but ultimately wouldn't be. Suddenly, Aidan roared out of the parking lot, as fast as the powerful V8 would take them. A mob of perhaps twenty, dirty and wasted and wretched, carrying pickaxes and cudgels, a couple with chains swinging them like lassos, disappeared in the rearview mirror.

He let out a tense breath.

"What's the matta'?" asked Mally.

"An angry mob, that's what's the matter. Miscreants. Or maybe just hungry," Aidan paused, "but you know, I don't think it matters which they are."

They continued to traverse south from the crossroads.

Toward the end of the world and whatever awaited them there.

» Chapter Fourteen

Sawnee Mountain, Georgia:
Evil Dwellers 'HQ

A Problem of Their Own Making

Mission accomplished, the pair returned with the generators, hoping Queen Gertrude would be pleased. Didn't mean she would be, or would show it if she were, but one could always hope. They delivered the generators to the rear of the mansion to be installed on a concrete pad next to the propane tank. One of the queen's sycophants, an engineer in his former life, met them to perform the technological connections.

Once installed, the mansion would be assured of electricity even after the world went dark. And one of the best features of the portable units was their ability to direct their output at specific functions, so they wouldn't have to waste power on unnecessary appliances or functions like the maintenance of the swimming pool or operating the fountain in the center of the circular drive. Those might be nice for greeting guests but probably would be used seldom, if at all, during an apocalypse.

A defense mechanism Queen Gertrude had ordered was a wire fence wall, twenty feet high, around the perimeter of the mansion's grounds and topped with floodlights. Generators would power them so they would turn on when movement was detected. Even at the expense of scaring the shit out of the occasional small black bear.

« Chapter Fifteen

Cumming, Georgia:
The Good Guys 'HQ

Memories

A knock at the door. Through the textured cut glass Patrick could see his old friend Bill Crain. He glanced quickly to be sure there were no threats in the shrubs and greeted his friend with a bear hug.

"I would have called if phones still worked. Duncan said you needed my help. What's up?" Bill said, stepping inside.

"The Reckoning."

"Well, that sucks." He remembered their battle with the Dwellers almost a decade before.

"Yeah, and that's not the worst of it."

"What could be worse than mutants rising up all over the world and trying to take over?"

Speaking quietly, Patrick said, "Trudy is their leader."

"What the fuck? I thought she was —"

"Yeah, dead. We both did."

"So, what are we going to do?"

"That means you're in?"

"Are you kidding? I can't let you battle a threat to the survival of all humanity without me," Crain said, holding out two fists.

They fist-bumped as Patrick said, "That's my man."

"Have you got a plan?"

"Me? That's what I needed you for. You were the army strategist, Colonel."

"I was afraid you were going to say that. It always worries me when you call me Colonel."

"Afraid? Worried? Colonel Bill Crain's not afraid of anything."

Bill had to grin at that. "Well, what about Duncan? Have you thalked to him about this?"

"How do you think I know about The Reckoning? Apparently they forgot about him and how he has the same telepathic ability as them."

"Thank God for that."

"I'll say."

"So, do you have any idea where they are…or how to find them?"

"No. But…wait a second. Duncan was just listening to us. He just told me he was doing some eavesdropping on the bad guys. That Trudy and her main group are holed up in that mansion atop Sawnee Mountain."

"Cool. That's not far at all. We could walk it if we had to."

"Hopefully we won't need to. I filled up the Lexus' tank when this started and I'm sure we can siphon some out of underground tanks at any service station if we need to."

Σ Chapter Sixteen

Philadelphia, Pennsylvania:
Destination — Georgia Guidestones

Slow Progress

"I went into medicine because I wanted to help people. I became a surgeon because I wanted to save people's lives. This is killing me! I can't do anything." Rocking, hands clenched between her knees, torment on her face, Lace stared at the battered bodies that crashed onto the car's hood.

Cody tried to comfort her by stroking her hair and smoothing it behind her ear.

Lace pushed her hand away a bit more aggressively than she'd intended.

Z Chapter Seventeen

England:
Destination — Stonehenge

Sets In

Aidan coughed.

Mally and Jeanette withdrew in horror.

"What? It's nothin'."

Jeanette said "You aren't taking ill, are you?"

Then Mally coughed.

Aidan laughed. "See? Nothin'," welcoming the perfect timing of Mally's own cough.

The further they made their way into England, the slower was the going what with the increasing number of disabled vehicles clogging the narrow artery. Firmament, ground, freeway, all lonely lugubrious grey. From morning's light 'til evenfall. The color never changed at all.

"Do you think we'll run into anymore gangs?" Jeanette asked.

"I think you can count on it." Aidan really didn't want to act like a grinch, but he didn't have the time or energy to think of a better answer.

Mid-afternoon in late October and whatever UK sun remained, the lonely surfeit of grey shadowing was turning a deeper shade. Rural England could be both comforting and off-putting. Now, it was just scary. As they bore south it became even more rural and all they saw was the occasional farmhouse and barn. All dark.

» Chapter Eighteen

Sawnee Mountain, Georgia:
Evil Dwellers 'HQ

Rallying The Troops

Queen Gertrude summoned Drummond and Bad Penny to her aerie on the fourth floor. The small terrace was barely able to accommodate a round table and four wrought iron chairs for when she wanted to conduct a private meeting. At least as private as it could be when nearly everyone could read minds. But she had made it clear that anyone detected trying to read her mind or eavesdrop on her meetings would literally pay with their heads. His sword skills had been one of the primary reasons she'd wanted Drummond to join them, to serve as her bodyguard and personal executioner.

Others thought his skill ghastly. She deemed it a magnificent sine qua non.

"I'm concerned someone may well rise up against us in other parts of the world. I want you to reach out to our friends everywhere and find out if I'm right. If they're hearing anything."

Since the trauma of dying in Patrick's arms she had lost all memory of her marriage to him or she would have known to have someone read her former husband's thoughts and have been able to head off the most likely attack.

"Any place specifically? Particularly worrisome?" asked Drummond.

"Not really. It's just a feeling I have. But I would say look at where you're from. Try England...The UK."

"We'll get right on it," Drummond said.

They returned to the first floor level referred to as the common room. It featured a billiard table; a green felt-topped card table where they played poker, although even they had to admit that money was less important now; and a large screen tv which no longer broadcast anything, including sports, since no one was working at any of the networks. The NFL had already cancelled the second half of its season and college football had followed suit. The room's large windows overlooked a once-pristine swimming pool now turning shades of green, the result of no skimmer or chemicals. It was only used by a couple of the Bottom Dwellers.

Drummond sat on an expensive burnished leather sofa that came with the mansion and, as he'd been taught, began to focus his thoughts at certain counterpart Dwellers in the UK. It seemed that since his death at the hands of Detective Holmes he had been imbued with some of the same powers as the ones that had been communicating with him for years, including his new partner, Bad Penny.

« Chapter Nineteen

Cumming, Georgia:
The Good Guys 'HQ

Reconnaissance

Patrick concentrated on Duncan, who responded telepathically. Since cellphones weren't working, Patrick asked his cousin to thalk to friend and former sheriff's deputy, the all-American college defensive end and all around bad ass, Jeff Byrd.

Patrick and Jeff had stood up to home invaders who were assaulting vacationers in their rental cabins in the North Georgia mountains and killed two of them. That had been when they'd encountered the Trail Dwellers, selected Southeast Indians who had died on the Trail of Tears. The ones who had murdered but not murdered Trudy. The White County sheriff had referred to Patrick and Jeff as a one-man wrecking crew. Patrick corrected the Sheriff by saying, "Two man". The Sheriff called Patrick a smartass.

Not long after dusk, the sound of a motorcycle engine echoed off the glass of the huge front windows of Patrick's luxurious home. A long leather scabbard on the side of the Harley's shiny midnight blue gas tank held a lethal-lookin' shotgun. The lean six foot-six-inch man who moved like an athlete withdrew the weapon as he climbed off the Hog. When he took off the full black helmet, a long brown ponytail dropped out. His grin displayed huge dimples as he ambled to the double front doors with cut-glass panes. He knew he was being watched from inside. He displayed the look that a sportswriter once described as "cooler than the other side of the pillow."

Patrick opened the door before his friend reached it. "You don't have to strut for the neighbors. Most of them are already dead, anyway."

"Have to stay in practice. You never know what's going to happen."

"Same old Big Byrd."

"You wouldn't want me to change, would you?" He flashed the mischievous smirk that drew the affection of coeds throughout the ACC when he played defense for the University of Virginia. "And you know, you and the sports writers in college are the only ones who've ever called me Big Byrd."

Ignoring his friend's comment, Patrick asked, "So, are you ready?"

"For those Dwellers sons of bitches? Ha, those assholes are the ones that better be ready."

"That's the spirit."

Patrick was covering up for how he really felt about knowing that Trudy was one of the undead. The sole thought that gave him comfort was that she hadn't become one of them by choice. They'd murdered her, taken her, made her one of them. And if she hadn't been so intelligent, brave, and determined, they wouldn't have wanted her. And now she was their leader.

Worse. Their queen.

He led his good friend and former investigative partner to the study they converted to their Intelligence HQ. "You haven't met my friend, Colonel Bill Crain," he said, gesturing toward his massive mahogany desk. Crain had commandeered Patrick's chair and sat checking the magazine on a Colt AR-15.

"He's much too formal. Besides, I'm retired. Call me Bill." At five-foot-eight he didn't even rise to the shoulder of the six-four Dylan or the six-six Byrd.

Jeff extended his large hand and said, "Byrd, Jeff Byrd."

Patrick said, "Following the army's recommendation I think we should get a couple of hours of rest before the mission. Do you agree, Bill?"

The retired colonel did. "And by the by, are you going to get your cousin to help us?"

"Absolutely, but as you know he has to limit his time out of water. But I can call him when we're ready to execute and see what he knows."

"Sounds good."

Crain lay down on one of the two sofas facing each other in the living room overlooking the dark rear lawn. Byrd took the other, his length barely able to fit. Illuminated by a streetlamp, Patrick slumped in the leather chair in his study on the front of the house.

"So we're really going to do this?" Byrd asked.

"Desperate times. Desperate measures," Patrick paraphrased.

"I'm with you. But seems like this is way past desperate to me."

"Come on, man. It's always darkest before the dawn."

"We're just full of tired old sayings, aren't we?"

"Byrd, we're full of something."

Σ Chapter Twenty

Philadelphia, Pennsylvania:
Destination — Georgia Guidestones

Home Calls

"I think we should try and get some gas before we get too low," said Strange.

"How?" asked Fleetwood.

"I've been thinking about it and considering all the abandoned vehicles we've seen I bet at some point we'll run across a gasoline truck on the busiest highway in the country and can just take what we want."

"Sounds like a plan." Fleetwood paused. "But, a milk truck might be better."

"Only if we find an Entenmann's to go with it." Strange and Fleetwood laughed.

"How can you guys make jokes at a time like this? After what we've seen?" Lace said, still sniffling and upset about the baby and mother that died.

"Sorry, Lace," said Strange, "I'm trying to keep from thinking about it. I'm as upset about this as you are. Believe me. Anyway, this was a mistake. Philly seems as bad as The Big Apple. We'll make our way back to the turnpike and point toward Baltimore and DC. We'll find somewhere to sleep in that area." Strange got quiet for a moment, then, "Whenever I get south of DC, I start thinking about Tennessee and home. I guess what they say is true — one can never leave home completely behind. And I don't even like it anymore." He shrugged at the irony of what he'd said.

Back on the turnpike, reaching speeds as high as twenty miles per hour in some stretches, before the congestion of disabled vehicles brought them to a full stop, Lace took it upon herself to pass out bags of chips and sandwiches she'd had the foresight to bag up the night before.

Cody, ripping into a bag of Gardetto's garlic chips, said, "Look! Snow."

"I think those are technically called flurries," said Strange. "I used to love snow back in the hills of Tennessee when I was a kid."

"Yeah, before you moved to New York where all we have is piles of frozen gray slush all winter."

"Tell me about it. But Tennessee's mountains and hills are beautiful covered in their white blankets.

"I bet they are," said Cody.

Fleetwood asked, "So, what are you thinking about for a place to spend the night?"

"I have some ideas, but I'd like to know what you guys think. And I'd like to get closer to DC, before we look for a place."

"One thing is for sure," said Strange, "if there are no signs of life in the nation's capitol, it really is the end of the world. The government always keeps going."

"I hear you," said Fleet.

Proving the maxim the government always keeps going, a short time later, two Navy fighter jets appeared in the mournful sky.

Cody said, "Probably under the command of Homeland Security, which is under the direct command of the President himself."

In addition to her mid-day deejay duties, she'd acted as WAYN's political correspondent and was still turned on by Washington politics, even though she'd been at it for over half a decade. Just hearing the pure roaring resonance of them was comforting, as were the contrails reminiscent of a large checkerboard crisscrossing the unconcerned sky.

"See, the president must still be alive," said Strange.

"Maybe. Or a majority of congress?" said Cody.

"Republican or Democrat?" quipped Strange.

"Funny, dude. Either way at least we have some semblance of a government," Fleet said, "and that's got to be a good thing."

"Yeah, right," grumbled Strange who, true to his Tennessee hills roots, wasn't wild about the federal government. "All it means is everything hasn't crumbled yet. At least they had someone to fill up the aircraft with fuel and someone to fly them. There might not even be any control tower workers. They could literally be flying by the seat of their pants."

"Those jets are amazing," said Cody. "They can fly from DC to The Big Apple and back in under thirty minutes. So they're probably keeping lookout over the entire Eastern Seaboard. You never know. One of our enemies might try and take advantage of a dire situation."

"I hope they're keeping watch over us," Lace said. "We need somebody to."

"And too bad for them it's the end of the world," said Fleet. "In a few years those guys could be flying for American or Delta, making huge dollars."

"That's all you think about, Fleet, the dollars. Pretty soon they won't be all that important," Cody said.

"I worked for you, so I can't be all about the dollars. So, what do you think it's gonna be? Survival of the fittest?"

With an unenthusiastic shrug, Strange said, "Maybe."

Z Chapter Twenty-One

Unknown Shires of England:
Destination — Stonehenge

Reality Sets In

"I think maybe we should find a place to bed down since these dead cars have slowed us down so much." Aidan was more concerned about their situation than he let on.

"What are you thinking?" asked Mally.

"I've been thinking about one of these barns we've been seeing along the way. What do you think?" Like a good commander he asked his charges their opinion, but knew he had the confidence of command to make the decision.

"Brilliant."

"That's it, then. Keep your eyes peeled."

It wasn't long before they saw in the distance a mid-century clapboard cottage. No lights on. Behind it an ancient barn with wood turning to gray. With the approaching sunset everything was grey. Barn, house, earth, trees, sky. The world. The elegiac grey of ash, dust, weather, and unspeakable gloom. The house needed paint but looked otherwise maintained.

"That looks like the answer," said Aidan. He turned off the vehicle's lights and turned into the drive — well-worn, deeply rutted two-track, dirt — that led to the house two kilometers away.

"If we aren't greeted with a shotgun, Jeanette can knock on the door. Her appearance will be less threatening. Mally, you can cover her with the pistol, just in case. And if no one's there we'll take over the barn."

"Sounds like a plan," said Mally.

"I'm glad somebody thinks so." Jeanette looked as if she weren't sure.

Still some distance from the house, and putting a copse of trees between them, Aidan came softly to a stop trying to reduce tire noise on the mixture of dirt and gravel. Mally climbed out quietly while trying first to hide the interior light with his hand. He helped Jeanette out of the backseat. She approached the farmhouse, shrinking into herself, looking not unlike a poverty-stricken guttersnipe.

The ancient revolver was tucked into the waist of Mally's trousers. "I'll make sure nothing happens to you," he said, confidently touching the stock above his belt line.

He followed her as far as the front porch then dropped to his stomach on the damp ground below the stoop's surface, the mouth of the barrel pointing toward where she meekly knuckled the door three times. The ground was uncomfortably cold.

No response. She rapped again. With more meaning. The frosted pane rattled from her touch. No response again. Aidan quickly but stealthily exited the Range Rover before pausing to extract a lug wrench from the back. Just in case it was needed as a weapon. He joined Mally on the porch and with a quick shrewd glance between the two, using the tire wrench like a pry bar, he firmly, but softly, forced the loose-fitting door inward until it stopped against the foot of a tiny corpse. An elderly woman. In a dull-colored house dress and a brown cardigan sweater buttoned to the throat.

The body was festered and the level of decomposition looked like she'd died before The Plague started. Still smelled. The corpse wasn't yet desiccated, but soon would be. The eyes sunk into their sockets and the skin stretched over her head made it look more like a skull than a face. Had probably just been her time. Anyone who cared enough to check on her had probably died before they could get to her. Lucky for her she wouldn't have to go through the cataclysm that was the end of the world. It was ironic, morbidly so, that one could live that long and miss seeing the world end.

"I'm going to be sick," said Jeanette, turning green.

"I guess we can be sure no one else is here," Aidan observed.

They stepped around the body and went inside. The wood-paneled parlor had the dated look of a different century. Except for the dead woman's corpse and old framed photos on every surface — mostly young lads and lasses, probably grandchildren or greats — the small house was tidy. Hopefully it meant the barn would be as well.

"The barn is where we spend the night," said Mally.

"Are you sure?" Jeanette was still a wee bit wobbly after her role in the scene and seeing the body.

Mally assured her that all would be fine. "Think of it as an adventure. Like we're camping out."

That didn't even sound plausible to him. But he had to at least try to reassure her. She was his responsibility. A job he accepted lovingly. The most important job he'd ever held. Mally might have appeared Falstaffian in look, demeanor, and appetites, but he was more Sir Galahad in manner, gallantry, and accepting of responsibilities, especially when it came to his beloved. But his sainted mother wouldn't have approved of a comparison of him to the illegitimate son of Sir Lancelot and Elaine of Corbenic, no matter it were with one so noble.

"I'm going to pull the Rover around to the back of the barn. No sense drawing attention to ourselves if we can keep from it," Aidan said when they returned. If anyone does show up, he hoped they wouldn't notice the tire tracks in the mud. He returned carrying an old red plastic bucket. He jerked a thumb over his shoulder. "I found a well and filled this bucket. We need to fill everything we can find with water. Has a hand pump. Water comes out of a pipe that resembles a kitchen faucet."

The barn was old but clean; somewhat fresh hay covered almost every bit of the floor. Somebody, maybe a younger son or son-in-law, had maintained the barn for the old woman. It still smelt unsullied. It hadn't been long cleaned. They chose a stall about fifteen feet square. Using a clean muck fork and their hands, they scooped up as much straw as they could gather to cushion the hard dirt floor beneath their bedding, then arranged blankets, sleeping bags, and pillows. Mally and Jeanette's blankets were close together; shared body heat was the best way to keep warm.

After preparing their bedding they took to exploring the rest of the structure on a mission of collecting things that might be helpful in their quest. Most welcoming was a concrete manger in the nearest stall in which they could build a fire to heat the cans of veggies they'd procured.

Mally found a long coil of rope. "I'm sure we can use this," he said, and pulled down the heavy hemp from a hook on the wall.

"Splendid," said Aidan.

"Could we use a pitchfork?" asked Jeanette, holding one high.

"You never know," said her husband. "Probably should take it."

"Here, allow me," said Aidan taking the pitchfork from her.

He lay it next to the manger. "There. Place it with the tines over the flames and that will be a proper grill on which to cook."

Mally disappeared to the rear of the barn. Quoting the well-known Old Testament scripture, he called out, "Hey! You think we could beat this plowshare into swords?"

"Only if we had enough time," said Aidan.

"We need a starter and some wood," said Mally.

Jeanette said, "Let's go," and started for the big barn doors. "What?" she said, when Mally looked at her incredulously. "You men just go about collecting your wood and I'll find the kindling." As she walked gingerly in her cute sneakers across the damp ground trending to mud, the men tramped off in different directions.

Mally looked at Aidan and shrugged sheepishly. "She's been bossing me around for over thirty years, so I don't know why I thought an apocalypse would stop her."

He had the build of a prop, the largest man on a rugby team, the position he'd played in primary school, but his tiny wife could keep him in line. He remembered his days on the pitch fondly. His team, like his school, had been made up of wee children from the mostly blue collar and somewhat less than posh neighborhood. All of them with dreams of playing professionally with accompanying fame and real fortune delivering them from their predestined working class existences. Mally's family a wee bit less than distinguished, but nonetheless, prideful. Being the funny one, he'd been well-liked by his mates on the team, even though he'd been no more than a substitute. The handsome, blonde-haired young lad he backed up went on to play at university and even won a tryout with the Heart of Midlothian Football Club of the Scottish Professional Football League. Would such a life ever be again?

Under the tall bare trees, it smelt of wet loam and huge flat-topped dark mushrooms; unfortunately for their shrinking stomachs, none of the fungi appeared esculent. The only reality that could be heard was the sound of permanence in the trees. The permanence of cold. The permanence of evil. The permanence of death.

It wasn't long before they rendezvoused, the men with armfuls of dead branches and Jeanette carrying twigs, small limbs, and pinecone pieces. The recent inclement weather had deposited all they needed on the ground. Her cute canvas sneakers were covered in mud. The Oxford Uni logo on her sweatshirt was obscured by dirt and detritus from the cones and small limbs she hugged to her body like treasure.

Mally's and Aidan's leather boots were covered in mud, too, but sturdier in construction so it didn't matter as much. She'd have to do something about her shoes before they got worse.

"Looks like we have the makings of a proper cook-fire," Aidan said.

"Indubitably," said Mally and headed to the Range Rover to get some canned vegetables.

"One more thing," said Jeanette. She gathered up an armful of fresh, dry hay to serve as a perfect starter.

"Now, we're ready," she said.

Using two wooden matches from a small box, Aidan lighted the pile of yellow straw in the manger. Little by little he placed small pieces of wood and pinecones atop the flames. Mally returned with an assortment of cans. Before long a hot healthy flame beckoned cans of food while Jeanette sorted the cans into a proper meal. She examined the tins for damage in an attempt to keep them all from getting sick. She threw out a dented can of asparagus. She didn't think they looked appetizing, anyway.

Lima beans, green beans, baby carrots, and yellow corn was a great start for a proper succotash. "If only we had some bacon and onions," Jeanette sighed.

"And salt," Mally added.

"You couldn't have it anyway. You know what the doctor said about your heart." Jeanette made sure Mally knew that even if it were the end of the world, he couldn't eat whatever the hell he wanted. Not as long as she was around, anyway.

"Ahh, what does that quack know, anyhow, with his fancy education and certificates and diplomas decorating the walls? No offense, Professor."

"Quite alright. None taken."

"And you couldn't have the bacon either, for that matter," she threw in for good measure.

Aidan said, "Let's go back to the house, find a pot or two and dishes and proper eating tools."

"I'll go," said Mally.

"It's getting darker. We should all stick close together for the time being. Just until we see how things shake out." Aidan was still worried about who or what they might encounter.

"Good idea," Mally agreed and the three tramped to the house. They held their breath and silently prayed for the old woman as they quickly stepped around her. They went to the kitchen.

"These dishes are too lovely to use in a manger in a barn," said Jeanette, peering into the cupboards, where she also found an assortment of spoons, forks and knives, and cloth napkins. And candles.

"You're such a girl, you are," said Mally.

"You wouldn't like me if I were a man," she said.

"No truer statement was ever said," he said honestly.

"Look, canned tuna," said Aidan. Verily, there were a half dozen cans in the pantry. He stacked them in his arm. "Let's get back to the barn," he said. "I'm not comfortable in here. It's like being in a tomb."

"Wait," said Mally. "Let's see if we can find some blankets."

"Can't hurt," said Jeanette. Aidan nodded.

In a small bedroom off the tidy parlour they found three heavy quilts stacked neatly on a large chair. These would come in handy, Jeanette thought as she picked them up. She noticed the uneven yet fine and close stitching and knew immediately these were hand stitched works of art. It took hundreds of hours to put together these intricate patterns and wondered about the meaning behind the squares. Were any made to remember the births of her children and grandchildren? Glancing around the room, she found what she expected: A quilter's frame attached to the ceiling and covered in a layer of dust. Somehow it was this quilting frame from a different era that made her want to cry more than all the death and destruction she'd recently witnessed.

They returned to the old barn and the straw, twigs, and small limbs they'd collected had grown to a substantial fire in the manger. Jeanette placed a large pot on the curved tines of the pitchfork, positioned it over the blaze and emptied the cans into the steaming vessel. The assorted vegetables began to give off heavenly smells. She seasoned the pot with black pepper from the original tin with the perforated lid she'd found in the cupboard. It was all she had. While the meal heated, she lit two candles. They must have been hungry to think the meager meal smelt that good. Jeanette filled bowls, pushed spoons into the succotash, and passed them to the men. Then served herself one. By flickering candlelight, in an ethereal, unsettling way, the dim scene was almost romantic.

Jeanette retained impeccable manners while eating, using a small spoon delicately and dabbing daintily at the corners of her mouth with a cloth napkin. Mally shoveled his. Aidan's manners were somewhere between the two. Not perfectly proper, but not like a mine worker's either.

"Damn," he said, softly. Even though the vegetables were softened, they still hurt Aidan's tooth; a canine on the upper right side.

"Do you know what would make this lovely?" Jeanette asked. "A nice bottle of champers."

Aidan said, "This could use a wee bit of salt, but I have to agree. A proper glass of the bubbly would be splendid. And it might stop this tooth from hurting." He rubbed the spot.

Mally chimed in. "I could do with a boilermaker, I could," his frayed blue collar showing. Jeanette flashed him a look that could kill. Of course he had probably said it only to get under her skin. And it had worked. But he did fancy his whisky and a pint.

"By the bye, the mathematician in my soul has been running some numbers," Aidan said.

"Do tell." Jeannette knew how he was when he got this way and the best way to deal with him was to just hear him out.

"There are roughly sixty-five million people in the U.K. It's over two-hundred and forty-two thousand square kilometers. That's around two-hundred and seventy-four people per square kilometer with a majority of those in five cities. Apparently, if the reports we heard before we left are accurate, a lot of them have died. So, the upshot is, we're not going to run into many people."

Jeanette said, "We'll take your word for it."

Mally said, "That's good news for us. But probably a lot of people that are still alive aren't dealing with the end of the world well and could be dangerous."

Σ Chapter Twenty-Two

Maryland:
Destination — Georgia Guidestones

Not The Ritz

"We need to find somewhere to spend the night," Strange announced.

After a short time in Delaware, they crossed the Mason Dixon Line and entered Maryland. He felt responsible for this little nomadic band and would do his best to make sure they were taken care of. A blue interstate sign read 'Maryland welcomes you' with the soft admonition to 'Please drive gently.'

"I'm going to try the first exit," said Strange.

And in perfect synchronicity, a moment later, immediately upon leaving the freeway, three economy hotels appeared. One even advertised in its name how comfortable you'd be, but even Comfort Inn appeared desolate.

"I don't think it matters which one we try," Strange said. With the hope of calling the least amount of attention to their presence, he pulled around back into the one furthest from the turnpike and parked. The rooms faced dark Maryland wilderness. They could only hope nothing desperate lurked there. Fleetwood rifled through the rear of the aging SUV searching for something they could use as a weapon or to break down a door. They walked toward the bank of rooms. He figured even the steel doors wouldn't stand up to the heavy crowbar he carried with a freshly born swag.

"Look," Cody said, pointing at an open door. Inside, a freshly-made room with two double beds; apparently housekeeping had decided there were more important things to do than make beds and vacuum hotel rooms at the end of the world. It looked as if they stopped in the middle of their chores. Strange and Fleet would take one bed, and Cody and Lace the other. Lugging gear into the room, they dropped it on the beds and floor.

"Let's see if there are anymore drink machines, or anything else we can get." In the breezeway between the rooms and the office-lobby was another soda machine with Pepsi products. They broke it open and picked the ones they wanted.

"Let's check out the kitchen. See what else we can find," said Lace. Unspeaking, Cody appeared almost comatose. A glass door to the rear of the hotel's lobby was locked, but the glass was shattered, allowing them easy entrance. But a male corpse lay on the floor behind the check-in desk. And it stunk. White maggots, each no more than a half an inch long, were feasting on the body, crawling in and out of the mouth, nose and eyes. The cash register drawer was fully open, cash slots empty. Probably hadn't held much anyway since most travelers paid by credit card.

But what good was money at the end of the world?

« Chapter Twenty-Three

Cumming, Georgia:
The Good Guys 'HQ

Reconnaissance

It was an hour before midnight when Patrick awoke. He didn't need an alarm clock. He was awakened by the internal clock he'd set.

"Guys, wake up." Without waking, Jeff snorted an unconscious response. Patrick kicked Jeff's foot. "Come on. Let's move."

Jeff and Bill shook their heads to stir the cobwebs.

"I'm ready," said Jeff.

"Me too," replied Bill, mechanically.

"We'll take my ride," said Patrick. They didn't want the Dwellers to hear them coming, so taking his Lexus SUV would be quieter than Bill's American-made pickup with its large V-8. Or Jeff's Hog, couldn't have him roaring on that.

Jeff said, "I don't know if I can ride in something that has four tires."

"We all must sacrifice something," Patrick laughed. "Let me thalk to Duncan before we go. Get him to eavesdrop on them, just in case." He concentrated on his cousin, and a moment later Duncan was there in his head, *"Hey, what's up?"*

"We're going to do a recon on the bad guys. Just wanted you to check on them, make sure everything's cool."

"We're thinking alike. I just was. They're not doing anything. Most of them are asleep. Even Dwellers need rest. Although we call it hibernation."

"Okay, cool. Thanks."

"Sure thing, Cuz. But, hey, watch your asses anyway."

"Will do. Thalk soon."

"I'll keep an 'ear' on you. I'd go with you, but we probably need to keep me hush-hush as long as we can. Kind of like your very own secret weapon."

"That's what I was thinking. We don't want them to go dark if they know you're out there." Patrick turned to Bill and Jeff. "Duncan says they're asleep. We're good to go."

Inside the SUV, Patrick plugged in the iPod which held nothing but classical music that the Dwellers hated. They hadn't needed it in years. "Just to make sure," he said.

"Better safe than sorry," Jeff agreed. "Best not to take chances with those dudes."

They headed west on Highway 20 until they came to a billboard advertising a school of Jiu Jitsu. It rose up over a squat small building housing a chiropractic clinic. The low building appeared to have been a barber shop in the Fifties. It was probable the physician opened the practice under the sign guessing that students would need treatments after the rigorous classes. It was likely neither the school nor clinic had much business during The Plague, even if the proprietors themselves were still alive. The covert team turned right next to the sign. The road meandered by a used car lot, then a now-silent cell tower, and eventually on past a small Baptist church before turning left on the rough two-lane road that rose almost straight up the rugged mountainside. The church had probably had a full house the previous Sunday. The end of the world is always good for the preaching business.

They didn't go too far before Bill said, "We park here. Hike the rest of the way. Quieter, no lights, and if they expect anything to happen they'd expect it to come from someone riding up the main road. Not skulking through the trees like wild animals."

"Sounds good," said Patrick, braking hard and jerking to a stop, cutting off the lights simultaneously. "Shut the doors softly. Animals don't usually close car doors. At least not loudly."

"Not funny, dude," Jeff said.

"I'd say leave them open if it weren't for the door lights," Patrick said, slapping his forehead. "I wasn't thinking. Should have disabled them."

Jeff uncoiled a rubberband from around his wrist, popping it as he did, then pulled his long brown hair back taut from his face into a ponytail, winding the rubberband around it. He was ready to go.

Z Chapter Twenty-Four

Unknown Shires of England:
Destination — Stonehenge

Day Two

Mally asked Jeanette for more vegetables.

She dished up a small bowl. "Get them while they're hot. We have plenty."

"Got to fill up on something since we're saving the tuna." He was a lifelong serious meat-eater and used the protein to build the muscle he had cultivated and was proud of.

"I know."

"How about me?" asked Aidan.

"Of course, sir," she joked. "How about the Chef's Special?"

"A wee bit, please. And by a wee bit I mean as much as you can spare," he said with a grin. "That would be lovely."

"You got it." She scooped more into the bowl he held out for her.

It didn't take long before they finished eating. Jeanette said, "I want to go back to the house and wash the dishes we used." She couldn't help it. She was old school. It was just the way she was raised. If she were going to break into someone's home, borrow dishes, and sleep in their barn, the least she could do was wash them. Especially since it would be considered rude to leave dirty dishes for all eternity.

"I'll go with you," Mally said. Always the dutiful husband, he helped her gather the dishes and take them inside. Aidan helped. Now that it was even darker, they certainly didn't want any of them to be alone. While inside, they used the toilet and brushed their teeth, then headed back to the barn to settle in next to the glow of the remaining fire's embers and the candles. Aidan mumbled a good night.

"'Night, boss," Jeanette said. She could just make out his scowl in the dim firelight. She carried a pair of lace-up boots she'd borrowed from the old woman's dark closet. They would probably be a wee bit small, but still better than her trainers. She had no idea just how much she would be walking and how much those boots would help more than her trainers.

"Goodnight, Professor," said Mally.

"Goodnight, mate," said Aidan. Spending extended time with the blue-collar Mally was beginning to loosen his tight arse up. In the deep dark of night, Aidan was awakened by a cough. It came from him. Startled, his pulse quickened. But his throat was scratchy and his patrician nose stuffy. Then he sneezed. A garden variety cold, it seemed, and not The Plague. Still, for a moment it chilled him to the marrow of his blue-blood bones. He hadn't slept outside since he was a mere lad. He didn't fancy it then and he didn't fancy it now.

Aidan looked at his SuperOcean Automatic 44 Breitling watch. The luminous face showed at least four hours until dawn. If they were going to make it to Stonehenge before nightfall they'd need to get an early start. He fluffed the hay beneath him and tried to tuck his blanket to seal out more of the cold. Jeanette snored softly. It sounded like a docile house cat's contented purring. But before he could return to slumber, a ghastly growl from the first layer of trees curdled his blood.

Mally was startled awake by it, too. Even though the barn door was shut, he was up with his rusted but trusty firearm at the ready. It occurred to Mally that if they all didn't die, he'd have to remember to clean the beloved heirloom when the trek was over. Aidan heard the click of metal against metal, loud in the dark, when Mally pulled the hammer back to cock the ancient Webley.

"What in the bloody hell was that?" Mally asked, not expecting an answer.

"I've never heard anything like that except at the London Zoo," said Aidan.

"Never heard a pissed off snarl like that at the zoo."

They both remained on high alert, glad to not hear the unnerving sound again.

The adrenalin rush kept Aidan awake. He pondered the end of humanity and postulated existentialism. He questioned Sartre. Sartre could always be counted on to put him to sleep. And eventually…it worked again; but not long after, the first dull light from the rising ill sun began to worm its way through slits of the wood-slatted barn wall that faced east. Still, it barely tampered with the heavy grey gloom.

Aidan rose with the groan of a man beginning to feel his forties, put his hands on his hips and bent at the waist, stretching in all directions. His joints popped like New Year's Eve fireworks or, since it was almost Halloween, the bones of a naughty skeleton. His back hurt from sleeping on the hay-covered hard dirt floor. He went outside with a bucket to get some more of the ice-cold well water for shaving and to brush his teeth. A dim but full moon resembling a failing overhead floodlight hung suspended above the black trees.

Aidan remembered it was almost Halloween. A bitter wind blew. The white of his breath scattered on the gust.

Σ Chapter Twenty-Five

Maryland:
Destination — Georgia Guidestones

Exploration

"Check that out," said Cody, pointing across the road to a liquor store that had partial electricity. The large sign above the entrance read World Beverage in four-foot tall letters, but because the neon letters were independently lighted, the 'Beve' in Beverage had gone dark so that the sign now read 'World   rage.' Then someone with a morbid sense of humor had painted 'of' between the two remaining words to make an apt and fitting title for an apocalypse.

World of rage.

Below the sign in front of the store, at this place between Genesis and the end of the world, two young men were tossing a football in the parking lot. Was it for exercise or to try and take their minds off death and destruction? Was this an attempt at normalcy to keep their sanity what with unpleasant death all but certain, but if they lived in a future that was unknown? Was it they who had been the artist whose creativity on the sign showed what they thought about the end times?

They stopped playing and turned to stare. No way to know if they were just surprised to see living people, or had nefarious ideas, but Strange wasn't going to wait to find out. He said, "I don't trust those two. Let's get out of here."

The four grabbed their belongings, threw themselves in the vehicle, and hauled ass as fast as the congested road would let them.

"Hey, Fleet. How about you crack the seal on that bottle of whiskey you got?"

"Sounds good to me." Fleet rummaged into his pack and pulled out the Bushmills.

Strange looked into the rearview at Cody and Lace. "Waaat aboyt de two av yer? Cud yer chucker wi' a wee sip av de Oirish?"

Spending all those years on radio and doing voiceovers for commercials meant his fake Irish accent wasn't half bad and made Lace and Cody smile; they shrugged in reluctant acceptance.

Speaking for both of them, Cody said, "Sure. Let me get some cups." She had picked some up from the hotel room. Fleet poured two fingers in each cup.

"Ice sure would be nice right now," Strange said, one hand on the wheel. He tilted the plastic cup at the group and made a toast. "In any case, here's to not having ice, the end of the world, and a successful conclusion to our trip."

They raised their cups. "I got your back, man," Fleetwood said.

"Draink 'eartily, boys an' birds," Strange said. Fleetwood tilted his glass and gave him a wink and a nod. Then the four momentarily got lost in the peace of the rich amber liquid, forgetting about the world around them just for a moment, then returning to think of the coming what-ifs.

» Chapter Twenty-Six

Sawnee Mountain, Georgia:
Evil Dwellers 'HQ

Deception

Drummond's concentration paid off as counterparts in England were summoned. He asked if they were getting any significant pushback.

One of the Dwellers in the River Thames thalked back. *"We're misleading a small group from Edinburgh University. They think they can end The Plague by praying before Stonehenge, so we're encouraging them, making them think they're on to something. It won't do shit. Just a little misdirection."*

"Sounds like a splendid plan. I'll inform Queen Gertrude. She'll be pleased," thalked Drummond. What Drummond didn't say was that not much pleased Queen Gertrude. But it was unnecessary to dash a lackey's hopes. The large room he was in was filled with the latest technology and served as the nerve center for the Dwellers' operation.

"The perimeter is secure?" thalked Queen Gertrude to the men watching the CCTV screens.

"Yes, Your Majesty. The only problem is animals. Even small rodents are setting off the perimeter lights."

"Can the sensitivity be turned down?"

"Certainly, we just don't want to go too far with it."

"Use your own judgment." What she blocked him from hearing was "But it's your ass if anything goes wrong."

"Thank you, Your Majesty."

« Chapter Twenty-Seven

Sawnee Mountain, Georgia:
Evil Dwellers 'HQ

The Good Guys: Recon

The covert team exited the luxury Lexus quietly. Patrick's beloved dead wife, Trudy, now known as Queen Gertrude, was in the highest point of the mansion. They could see the tip above the trees against the dark sky.

Taking the lead up a path made by large animals, Patrick paused and said *sotto voce*, "Bill, I just thought of something. I know how to kill undeads one at a time. But how do you kill a bunch of them?"

Colonel Crain said, "The army can help us with that."

"Sweet. I hoped you would come up with something."

They followed the red clay path, though it wasn't highly visible in the moonlight diffused as it was by the dark evergreen canopy. Three steps further and bright floodlights turned night into day. A heartbeat later followed the angry loud rhythm of automatic gunfire cutting into the tree trunks. They dove to the ground and let the deadly fire pass over them. The guards had fired at random. They couldn't see the invaders and fired indiscriminately, but they could still get lucky. Crain gave a barely visible hand signal to saddle up and get back to the vehicle double-time. They belly crawled scrambling down the hill collecting brambles, scratches, and red clay as they went.

They jumped in the SUV and slammed doors with Patrick simultaneously starting the engine, engaging gears, and spinning the vehicle around to head back down the mountain. Patrick said, "I guess that's enough recon, huh?"

They were back at his home before zero three hundred hours.

Resuming their positions on the two sofas and the leather chair, though unhappy they were back so soon, they slept the sleep of the dead. Morning's light did nothing to rouse them. Patrick gained consciousness at eleven and started coffee on his camp stove. Jeff and Bill were awakened by the glorious aroma. Bill, like many current and former members of the military, drank his black. Jeff and Patrick both hurt the coffee's feelings by adding cream from the last bottle Patrick had drowning in melting slushy ice in a Styrofoam ice chest.

Gesturing with his mug, Jeff said, "You're going to make somebody a good wife." He blew on his hot caffeine before sipping.

"Smart ass. You never change."

"You wouldn't know what to do if I did. But I do think I've finally unpuckered," he added.

"I wish I had," Bill said, chiming in, "I've been shot at hundreds of times. I never get used to it."

"I'm with you, Bill," Patrick said. "I've never been shot at before, but I can tell you right now, I do not like it and hope it never happens again."

"So what's next?" Jeff asked.

Bill answered. "Well, one thing's for sure, we don't have to be in a hurry. They already launched The Plague, so can't stop that. Unless I'm wrong, we've got a revenge mission going on here."

Seeking revenge on his wife, Patrick thought. He hated it. She had been his love like no other; but she had ceased to be his beloved Trudy when she was tortured, killed, kidnapped, then coopted by the Dwellers. "You aren't wrong, Bill," Patrick said sadly.

Z Chapter Twenty-Eight

Unknown Shires of England:
Destination — Stonehenge

A Change in Plans

Aidan's icy well-water shave was invigorating. It did what he had intended and served to motivate him and get him ready to start moving in the cold of early morning. Fortunately, he'd thought to put a new five-blade cartridge in his razor before they got the hell out of Dodge. He didn't know how long the blades would last. He usually swapped them out twice a week even though they would have given a clean shave for longer.

He poured a bucket of cold water over his head washing his body in a concrete-floored stall where horses would have been washed. He wondered where they were. Had someone set them free? He hoped so. Even so, it was probable they were dead by now. Even though it offended his senses, he dressed in the previous day's clothes then joined Mally and Jeanette heating more veggies over the fire. Jeanette was unwilling to dirty more dishes and have to wash them, so they ate from the hot tins with their fingers. They too, had put on the previous day's clothes. Except Jeanette who had laced on her borrowed boots.

They finished their food less enthusiastically than the night before, put out the fire, and gathered their belongings.

Aidan said, "I'll go warm up the Rover and turn on the heated seats so it won't be so cold. Then we'll be off. Early bird catches the worm and all that rot."

Mally said, "Or maybe the early bird gets the worms."

"Couldn't be as bad as The Plague," he said, and headed out of the barn.

Jeanette said, "Mally, speaking of birds. I miss their singing."

Mally listened and, indeed, there were no sounds at all except for their voices. All around them nothing but the somber sound of death. "I miss the sounds of everything. All we ever hear is the goddamn wind."

In the SUV, Aidan hit the ignition and it hesitated. Held his breath. And though not a religious man, he mouthed a silent prayer. It finally caught. "Thank you, Lord," he said out loud. Thankful for his childhood catechism classes, he made the sign of the cross, and even threw in a grateful Hail Mary. He turned on the seat heaters, gave the petrol pedal a couple of vigorous pumps, then left the engine running while he went to help Jeannette and Mally bring the rest of their stuff. He wasn't worried about anyone stealing his pride and joy.

Back on the road, rural England was even less congested than what they'd already seen. And that had been very little. A hundred kilometers and an hour later the big SUV's engine sputtered twice and fell as silent as the breathless world. When the power steering shut down Aidan was barely able to muscle it to the side of the road. He managed however, to get it to the weedy grass, off the highway. Even though he knew what it would say, he glanced at the fuel gauge. It showed an almost full tank. He bumped the key and got nothing for his trouble, not even a click.

"Let's give it a look," said Mally, opening the door. Aidan popped the hood. Battery cables looked fine, they were clean and nothing else was obviously wrong.

"Probably the alternator," Mally said.

"Shite," Aidan shouted. "We're done for if that's the case." He stared at the dead SUV, then turned to Jeannette and Mally. "I guess you guys have a decision to make. To wander around to our goal was not my first choice. Nonetheless, I will carry on. I must, even if I have to trod the rest of the way. It will probably take a couple of months, but I feel like I have to do it for all of man."

Jeanette said, "I certainly didn't plan on walking to Stonehenge, but we're with you. What are we going to do? Walk back?"

"She's the boss," said Mally.

"I like your attitude," said Aidan. He only hoped the Range Rover would be there when they got back.

If they got back.

Σ Chapter Twenty-Nine

Maryland:
Destination — Georgia Guidestones

A New Dawn, A New Day

Strange was the only one whose head wasn't pounding from too much Irish whiskey. Then again, it was probably because he was the only one used to over-imbibing in God's gift to the Emerald Isle, the Black Rose country. He awoke to the moans of the others.

"I should know better," whined Lace, "I'm a doctor, for God's sake. I know what alcohol does to your brain." Her already strident voice was particularly astringent.

Cody said, "I love you, Lace, but please…be quiet."

Lace began to cry. That upset Cody because she knew it was a natural reaction to all the death around them, and probably their own in the not too distant future. Fleet and Strange had slept in their street clothes. They stepped outside to let Cody and Lace have some privacy to get dressed. To ward off the early morning cold, they sat in Strange's Toyota but didn't start the engine, even though they would have liked heat. But gas had to be conserved. An hour later they knocked on the door to the room. Cody opened it, dressed in clean clothes, smelling of perfume and said, "We're ready." Lace had done the same. They were girls, after all.

Strange said, "Good. Let's take this show on the road."

Cody said, "Come on, Lace; before Strange has a fit. We have a date with destiny."

Lace shouldered her duffel but wasn't as enthusiastic about it as Cody sounded.

Before they pulled out of the parking lot, Strange asked, "How about some music?" The old Toyota was dated, thus it had only a radio and a cassette player. He shuffled through a vinyl-covered box, before pulling out a cassette. Holding it aloft, like a sought after prize, he said, "Look, The Cranberries. How about *Zombie*? I think that's appropriate for the end of the world."

Everybody thought he'd crossed over a big bold line with that one. Fleetwood made sure he knew it. "Dude, this is some serious shit. Even if we don't die, the world as we know it is over. Why don't you ease up on the goddamn Armageddon jokes?"

"Sorry, man. No prob. Sorry, Cody, Lace."

"It's okay," Lace said. "I'll be fine."

"Then let's do it." Properly chastised, Strange was still in a rush to get down the road. He pulled out of the parking lot and drove slowly through an intersection formerly congested with traffic, now congested with disabled vehicles. As he negotiated the obstacles, two young men ran up to their vehicle, pounding the windows with their fists. Seems the cars had not been as disabled and random as they appeared and had been moved there strategically in a calculated plan to commit mayhem.

Strange stayed focused, ignored the threat, cleared the junction and sped away, one of the two clinging to the roof rack until he was able to shake him loose by swerving and hitting the brakes. He watched him tumble to a stop on the pavement in the rearview mirror.

"That was scary," said Lace.

"I'll say," said Fleetwood. "It was my window he was trying to break."

"And they looked pretty normal," said Cody.

This time it was Fleetwood who said, "What did you expect? For them to look like zombies?"

Lace could have throttled him. Abnormally calm, Strange said, "Baltimore calls."

They made their way to the entrance ramp to continue south on I-85. The nearer to Baltimore they got the more choked the freeway became with disabled and abandoned vehicles. He was rarely able to shift the five speed standard transmission out of second gear.

A flying vee of geese migrating south for the winter soared silently high overhead. The geese were undisturbed by a squad of fighter jets flying even higher with their white contrails of condensed water forming a giant tic-tac-toe square covering hundreds of miles as they kept watch over the Eastern Seaboard. The sky, though, was indifferent to the reason for a dearth of aircraft high above the world's busiest airspace.

The Baltimore skyline drew nearer on the right. Lace said, "Some Baltimore crab cakes sure would be good."

"Sure would, but you shouldn't torture yourself," Cody agreed, smoothing Lace's hair.

"I'd like some New England-style clam chowder," said Fleetwood.

"What about you, Strange? What would you like to eat?" he asked.

"A Nathan's Famous Red Hot at Yankee Stadium during the World Series, because that would mean the world was normal."

They all agreed that would be the best. Strange decided to stick to the interstate that mostly bypassed Baltimore, or at the very least only brushed the outskirts, since the entire East Coast was mostly urban. He didn't think it was worth the risk of encountering more survivors with bad intentions.

A gray ash covered every surface. Although there had been no fire, nuclear explosion, or man made catastrophe of any sort, it appeared that the entire earth, or at least as much of it as they could see, was turning forever gray. Maudlin, leaden clouds obscured the dirge-like sky.

It started to rain, turning the ash to mush. Lace began to cry.

Fleetwood said, "What's the matter? Why are you crying?"

"What's the matter? What's the matter? Everything's the matter." With fists balled, Lace pounded the back of the seat in front of her with each statement. "It's starting to rain. It's the end of the world. Armageddon. Whatever the fuck you want to call the end of mankind. We. Are. All. Going to die, for God's sake. I've got a better question. Why aren't you crying?"

Cody tried to calm Lace, but Fleetwood snapping back at her didn't help matters much. "Thanks for reminding me. Appreciate it. Really, I needed that."

Strange hollered, "Hey! Everybody stay calm. At least until it's time not to be calm."

"And when will that be?" asked Lace and turned to cry on Cody's shoulder.

Strange took a deep breath to buy a moment of time before answering. Recalling the two that had attacked the truck, he said, "I guess if we see gangs of bad guys coming after us." Seeing the sudden look of despair appear on Lace's face, he quickly added, "But, I'm not saying we will."

» Chapter Thirty

Sawnee Mountain, Georgia:
Evil Dwellers 'HQ

Discovery

"What the fuck is going on?" Queen Gertrude thalked to the man monitoring the perimeter defenses.

"Don't know yet, Your Majesty, but probably just a medium-sized animal," the bespectacled creature of unknown previous origin thalked back.

"For your sake you better hope to hell it is."

What the queen conveniently forgot was she'd been the one who suggested changing the sensitivity. Then again, facts didn't matter when it came to doling out punishment. It was the first time he'd been on the receiving end of the ire he'd only heard rumors about, and he didn't want to experience it again. Queen Gertrude instructed Drummond and Bad Penny to dispatch a team to search the grounds at morning's first light. Find out what the hell the disturbance was.

At daybreak, Drummond and Bad Penny searched the circumference until they found the path Patrick's crew had belly-crawled down back to their vehicle. Gravel had been scattered when the vehicle peeled out. Putting it mildly, Queen Gertrude would not be pleased.

Bad Penny confronted the security team as soon as they returned. *"Well?"* His tone almost made them piss their pants. *"Somebody was out there. We saw where they crawled to avoid the gunfire and where their vehicle was parked. Something big. She Who Must Be Feared won't be happy we were almost breached."*

"That's not my fault," said the team leader.

"Quit your whining, bitch." Bad Penny could be as hard as the queen, and it pleased him.

« Chapter Thirty-One

Cumming, Georgia:
The Good Guys 'HQ

Reassessing

"I've been thinking."

Patrick quipped, "Isn't that something you never want to hear from military intelligence?"

"Do you know how many times I've heard that?" the Colonel said. "Anyway, rocket launchers, sure would come in handy."

"Love it," said Jeff.

"While I don't share his enthusiasm, I'm keeping an open mind," said Patrick.

"We can make a trip to Fort McPherson. Quick trip to south side of Atlanta near East Point. Hopefully everyone's dead and we can just stroll in and take whatever we want."

"Brilliant," said Jeff. "If only it would be that easy."

"Again, I don't share his enthusiasm, but I can see where that could work."

"Then we leave early in the morning. Might take most of the day. We'll need as many of those bad boys as we can find. Put them in my pickup's bed. Not to mention anything else we might can find that will help us."

"Sounds like a plan," said Patrick.

Jeff and Patrick spent the afternoon working out. Pushups, body weight squats, jumping jacks, anything they could think of to get their blood moving. Having gotten the lay of the land the night before, Bill began strategizing their next assault on the mansion.

Z Chapter Thirty-Two

Unknown Shires of England:
Destination — Stonehenge

On Foot

"Get everything you can carry. It's possible we could need anything."

Aidan grabbed a bound leather notebook and pen from the glove box before he emptied his toolbox in the rear storage compartment of the SUV. They stashed tools in every pocket. Screwdrivers, hammers, wrenches, pliers, wire cutters. A tire-tool would make a capable weapon. Writing his daily thoughts in a journal might form the basis of a book if he — and the world — survived this. If not, it would help them keep track of tasks they should do as they traversed to Stonehenge to meet their goal of saving the world.

The last item he grabbed was his iPad. It was his security blanket, even though he wouldn't be able to use it for long with its battery soon to die and the Internet a rapidly fading memory and soon to be thought of as a disinvention. He'd had it for so long he couldn't take a step without it. A psychologically necessary crutch. Everybody had one, and so did Aidan.

It wasn't possible to predict everything they might need. Each clutched a triple-lined plastic trash bag filled with their bedding and clothes. They stuffed overnight bags with cans of food and stuffed their backpacks full as well. Aidan pushed the button on his key fob to lock the doors to his pride and joy — the yellow parking lights flashed in reply at him through the fog and the mist — and they set off plodding south at a slow but committed pace.

The planet smelt of mouldy grey death.

Angry with his expensive SUV for breaking down, frustrated and scared at the end of humanity, Aidan dug in his pack until he found a heavy tin can of red beans. Examining the label thoughtfully, he wrapped his long fingers angrily around it and threw it at the glass windscreen with all the force he could muster. It clunked away in beaten despair.

A cold wind began to blow as they walked. Denuded trees with lonely conifers interspersed among them rose above a low underbrush wall encroaching on both sides of the road. The gentle quiet wind scattered trash, soda cans, and bits of paper on the road. The soft sound of the wind and swirling trash on the pavement were somehow comforting, vanquishing the prevailing ghastly silence that overarched all. Like people were present. Like life was normal. Whatever that was these days.

The land was mostly flat with a few gently rolling hills. If indeed they made it to Stonehenge and if one believed one gets a limited number of steps in life, then they could be assured of using their allotment before their time was ended.

Σ Chapter Thirty-Three

The District of Columbia:
Destination — Georgia Guidestones

The Capitol

South of Baltimore, DC was next. Two more pair of fighter jets flew high overhead. Cody said, "I think that's proof the President is still alive."

"Big deal," said Strange. "What can he do?"

"Well, I hope he can get The Centers For Disease Control down in Atlanta working on it, if they aren't already. Those scientists at the CDC are geniuses."

Strange said, "They might be good, if any are even still alive, but I think what we're going to do has a better chance of stopping The Plague than they do."

"I hope you're right," said Cody.

"Of course, I don't have any other fuckin' clue what might work."

"If *we* are mankind's best hope, then I'm really frightened," Lace moaned.

« Chapter Thirty-Four

Greater Atlanta:
The Good Guys

Acquisitions

On a typical day the trip from Cumming, on the northern reaches of Atlanta, to East Point, Georgia, where Fort McPherson is located south of the ATL, could take anywhere from just over an hour to almost two, depending on the time of day and traffic. Today, with abandoned vehicles and vehicular coffins littering every mile of the way, it took over three and a half hours to make the less than fifty mile one-way trip.

Having left before breakfast at eight a.m., Jeff was hungry. "I sure could use a Whopper," he said.

"What, no fries?" Patrick couldn't help throwing some shade his friend's way.

"No, dude. You know I've got to stay in fighting condition to do battle with the Dwellers."

"Is that anything like football condition?"

"Almost exactly the same."

"Okay, just checking."

The gate entering the base was locked and chained and the guard shack empty. Bill stopped short of it. Looked like the United States Army had closed up shop and gone home.

"You got a tire tool?" Jeff asked.

"In the toolbox in back. Whatcha gonna do?"

"Just stand back and watch."

Patrick grinned while Bill wondered if the tire tool would come back in one piece. They heard metal clanking against metal as Jeff dug around in the huge lidded container. A second later his head popped up, a proud grin spreading across his face. He jogged to the gate and wedged the flat end of the tool between the heavy steel fingers of the lock. Using his two-hundred sixty pounds of muscle, he snapped it in a matter of seconds and swung the gate open leaving the heavy link chain hanging. When he turned around his grin was even bigger. Jeff hopped in the big white pickup.

"I haven't been here in awhile," Bill pointed, "but if I remember correctly we follow this road around back to the left. Ammo depot is in a concrete front building that looks like a huge Quonset hut the size of a football field. We're lucky we have Jeff here for his expertise with locks."

They followed the perfectly maintained road lined with trees draped in fall colors until they came upon the large building on the right he described. Having never been in the military, Jeff and Patrick were surprised at just how tidy and neat everything appeared, especially during Armageddon. Grass shorn, shrubs trimmed, trees pruned. Pretty, even under the heavy gray, indifferent sky. Apparently it had just been maintained right before people started dying.

Bill pulled to a stop in front of a single steel door. "Okay, Jeff, do your thing."

This time Jeff took the heavy iron tire tool and pounded until it swung open. Glistening in cool sweat, he stepped to the side, sweeping his hand like Vanna White unveiling a new car, to let Bill and Patrick do the honor of passing through first. He followed them as they entered the medium-sized front office area. It contained two wooden desks, still strewn with papers from the last day their occupants worked. They passed through a short, slatted swinging door, past the desks, to a glass-paned door to the warehouse.

Bill said, "Small arms and ammo in the front, ending with the largest ordnance at the rear. What we're looking for — weapons and shells — should be about midway."

Indeed, halfway to the rear on the left side were long wooden crates labeled with a series of letters and numbers that indicated to the colonel they contained the weapons they coveted. Jeff cracked open a wooden crate and, at Bill's urging, they took two cases of the M-16s. Patrick and Jeff cocked their heads and raised their eyebrows as if asking if a dozen high-powered semi-automatic rifles with rocket launchers attached were necessary. The retired colonel noted their looks of question and said, "An old army axiom. Better to have it and not need it than to need it and not have it."

Jeff and Patrick had to nod in agreement. Patrick laid the crates on a flatbed pushcart, then gently placed four smaller boxes, each containing a dozen rockets, on a nearby hand truck. Wouldn't want to jostle them in a warehouse full of thousands of tons of lethal explosives.

It felt like they were collecting needed items for the house at The Home Depot. Next to the rockets was a case of a dozen flare guns.

"I've always wanted to play with one of those," Jeff said.

"Let's get some, then," said Bill, picking up the box and putting it on the hand truck. "Really?" Jeff's eyes lit up like a kid's.

"Why not?"

"Awesome! I always wondered what would happen if you shot somebody in the gut with one of these. Flames and sparks going everywhere. Catching shit on fire."

"Maybe you'll get to find out," Bill said quietly.

Returning to the front of the ammo depot, they gathered as much 9mm ammo as they could carry. At the front they also located a store of jungle camouflage BDUs and got two XXL sets and one small one. They were lucky to find sizes to fit Jeff and Patrick. With their acquisitions they probably thought they were prepared for a war with Rhode Island.

Back in the truck, Jeff said, "How about some lunch? I'm buying."

"Is food all you think about?" Patrick knew his friend had a high metabolism from his days as a college football All-American.

"No, I think about beer, too."

"I remember. And if we find a Burger King with workers that are still alive we'll take you up on your offer."

"Maybe we'll find one with a skeleton crew," Jeff said, with a smart-ass grin.

Bill Crain groaned. "Man, I can't believe he said that."

"Really," agreed Patrick.

» Chapter Thirty-Five
Sawnee Mountain, Georgia:
Evil Dwellers 'HQ

Hell To Pay

Queen Gertrude was in no better mood with daylight's arrival. Bad Penny gave her the news that the search team had found evidence of intruders.

"Fuckin' mouth-talkers." It was a derogatory term they'd come up with for those people who believed Dwellers weren't as evolved as normal humans yet were unable to communicate by merely thinking. *"So, who the fuck were they?"*

"I'm sorry, Your Majesty. There's no way of knowing."

"Well by God, somebody better find out or their ass is mine."

***

Bad Penny found Drummond relaxing in the common room. *"That certainly wasn't fun."*

"What wasn't fun?"

"Telling the Queen we had intruders last night."

"Better you than me."

"Thanks a lot."

Z Chapter Thirty-Six

Unknown Shires of England:
Destination — Stonehenge

Reality

Aidan had wanted the expensive SUV for as long as he could remember. Truth was, though, it was only a car. If it's not the end of the world he'd get another one. If it is the end, it won't matter anyway.

"So how long do you think it will take us to get to the Henge?" Jeanette asked, not sure if she wanted to know.

"I think we can make it by Christmas. Which would be an appropriate time to save the planet, don't you think?"

"Two whole months?" Jeanette said forlornly. "I don't think I'll make it."

"I'll carry you if I have to," said Mally comfortingly.

"If there's one thing I've learned from running marathons, it's don't think about all the steps. Just take one more," Aidan advised.

"I'll try," she sighed.

"Good girl," said Mally, taking her by the hand.

Aidan gazed skyward, a dour look on his face. A white-tailed eagle with its eight-foot wingspan sailed on the breeze. Beautiful but deadly. He hoped it wasn't planning on picking their bones when they were dead. Taking their remains back to his eyrie to share with the young in his care. That thought served as added motivation to stay alive. They walked along the two-lane road lined on both sides with almost-bare hardwood trees.

"What do you remember about the night we met?" Mally asked Jeanette, trying to keep her mind off her fears.

She smiled. "Ah. It was Saint Patrick's Day. How handsome you looked in your Kelly green double-breasted suit. And you had a fresh haircut. You looked quite spivvy. I was immediately smitten." She added sarcastically, "I promised I would never tell Aidan about that suit and I won't."

"Thanks luv. And you were beautiful in a pink dress."

"It was yellow."

"What, dear?"

"The dress. It was yellow."

Aidan fought unsuccessfully to wipe the grin away, while he shook his head. He tried to save the conversation in his grey matter so he could record it in the journal once settled down for the night.

"I was just kidding. I knew it was yellow."

Jeanette gave him that look. "Yes dear, sure you did."

Even though he struggled with the bag, Mally raised his right hand as if he was swearing an oath. Jeanette looked at him doubtfully. Truth was, Mally had been smitten hard. Being wayward would have never entered his mind. To that very day he had never strayed. Before long, in the face of God-only-knows-what, all three were laughing. And their pace quickened with their laughter, which was good, because the longer they walked the slower the pace would be. So putting pavement behind them while they could was important.

A light, cold rain began to fall. Mally tried to hold his backpack above Jeanette to afford her protection, but even with his large muscles, the bag, laden as it was, quickly became too heavy for him to hold aloft. They struggled to continue.

Jeanette's tears mixed with the rain. Even for Aidan, a triathlete, it was all he could do to keep from succumbing to the cold and rain. A small animal skittered through the dying underbrush beneath the trees, drawing Mally's attention. Not usually one to be jumpy, the probable end of the world had even the strong man on edge. For hours they walked south, the callous grey sky pregnant with more rain and darkening with the approaching end of day.

The days of autumn were growing shorter. Worse yet they hadn't seen the bright shining sun for a while. At this rate, day and night would soon look no different. Rain made the crumbling macadam roadway slippery. It was harder to continue.

"The next abandoned house we see we should probably stop for the night."

Jeanette groaned, "Thank God."

Mally said, "You'll be fine once you have some food and rest."

"I doubt I'll ever be fine again."

Σ Chapter Thirty-Seven

District of Columbia:
Destination — Georgia Guidestones

The Seat Of Government

The freeway passed near enough to the city to see the Capitol's dome.

"Tell me I'm imagining it, but does the dome look dusty, like it's covered in ash?"

"You're not imagining it, Cody. I think all the death happening on the planet, human and other, it's fucking up the environment. Who knows? If The Plague doesn't get us, Mother Nature might."

"Thanks, Strange," Cody said. She gave him a look that could kill.

"Sure, anytime." Then it dawned on him what she meant. "Oops, sorry."

"But don't you think that the president has a special group working on this, trying to come up with a cure, a vaccination — something to stop it. I mean this is the U.S. Government. They have the smartest minds on the planet available to them, just to think shit up." Cody had thought it through logically. "And they double up on everything. They probably have another group sitting around thinking shit up backing up the first group."

"For God's sake, I hope so," Strange said. "But until then I still think *we* are the best chance the world has."

Lace shouted, "Then the world is truly fucked."

« Chapter Thirty-Eight

Cumming, Georgia:
The Good Guys 'HQ

Prepare For War

Over morning's coffee on the outdoor terrace, Crain said, "I have a plan. So I need you guys to shoot holes in it."

"We can do that," said Patrick.

"Who can you count on, if not your friends," Bill agreed. "Thanks a lot."

"We got your back, Colonel," said Jeff.

"Anyway, we attack during the day. We know they guard the perimeter at night. We've got our camouflage. We should be able to get close enough to use the rocket launchers to take out the machine gun sites and crumble the mansion. Then — and this is where the fun starts — we go in with small arms fire and we eliminate all resistance."

"Fun?" Jeff said.

Patrick said, "I like it…until the part where we go in with small arms fire. Jeff used to be a deputy but he and I aren't soldiers, remember?"

"Then I feel even better since he was a deputy, and I have faith in you guys. I'll train you. We'll set up a range on your back lawn. I don't think you have any neighbors left to complain and I'll have you experts in shooting in a week's time."

Patrick looked skeptical, but said, "You know I have faith in you, Bill. If you say you can do it, then I believe it."

» Chapter Thirty-Nine

Sawnee Mountain, Georgia:
Evil Dwellers 'HQ

Double Down

"That cannot happen again." Queen Gertrude spewed venom to the intelligent creatures manning the CCTV stations. Nobody had ever seen her like this. *"We expand the perimeter, turn up the sensitivity on the floodlights and double the manpower at night. No offense to you non-humans."*

Everybody in the basement command center, human and non-human alike, fidgeted after that comment. No further intrusions occurred during the nights to follow. Even forest creatures, some probably no more than two generations removed from some of the more animalistic Dwellers, seemed to have gotten word they shouldn't run afoul of Queen Gertrude. Which was just fine with her.

"I'm calling a conference with the heads in Europe," she thalked to Drummond and Bad Penny. *"I want to hear directly from them how things are going over there."*

"Sounds like a splendid idea, Your Majesty," thalked Drummond. He couldn't help laying it on thick, it was simply his proper British upbringing.

"I need good news. Sometimes they think they can do their own thing and I need to make sure they know who's in charge from time to time."

"I'm sure they know you're the boss, Your Majesty," Bad Penny said quietly.

"Thank you, Penny. And that's why you're my favorite."

Bad Penny beamed while stealing a quick glance at Drummond. Everyone wanted to curry favor with the Queen. Even a badass who never kissed anybody's ass; it could mean the difference in life and death.

"So Professor, can we thalk about your contacts in England and what they told you?"

"Absolutely, Your Majesty. Is now good for you?"

"I'll let you know when I'm available."

If one kissed her ass too much she didn't like it.

Z Chapter Forty

Unknown Shires of England: Destination — Stonehenge

The Trek Continues

A farmhouse appeared on the left. They crossed the highway to get a closer look.

"No good," Aidan said, "An oil lamp burning in the front window."

"But there aren't any cars," Mally said.

"Their barn certainly looks warm," Aidan added. "It's certainly worth a try."

With that, all three crouched and moved as fast as they were able. The dark and cold rain grew heavier as they ran. They reached the small porch illuminated by the warm yellow glow of a lamp perched on a small table centered in an unmullioned parlor window.

Mally withdrew the old Webley from his belt and Aidan grabbed a large stainless steel crescent wrench from his waistband. Aidan couldn't believe how he, a gentle man, could so quickly devolve into someone who would wield a seven pound wrench, perfectly willing to cave in somebody's skull if push came to shove. He keeked into a small window in the door and, seeing no one, risked a light rap on the delicate door. An officer in command leading his troops.

No response.

Aidan took the wrench from his waistband and shattered the small window, reaching inside to unlock the door. Slowly entering the house, it smelt stale, or maybe it just smelt like an old person. They went straight to the kitchen where they found a treasure trove of canned meats, meatballs in tomato sauce, jumbo hotdogs, and even Spam.

"Let's retire to the darker environs of the barn. I think it'll be safer than taking up residence in the house if anyone should come home unexpectedly."

The barn wasn't as well cared for as the one of the previous night. The hay not as clean and the concrete a wee bit stained. But it would keep the rain and the wind off them.

"What in bloody hell is that odor?" asked Mally.

"I don't know, but it smells like shite." Aidan didn't have a strong stomach.

They collected wet wood for a fire and after getting inside found two dark corners to strip out of their soaked clothing and change into fresh dry clothes. It took awhile, but finally they got a fire ignited in the center of a concrete floored stall. Each squeezed the water out of their sodden clothing, heavy with rain, and laid them to dry as near to the blaze as they were able.

Aidan swung his torch's light around the barn. "There's the source of the smell." Dung-dripping yellow-eyed fat black bats hung from the rafters. Aidan scratched an itch on the back of his neck as he stared upward, squinting.

Jeanette gazed up at the bats, then down at their clothes by the fire. "I just don't understand what we're doing," she sobbed.

"We're staying alive," said Mally, firmly but comfortingly.

"Mally's right. Don't lose sight of that," said Aidan. "As long as we keep moving, find food and water and a warm place to stay at night, we'll be fine."

"But I can't live the life of a mendicant. This isn't living," wailed Jeanette. "I want wine and clean clothes and clean sheets. I don't want to sleep on straw. I want to be warm and dry."

Mally hugged her close. "I'll keep you warm."

"But I'm not made for this. It shall drive me mad."

"There, there," he said into the cold pale grey skin of her delicate neck.

He felt her entire body shiver. Only there was no way for him to know if it was from cold or fear. Like the night before, they huddled around the fire and sorted through the tins of vegetables. This time, though, after opening the cans, they placed the assortment of vegetables and canned meats on the open coals of the fire to heat them, making sure not to let them cook too long, lest they burn. Using needle-nosed pliers, Jeanette removed cans of yellow corn, green beans, Lima beans, and meatballs from the hot fire, and sat them where they could each easily get to them.

"I'm looking forward to finally getting some meat," said Mally.

"Well, now you've got it," Jeanette said to her husband. She looked around and said, "Oh dear, what are we going to eat with?"

Aidan said, "I knew you wouldn't approve so I didn't mention it, but I borrowed these," holding aloft three sets of flatware.

Jeanette smiled, happy that he'd absconded with the eating tools. At least she would feel only a wee bit less than human dining with proper flatware.

Finished eating and after fluffing his bed on a pile of hay, Aidan helped with the cleanup. He washed the forks and spoons under runoff rain from the barn roof. Aidan walked outside to tend to his evening ablutions. He regarded the stygian night sky hiding the morose conquered moon and vanquished stars. Aidan missed the pinpoints of light twinkling through their thousands of light years long trip across the universe to reach their appointed places above the planet.

Growing accustomed to the malignancy of gray, Aidan was afraid he would never be able to bear full color again. That he would abhor the abundancy of the living spectrum. The stain too great upon his eyes.

And yet it wasn't the color or the colorlessness of the grey that was so affirming; it was the solitary sound of it, the depth of its finality, the inalienable permanence of its evil. All comforting to one who believed himself all but dead in a dying world. At the same time, all too real rather than more existential. And with even greater trepidation, he dreaded the possibility of a sound louder than a soft voice or a leaf's gentle rustle. Afraid of the disquietude piercing his ears with the exquisite agony of a dagger. It was amazing what one could get used to if one only must.

Sparse grass crunched stiffly under his comfortable boots, a nod to the early third season freeze. The autumn mist of fog and dew on the needles of the conifers was frozen white, and although a late October arrival would be unusual for the Queen's land, the cold carried with it a hint of snow. As far as the eye could see, other than in the little house, no light shone from any source. Neither hamlet nor burg. Nothing in the unknown shire. The aromatic fragrance of Scots pine and fresh loam enveloped him.

Alone with his thoughts, Aidan felt like he couldn't let on for Jeanette's sake, but truth was he was nettled by events he had no control over. He was doing his best to maintain his own soundness of mind. He went to a line of trees to take care of his business, then returned to the old cave of a barn and shut the door behind him. Mally snorted. Except to slumber, not much to do at night without electricity.

The fire had almost burnt out. He'd let it die. Heat would be good but not attracting unwanted attention would be better. Sometime after midnight muffled voices, thuds and creaking boards woke them. Aidan snuck a peek through a part in the barn doors, as eight to ten armed men dressed in shabby well-worn black, stormed the porch at the house.

Aidan whispered loudly over his shoulder, "Upstairs, get to the loft."

Jeanette and Mally hesitated, and Aidan shouted a whisper, "Now. Quietly!"

Jeanette said something Aidan couldn't make out, but even in the dark the look of fear on her face showed she was terrified. They ran quietly to the other side of the barn. Mally pushed Jeanette ahead of him as they scrambled up the attached wooden ladder. Mally climbed with the old Webley in his hand. Aidan was glad he'd brought it and followed close behind. Watching Mally's protective concern for Jeanette, he felt a twinge of jealousy at what they had, wishing he could feel that smitten with someone. Alas, now that was all but guaranteed not to happen. It would be hard to find romance at the world's end.

They lay face down in the straw covering the loft's ancient wood-plank floor. Aidan fingered the long splintered handle of a pitchfork lying next to him. Mally slowly rotated the cylinder of the ancient blue steel revolver. Caressing the full complement of six shells gave him comfort. He wiped cold sweat from his face with short thick fingers good for making a fist.

The sounds of the mob ransacking the humble home sent chills down their spines. The accented voices were from other countries as England was a large melting pot for the rest of the world. They, like most people would, had banded together desiring to be unalone during uncertain times. But this? This sounded like they were enjoying themselves; doing it just for the fun it gave them.

Huddled on the floor of the loft, Mally said, *sotto voce*, "Hopefully they'll just leave after they have their fill."

"Hopefully," Aidan said.

After what seemed like an eternity, it grew suddenly quiet. A moment later the old wooden barn door slowly creaked open. Muffled accented voices wafted upward. Intruders spun off in different directions. Even in the darkened barn, they'd seen the makeshift bedding and smelt the remains of the cook fire. All wielded heavy implements or crudely fashioned homemade weapons. They appeared well-fed, or at least like they weren't in a weakened state yet, which hinted at the notion they were feeding off the misfortune of others.

To Aidan and Jeanette, Mally appeared confident, but to himself his beating heart echoed like it was contained in a huge hollow oil drum. He moved to position himself less than six feet from the top of the ladder for a clear shot at anyone ascending, but that dislodged hay that floated to the barn floor when he did.

"Hey, who's up there?" one of the itinerant thugs shouted. "Get your fockin' limey ass down here. Don't make us come up and get you." Hearing him, the other invaders came running. "Somebody's up there. Go get 'em," he shouted in heavily Middle-Eastern accented Cockney English.

"Get him. Get him," the others shouted in other accents, joining the lone man in his refrain.

Two mounted the ladder. Mally clenched the old gun tightly in his nervous sweaty palm and pointed the weapon in the direction to where the first crested the top. The tip of a rusty machete showed first. Then the unwelcome invader took a deep breath and the sudden grimace that showed on his face telegraphed his intent to leap onto the loft.

"Call me a goddamn limey, ya' stoopid fookin' immigrant. I'm a Scot," Mally shouted and fired. The intruder was met with a .45 slug entering his right eye, splattering eyeball, eggshell-colored heavy skull fragments, grey matter, and large amounts of blood all over his trailing compatriot. The strong smell of burnt gunpowder mixed with the pungent hot smell of blood filled the barn. The second guy shoved the first's dead body off himself, and let it tumble down.

Proving the truism that most low-rent thugs aren't rocket scientists, he continued the climb. Arriving at the top with a sledgehammer in hand, he too, looked down the unblinking eye of the huge 45. Mally fired. He was rewarded with nothing but a desperate click for his trouble. Apparently the decades old ammo was less than reliable.

Aidan, crouched behind him and literally having Mally's back, was able to control his shaking long enough to take action. Using the bad guy's momentum against him, Aidan thrust four thick and sharp daggers of the pitchfork deep into his throat just as he attempted to rush. Impaled, blood sprayed through a blood-gargling scream. The mounted head and collapsing body would have clobbered anybody unfortunate enough to be following below.

Aidan was aghast at what he'd done, but at the same time pleased with himself in a macho way at how he'd performed. He'd have to remember how the emotion felt to capture it in his journal later. Mally raised his eyebrows and shrugged nonchalantly at the gruesome result of

Aidan's handiwork. Instant Karma's gonna get you, he thought, recalling the John Lennon hit.

Other assailants started to collect the two bodies, but the apparent leader, showing that they had no loyalties to one another, shouted from a safe distance across the barn floor, "Fock 'em. Let's get the fock out of here." They looked relieved since it appeared that no one really wanted to carry the bloody bodies anyway.

The barn door shut. Jeanette released a blood curdling scream that had been building for two days. Mally attempted to comfort her, but she was inconsolable. Trying to wrap his arms around her, she beat his barrel chest with her fists and kept screaming.

He finally managed to hold her tight so she couldn't beat him any longer. He told her and Aidan, "We got to get practical, here. We should set up an hourly watch to make sure those losers don't come back."

"Good idea," said Aidan. "You and I will alternate until daybreak. Hour shifts so the other can sleep."

"What about me?" Jeanette cried. "I can watch, too, you know. I will never be able to sleep again. You two just killed those men. I don't know how you cope with that. I can barely cope with seeing it."

What she didn't know was that, before they'd met, Mally had killed a man with his bare hands in a barroom rhubarb. It had been ruled self-defense, but he'd always known he could have stopped without killing the man if he'd wanted to — truth is, he just hadn't wanted to. Something inside him wouldn't let him. He'd been surprised at how good it felt. And he'd been proud of himself. Still, it wasn't something he'd want Jeanette to know. So, maybe somewhere deep inside he was a wee bit ashamed, which had to mean his soul could still be saved from eternal damnation. What he didn't know was, like a lot of women, Jeanette was attracted to what she detected but didn't actually know of the bad boy within him. She fell in love and stayed with him because of the sweet man that showed larger than the bad boy.

He consoled himself by saying that that had been a different life, a life before Jeanette. And yet, even now it gave him solace knowing he could call on that long-suppressed part of him if need be, to help them all survive. He didn't think their marriage was based on a lie by her not knowing. He'd never lied to her about it. He just hadn't told her.

But what they'd just done…whew. All three descended the two-by-four makeshift ladder. Back on the floor, they fluffed their bedding again from where it had been trampled by intruders. Mally and Jeanette lay down while Aidan positioned himself at the slatted barn door to take the first watch. He held Mally's old revolver and had his pitchfork just in case it didn't fire. None of them expected to sleep well.

In an hour, Mally tapped Aidan on the shoulder to relieve him. An hour later he wouldn't let Jeanette take over for him and stood her watch. Aidan took over. Then while Mally snored, she relieved Aidan. After an uneventful night, Aidan rose with the remorseful dim morning light. He decided against shaving. No one or nothing to shave for. He gathered his pile of dispirited clothes from the day before from where they dried by the fire. Not totally dry, but good enough to wear for the end of the world. Slightly damp with the comforting smell of woodsmoke.

Mally rose a few minutes later and shaved for Jeannette. He'd started sprouting a goatee once and she'd said, "Not if you ever want to kiss me again." Recalling that unpleasantness, he decided it best not to buck that horse again. Hoping the change would make them feel better, they both put on fresh clothes from the plastic garbage bags they carried.

Σ Chapter Forty-One

Virginia:
Destination — Georgia Guidestones

The Long Haul

"If we can't make more than ten mph it's gonna take us a week and a half to get to Georgia," said Strange.

The busiest interstate in the country connecting the populous East Coast's largest cities was clogged with cars full of bodies making anything more than a slow crawl impossible. "Look at it this way. At least there's nowhere else we need to be." Fleetwood's attempts at humor still weren't working.

"Has anyone ever told you you're goofy, Fleet?" Lace asked, not in a nice way.

"Not since I grew up and started shaving. Besides, brothers are never goofy. It's not in our DNA."

She rolled her eyes in response.

***

On the south-side of DC, Strange exited to Interstate 66 to the west. He hoped there would be fewer disabled vehicles in the Appalachian mountain area and they could make better time. Then, where it intersected with I-81, they would take it south to North Carolina and on to Georgia. It worked for the first hour or so. But the closer they got to its junction with 81, encounters with dead vehicles containing the dead became more frequent. It was then that Strange came up with the idea to take the Blue Ridge Parkway. It would be more pleasant driving through the mountains and was bound to be less congested.

Like most people who are wrapped up in their own lives and never notice what's going on around them, the increased potential for encounters with evil due to the isolation of backwoods mountain roads didn't occur to him. If it had, he would have heeded the banjo music.

« Chapter Forty-Two

Cumming, Georgia:
The Good Guys 'HQ

Shootists

Coffee was always first on the agenda before shooting. Of course, coffee before shooting was better than the old joke about whiskey before shooting. Making a pot, Patrick looked at the sink full of dirty dishes. It made him wonder if his housekeeper, a cute young woman from the Czech Republic, was still alive. Probably not working even if she were. She came in one day every other week. It was often enough to keep the place from getting out of hand. He was a single man, after all. It smelled better, too, after she had been there. They had to communicate through an app on her smart phone that they spoke into and it translated the words for each of them since her knowledge of English was limited and he understood no Czech at all.

After the first cup, Patrick retrieved travel mugs from a kitchen cabinet so they could take their second cups with them to the firing range Bill had set up on the rear lawn. Paper targets were set on bales of straw intermittently from five to thirty-three yards.

Even during the apocalypse the lawn was beautiful with a smattering of red and gold autumn leaves decorating the neatly mown grass. Patrick was glad he had had his lawn service scheduled to come for one last fall trimming before everything went to hell.

Bill issued final instructions. Patrick, with the Glock 9mm the colonel had loaned him, began from a kneeling position at five yards for five shots before hopping up and sprinting ten yards to the rear and changing to standing from fifteen yards and five more trigger pulls. Finally charging to thirty-three yards where he fell to prone and emptied the fifteen round magazine.

"Not bad," Bill said to his friend before turning to the other. "Jeff, you're next."

Jeff had his personal Glock .40. He eased back the slide to confirm the presence of a chambered round. He stepped confidently to the first firing line. He ran the course like he was running through blockers to get to the quarterback when he was a defensive end at The University of Virginia. A total of fifteen bullseyes.

"Excellent! You've done this before." It wasn't a question.

"Courtesy of the Forsyth County Sheriff's Department," he said giving credit to his training officer. "But I suppose I have a knack."

Bill said, "I suppose it's my turn although that's a tough act to follow." Indeed, he got only thirteen bullseyes.

After another round for each, with Patrick improving, Jeff duplicating perfect again, and Bill improving by one, they decided on lunch.

"Hungry?" asked Patrick.

Jeff said, "You know me."

"Yeah, I didn't even need to ask. What about you, Bill?"

"I could eat, but what have you got in mind?"

"As soon as the electricity started getting flaky I ran up to the convenience store at the top of the hill and got some ice before it could melt. I stuck it in the freezer with some T-bones. Door's been closed since. We can fire up the grill; it's charcoal, and I still have cold wine."

"Got any beer?" said Jeff.

"I can probably find one."

"Only one?"

"Okay, one six-pack."

"That's more like it."

Patrick got a bottle of Caymus Cabernet Sauvignon from the wine rack and put it in the freezer with the ice to cool down to sixty degrees — he'd stick a thermometer in to check. That was room temperature for castles where the notion of serving red wine at room temperature originated. And he got a bottle from a six-pack of SweetWater Pale Ale 420, a local Atlanta microbrew, for Jeff. Kept the six-pack within reach.

"Cool, one of my favorites," Jeff said.

"You sure know how to live, even if we're dying," said Bill, tilting his glass toward Patrick after he gave him a healthy pour of the Caymus.

"Isn't everyone?" said Patrick, tapping his friend's glass with his own.

» Chapter Forty-Three

Sawnee Mountain, Georgia:
Evil Dwellers 'HQ

Discovery

"Professor Drummond, I can see you now."
"Right away, Your Majesty. Bad Penny, too?"
"I think not."
"I'm on my way," he thalked.
"The door will be open."

Drummond rapped respectfully on the open door before he entered. Queen Gertrude stood on the small terrace of her suite taking in the view of the North Georgia mountains. It was her sanctuary. A place of peace. Today, she was deep in thought and pained. Wearing a long shear dressing gown, it was obvious she had no intention of leaving her rooms. Until he thalked, his presence didn't disturb her solitude.

"Queen? Your Majesty?"
"Oh...Professor...I didn't hear you come in," she said.
"Am I disturbing you?"
"Not at all. Remember, I requested your presence."
"Of course."
"Please, tell me what you heard from your homeland."
"There's a small group, but I don't want to overstate it, there are three people who have started making their way from Edinburgh — that's in Scotland — to Stonehenge. Apparently they believe they can prostrate themselves before the stones and end The Plague."
"I know where Edinburgh is,' she said with a huff, *"And what do you think we should do about them, if anything?"*
"With hundreds of kilometers to go there's no guarantee they'll even get there, but if it were me, I would encourage the others to keep doing as they are. Misdirecting, encouraging, misleading them. Something about them — I don't know what it is — makes me think if they find out about us they could be a pain in our arses."
"Then see that you take care of the situation."
"Shall do, Your Majesty."

Z Chapter Forty-Four

Unknown Shires of England:
Destination — Stonehenge

Voices

Before gathering their belongings, they decided to brew coffee on the makeshift cook stove. Rekindled a fire and set the old coffee pot which they'd used to catch rain, in the embers to heat. Nobody wanted to talk about the incident from the night before, so they avoided the subject.

"I had the strangest dream last night," said Aidan.

"I did, too," said Jeanette, "as if anything could be stranger than this," gesturing at their surroundings where they slept in the barn.

"What were your dreams about? Because I did, too," said Mally.

"Voices encouraging me to get to Stonehenge no matter what; that we would find the answer there."

"That was my dream, but somehow I didn't believe the voices. It seemed to me they were trying to deceive us," said Jeanette. Women were always the more discerning sex.

Mally said, "Same thing with me. And I'm with Jeanette. I don't buy it." Easy for him to agree with his wife, and better for marital tranquility.

Aidan said, "But how could we all have the same dream at the same time? It had to be something else. Something phantasmagoric."

"But what?" Jeanette asked.

"I've heard about something like this happening," Mally said, "We probably caused it ourselves, by talking about it, and since we all had it on our mind, it embedded itself in our subconscious."

"I think that's as good an explanation as any," Aidan said, tilting his coffee cup toward the large, sound-thinking man.

They carefully ignored the two bodies a few feet away.

Σ Chapter Forty-Five

Blue Ridge Parkway, Rural Virginia:
Destination — Georgia Guidestones

Hillbillies or Rednecks?

As it turned out the banjo music was only in their minds. But the rusted-out, green 1960s era American pickup that came up fast from out of nowhere and struck them from behind was real. Strange struggled to keep the aging Toyota under control. He thought it was unintentional when the face he couldn't make out through the dark glass backed the poor excuse for a vehicle off, but after he rammed them a second time he knew the guy did it on purpose.

"Shit! The son of a bitch is trying to run us off the goddamn road."

"You're from Tennessee. What do you do about backwoods mountain hillbillies?" Fleetwood yelled.

"If I'd been in Tennessee for the last twenty years instead of New York City, I'd pull out a fuckin' gun and back him off." Instead, he stomped on the gas pedal to try and coax more miles per hour out his old 4Runner, figuring that he could outrun the truck from five decades earlier, even if it were a V-8.

Cody and Lace sat in the back seat looking like they were going to be sick. Strange saw the speedometer's needle flirt with eighty before vibration in the steering wheel became too violent for comfort. But it was enough to leave the old pickup in their dust. It wasn't even in Strange's rearview mirror after he entered a large mountain curve, but then the broad curve constricted into an eye of the needle with an abandoned car in the middle of the road, he couldn't hold it in the narrow two-lane highway. The SUV plowed through scrub, brush, and small trees with trunks no bigger than a woman's wrist before it crunched to a stop against a small stump, engine racing and tires spinning in the wet earth.

When Strange roused, he shut off the ignition as the ancient rusted pickup was pulling to a stop next to them on the narrow road shoulder. He shook his head. Three gray-bearded men in overalls stopped short, shotguns raised. All three wore faded, filthy overalls. One wore an orange trucker's hat that read Buster's Feed and Seed on the front. The one that looked oldest, anger in his rheumy eyes, spoke through the shattered window on Strange's side.

"All right, climb on out, if yer able."

The middle one was bare-headed. The youngest, who looked like he was the scion of a clan whose mother was probably also his aunt, wore a dingy, faded green hat crowned with a yellow John Deere Tractor logo. They looked like they could be founding members of a peculiar clan that didn't believe in seeing dentists like some sects that don't believe in going to doctors.

"I can get out, but my friends need some help."

"Then hep 'em," he said, gesturing with the ancient shotgun.

Strange had banged his knee against the dash during the bumpy stop making it a challenge for him to move. "Fleet, wake up. Wake up. We've gotta get out. And we have to help Lace and Cody," he said urgently, slapping his friend's cheek. Fleetwood and the two women appeared to have been knocked unconscious during the bone-jarring stop.

Strange glanced over his shoulder at the three villains. He got the impression they'd have done this even if it weren't the end of the world. It was just a bad choice he'd made for him and his friends to come this way. My bad, he thought. Fleetwood came to; together they helped Cody and Lace out of the cramped back seat. Cody had a large egg-shaped lump on her head already turning blue, but Lace seemed uninjured.

"Climb on up in that there truck bed and lay down. And cover up with that ole tarp, and gimme those goddamned car keys."

Strange tossed the man the keys. With Strange and Fleetwood's help, the women reluctantly climbed into the back of the truck. The men followed. The tarp, stained reddish-brown, smelled of age, oil, slaughtered deer, and processed venison. Unless the pungent odor was from human remains. Nevertheless, following orders, they lay down flat and pulled the heavy canvas over them, up to their chins only, careful not to let the smelly blanket cover their noses. They could tell by the truck's movement that it bumped back onto the smooth roadway and without turning around, continued in the same direction. Except for Lace's soft mewling, they rode in silence for maybe a quarter of an hour.

The truck slowed to almost a full stop before making a hard right turn off the highway. They bumped on to a rough road, the sound of tires crunching on gravel told them where they were going was even more remote. After ten minutes on the rutted gravel two-track, the old pickup stopped. A door opened and a wooden gate swung wide with a strident squeak. The vehicle pulled up one car length and stopped again. They heard the gate squeak once more as it was closed, then the truck rocked when whoever it was bounced back in excitedly and the door slammed shut. Five more minutes on the bumpy two-track and the crappy truck stopped again. The old man shut off the engine.

Lace's mewling was louder and the tarp shook from her convulsing. This time Cody held her in her arms trying to comfort her. The two younger, father and son, yanked the tarp away exposing their captives.

"Come on, git on outta there," said the youngest.

As he helped Lace out, he said, "Can I have this one, Daddy, can I?"

"After I finish with her you can have her, Earl," the middle-aged one said.

"Oowee," said Earl, "I'm going to get me some pussy." His yellow-stained and missing teeth bared in a maniacal grin.

"Floyd, don't get the boy's hopes up," said the elder, "You know what happened the last time. Shit." He took off his hat and slapped his middle-aged son across the face with it.

"Yeah, I remember, Daddy. You and me fucked that one to death."

Lace sobbed and fell to her knees retching. God only knew how disgusting the act itself would be. She hoped they would just kill her.

"Gimme those goddamn handbags," the old man said to their female guests. He dumped them out on the filthy ground and pawed through the pile before finding a nail file and slid it into the bib pocket front of his overalls. Finding nothing else he thought could be used as a weapon, he tossed the bags on the dirty ground, then pointed toward a surprisingly sturdy old chicken house. The only part of it less than fifty years old was the heavy-duty, shiny stainless steel padlock, hanging from the door. Anyone naturally suspicious or a worrisome sort would be curious as to why such an old outbuilding for chickens would need such a formidable lock. The women picked up their bags, stuffing the contents back in and clutching them to their breasts.

"Now git," he said to the women. Lace and Cody held on to each other and cowered. "I said, git."

Strange and Fleetwood gently encouraged them with strong manly hands placed low on their backs. They hesitantly entered the tired shack smelling of chickens, chicken shit, and old hay. Without a word, their captors locked it and went in the direction of a small house that was even more decrepit-looking and older than the chicken house.

"What are we doing here," whined Lace not expecting an answer. "My head hurts where I bumped it," she said rubbing it, gently.

Strange said, "It'll be okay. I'll get us out of this." He didn't know if that was true, but he wanted to give her hope. To try and make up for all the bad end-of-the-world wisecracks he'd been making for the past two days

"Let's check this thing out," he said looking around the shack. "See if we can find anything we can use to get out of here."

They started examining all the nooks and crannies just to make sure their captors hadn't overlooked something they could use. Fleetwood helped Cody move a big piece of plywood to look behind it.

"Thank you, Fleetwood," she said formally. "You know, you've been a really good friend."

He looked aghast. "What do you mean 'been'? We're going to make it out of this."

"Do you really believe that?"

He paused to take a deep breath. "I have to."

« Chapter Forty-Six

Cumming, Georgia:
The Good Guys 'HQ

Preparing For The Worst

Patrick and his friends spent the next week shooting, working out, and preparing mentally for what could well be the fight of their lives. For payback. Nothing more. They didn't think anything they would do could change the fate of the world. It was for nothing more than revenge. They couldn't let them go unpunished. The Dwellers, and especially Trudy, had to understand that actions have consequences.

Tempers flared between the longtime friends because of the seriousness of their mission — and for Patrick because of the thought of what might happen if he came face-to-face with Trudy, his life's love.

He only hoped he wouldn't have to kill her. Could he kill her? Did he have it in him? Or could he get her back? Was it even possible to kill someone who is undead which by extrapolation also means alive?

The questions ripped him up inside.

Plus, they were getting tired of waiting. But they had to bide their time. The decision when to go had to be for the best outcome. For that reason and it alone.

>> Chapter Forty-Seven

Sawnee Mountain, Georgia:
Evil Dwellers 'HQ

Deception

Drummond talked to his contacts in the U.K. As the Queen's representative, he was authorized to tell them to step up their misdirection with the traveling nomads. They knew it was an order from on high. And coming from a Brit, one of their own, they were pleased to know he had such an important position with the queen.

After the excitement of the intruders, things had calmed down and were returning to normal. Even Queen Gertrude seemed less on edge, with a spring in her step and not exactly what one could call a smile gracing her face, but at least there wasn't a menacing scowl affecting it.

Z Chapter Forty-Eight
Unknown Shires of England:
Destination — Stonehenge

Seriousness Sets In

"I think we need to acquire some real weapons." Fighting with farm implements had worried Aidan.

"What do you have in mind?"

"The first town we reach, we go to the local gaol. Even though bobbies aren't armed they will have a storehouse of weapons just in case. We go in. Take what we want."

"Brilliant idea."

"No offense to your Webley, of course."

"None taken," said Mally.

A few kilometers south they ventured into an unknown hamlet.

"So how will we find the headquarters," asked Aidan.

"Look for a stone building with iron bars on the windows."

"You're joking, right?"

"No, most of them were built over a century ago and have never been updated. I think they look simply brill. Besides, cities figure those pounds could be better spent elsewhere."

Σ Chapter Forty-Nine

Virginia Backwoods:
Destination — Georgia Guidestones

Escape Plans

"See if you have anything we can use as weapons."

Strange had a small throwaway-type cigarette lighter. He didn't smoke but he'd taken it with him when he left figuring he could use it to start a cookfire if they needed to. He held it high and said, "Maybe we should just burn this shitty place to the ground. Hopefully living people would see the smoke and flames and come to help."

Lace found an old-style can of aerosol hairspray in her oversized bag, that she still used.

Strange said, "Let me have that. With my lighter we have the makings of a fine blowtorch."

"You can't be serious. You really want to burn it down with us in here?" said Lace, in shocked disbelief at what Strange had suggested.

"No, when one of them comes back I plan on setting him on fire."

"Great idea, Strange. That's why you make the big bucks," Fleetwood joshed.

"Indubitably. Anyway, let's think this thing through."

It was getting colder, so they huddled up in a small circle like they would around a campfire, wishing they had one.

The plan was this: Cody would pretend to be sick, drawing the attention of whomever they sent out to them. Then Strange would flick the lighter while simultaneously shooting a powerful spray at it and into the bad guy's face. A large fireball would engulf him. They hoped it would be the youngest one who appeared to be a halfwit. It was only natural to assume that he'd be the easiest one to hoodwink.

Cody and Lace were terrified about the plan, since they knew what would happen to them if it didn't succeed. For now, they waited.

>> Chapter Fifty

Sawnee Mountain, Georgia:
Evil Dwellers 'HQ

Better Than Hoped For Results

Queen Gertrude was ecstatic. She didn't call anyone away from their duties, but thalked to everyone at the same time.

"It appears, my friends, that our plan has been wildly successful; even more so than we expected. As near as our experts can estimate, over ninety per cent of the planet's population has already been exterminated and the remaining we anticipate to be gone in no more than a fortnight."

Her experts could thalk with her. But Earthwalkers, derogatorily referred to as mouth-talkers, didn't have thalking ability. With television, Internet, radio, and all other communications having failed, only Dwellers knew all countries in the world were afflicted. For all the Earthwalkers knew, all seemed to think they might be the only ones suffering.

Dwellers thalked their congratulations.

"That's awesome, Queen Gertrude."

"You're the greatest leader in the history of the world, Queen."

"All hail, Queen Gertrude."

On and on and on.

Z Chapter Fifty-One

Unknown Shires of England:
Destination — Stonehenge

A Cache Of Arms

"There it is," said Mally.

"Where?" asked Jeanette.

"Across the green."

Boarded up pubs and other closed small businesses dominated the square. He pointed across the large formerly well-kept lawn that was the center of the hamlet. All four streets surrounding the quad were congested with vehicles and bodies littered the sidewalks like so many dummy props from an M. Night Shyamalan horror film. They hurried to reach the gaol's unlocked door.

"The last one to leave didn't lock up," said Aidan.

"Probably in a hurry. Wanted to beat The Plague home," said Mally.

They pulled open the large double doors to a handful of bodies decorating the large open room. The unsurprising foul odor was unbearable. They let the room air for a moment.

"I wonder where the weapons will be," said Aidan looking around the big space.

"Probably in the cellar," said Mally.

Looking to corridors going in each direction to the rear, Aidan said, "Left or right?"

"Right," said Mally. "That's just a guess, though."

So they followed the green-tiled hallway to the rear. Passed the desk sergeant's large aerie of European oak. Mally stretched high on tiptoes to reach above the desk to dig in a fishbowl of colorfully-wrapped candies and pulled out a handful. Stuffed them in his pocket.

"I only thought I never had kids," said Jeanette, grinning.

"What?" he said when she smirked at him. "We might need them...you know...for energy." He unwrapped one and nonchalantly dropped the cellophane on the tile floor.

Then on past a wall of black-and-white eight-by-ten photos of men in dark suits and starched uniforms. A Chief, two captains, and four lieutenants, all middle-aged Caucasians and no females; not an exceedingly diverse force. Men's and women's loos preceded an elevator before arriving at a switchback stairway to the basement.

In the basement, the first door on the left was reinforced steel with a small face-high window buttressed with an elaborate reticulation of wire between two panes. But even though it had all that security, that door too had been left unlocked. Making it unnecessary to force it with a crowbar.

Mally's muscled right hand slowly turned the doorknob and with that simple twist they were given the proverbial key to the kingdom of weapons and ammunition. The room known in law enforcement circles worldwide as an armory.

A treasure trove of semi-automatics, carbines, and 9mm semi-auto handguns.

"We'll take two rifles, four pistols, and all the ammunition we can carry," Aidan said, pointing at the different store sections.

"Four?" Mally said.

"It doesn't hurt to have a spare."

"Do you really think this is necessary," asked Jeanette, disbelieving, looking from one to the other.

"Absolutely necessary," said Aidan. Mally nodded sadly.

Aidan draped a belt of .223mm ammo over each shoulder, crisscrossed from shoulder to hip, and clutched a weapon, morphing from university professor to Rambo in seconds.

They ran up the stairs to the front of the building; Aidan burst out the double doors landing in the squat of an alert predator between the swollen and bloated bodies of a man and woman, covered in flies and eyes pecked…or chewed, out. Her in a dress and heels, handbag at her side. Man wearing a dark suit and polished black Oxfords. Aidan's head rotated on a pivot in every direction. Mally and Jeanette followed close behind. Mally made sure Jeanette stayed between him and Aidan.

The only sounds were their footsteps, the rustle of their packs and weapons, and an evil wind carrying with it death.

« Chapter Fifty-Two

Cumming, Georgia:
The Good Guys 'HQ

Worse Than They Thought

"Cuz! Cuz! Can you hear me?" Duncan thalked to Patrick.

"Duncan, good to hear from you."

"Not so good, I'm afraid."

"What is it? What's up?"

"I was eavesdropping on the bad guys. Apparently over ninety per cent of the people on earth have died."

"Fuck."

"I couldn't put it better myself."

Patrick entered his study where Bill Crain had commandeered the proud leather-topped desk. He looked at home behind it, deep in thought.

"I hope you've been planning."

"Why? What's up?"

Patrick told the colonel about his cousin's report.

"Son of a bitch."

"I'll say."

Σ Chapter Fifty-Three

Virginia Backwoods:
Destination — Georgia Guidestones

Surviving The Night

Strange crouched in a corner of the shed and glanced at the fading brightness of the luminous dial on his watch. He strained to make out nine-fifteen. With so little light in the world, what the numbers and hands of his watch needed to refresh the strontium aluminate, they were losing their glow. He'd thought someone would have shown up by now. Just before nine-thirty, the expensive lock rattled on the door to the worn down shed. Cody dropped to the hay-covered dirt and Lace started the act by screaming in terror. "Help! We need help. Something's wrong with her." Fleetwood knelt beside her.

The slack-jawed mouth breather came in scanning the room with his shotgun. The older men obviously thought he could handle simple tasks.

"Don't just stand there. Come help me." Lace said while pounding professionally on Cody's chest.

He dawdled on his way over. He squatted, uncomprehending. The smell of cheap bourbon on his sour breath and in his foul sweat. Strange snuck up behind him, flicked the rough wheel of the cheap lighter and said, "Hey, asshole."

He waited for the half-wit to start to rise. Cody and Fleetwood yanked Lace to her feet and they moved off to the side. The man half-turned toward Strange. He sprayed the aerosol can toward the flame, engulfing the man's face in a huge fireball. It wouldn't make his looks any worse. The pungent recognizable scent of burning flesh and hair immediately filled the small space.

The man screamed, dropped the shotgun, and clutched his face with both palms. Strange grabbed the shotgun from where the inbred dropped it. He recognized the Remington 1100 twelve gauge semiautomatic. It had a twenty-eight inch barrel and held six shells. It was in surprisingly good condition. He presumed that mountain men would keep their guns in good working order and with a breech full of ammo. He hoped he was right about the weapon being fully loaded in the event he needed to use it again.

He watched the man stumbling around the enclosure, the fireball that had been a human of sorts, screaming in agony and considered putting him out of his misery. Send him straight to hell with a pull of a trigger. Then he shook his head and thought, No, I may need that shell later. Besides, he deserves to die in anguish.

Strange hoped the other two would hear the youngest's screams and come running.

He was still screaming, blindly bouncing headfirst off each wall. Then he passed out either from the pain, or the sight of his own face in his hands, and fell forward in the dirt, a smoldering heap. They didn't have to worry about hay catching fire and igniting the wooden enclosure.

And here they came. The door of their old shack opened and the two remaining hillbillies emerged with a torch afire. While the others hid further back, Strange, unseen in the dark, slid the barrel of the shotgun through a wide slat in the door. The rednecks ran side-by-side toward the coop. At twenty feet away Strange closed his left eye tight and lined up the sight with his right. It felt strangely familiar and comforting when he placed his cheek against the cool polished wood of the stock, just like when he was a kid hunting in the Tennessee hills. The eldest was the first target. Strange figured if the middle one knew he'd lost his son and his father there would be less fight in him.

An earth-shaking blast and a direct hit. The old man's head flew from his body in a bloody mess of leaking gray brain matter, stringy tendrils, and ivory-colored skull. The lower jaw pirouetted through the air in a different direction and the faded orange Buster's Feed And Seed hat fluttered even further. The neck opening of the headless body pointed toward the sad excuse for a house and the feet pointed toward the coop.

"Pawpaw! Pawpaw!" the last one screamed, leaning over him and vomiting into the gaping hole between the narrow shoulders where his father's head had once rested.

Strange shouted from the safety of the chicken shed, "Drop the shotgun or you get the next one."

Gripped by impotent rage, and in shock from seeing his daddy's head fly from his body right before his eyes, the middle-aged son did the only thing he could do and swiveled the weapon ineffectively toward the shack, firing wildly from the hip. There might not have been enough of the loose and cracked aged boards to shield a direct hit, but Strange got lucky. In the hillbilly's anger and sadness, and through the early evening fog, no shots even came close.

Strange returned fire killing the man with a direct blast to center mass, clean and neat, painting the night air behind him in an expanding mist of red. Then he paused long enough to feel his body for blood or holes to assure himself he hadn't been hit by a stray unfeeling pellet. After running his hands over his chest and stomach he decided he hadn't. He knew a leg wound would at least take time to kill him. He tasted the foulness of vomit rising into his mouth and tamped it back down.

Strange hadn't needed to kill the three so violently, but he wanted their souls. Trying to rain down misery on the miserable during a time like the end of the world, what they would have done to Cody and Lace, well…they deserved it. And yet he didn't feel like he'd lost his own being by killing them. He thought that maybe he'd saved it. He felt justified. That He, whoever He was and who judged all, would have mercy on him.

The sound of the blast and the smell of gunpowder took him back. Back to a time hunting dove, squirrel, and coon in the hills of Tennessee with his grandfather, and he thought even if it had been almost thirty years before, the skills he'd learned had paid off in a bigger way than he could ever have dreamed it would at the time. He would have hunted with the older man anyway because he genuinely liked spending time with the classically Southern Gentleman, but also because it got him out of the house and away from his old man, an alcoholic, who wasn't as good as his father. And apparently the apple hadn't fallen too far from the tree. At least that was who he blamed for his love of the Irish nectar.

When no more gunfire was heard, Cody, Lace, and Fleet peeked out, then ran to check on Strange.

» Chapter Fifty-Four

Sawnee Mountain, Georgia:
Evil Dwellers 'HQ

Proactive

Queen Gertrude's good mood hadn't lasted long. Even though she didn't have to, she called everyone together to ream them out. *"We need to speed this shit up. I don't have all the fuckin' time in the world."*

Everyone cringed at the sudden change in mood; that was extreme, even for her. No one could remember seeing her like this before.

"Divide up in small teams, use your powers to get wherever you need to, ASAP, and kill anybody you encounter. Drummond, Bad Penny, you are in charge. Make it happen."

"You heard the Queen," thalked Bad Penny. *"Five minutes. Be in the common room. And don't stop to take a piss. Oh yeah, I forgot. Some of you don't piss. Or you can piss in the woods. I crack myself up sometimes."*

Z Chapter Fifty-Five

Unknown Shires of England:
Destination — Stonehenge

Can It Be Done?

They crossed a small stone church's grounds, it's bright white steeple rising ceremoniously above the hamlet, and exited the town on the south side of the square. The cobblestone two-lane street meandered past the white stucco buildings that had been the homes of pubs, inns, and diners for centuries. All boarded up or windows shattered. The Cobblestone on which they trod was durable and would last for centuries more but still required routine maintenance. A couple of loose softball-sized stones would not be seeing maintenance anytime soon.

They slunk out of town, drawing as little attention as possible. They moved as quickly as they were able, but in their weakened state from insufficient food and too little water, that was not as fast as they wanted to go. Still, not even a hint of life was around to challenge or cause them concern.

"Damn," said Aidan.

"What's wrong?" Jeanette was accustomed to taking care of him at school and couldn't just turn it off.

"Just this damn tooth. Killing me. Mally, you still got those pliers?"

"Sure do. What you need 'em for?"

"Going to pull this damn tooth."

"Shit, you want me to do it? Might be easier to let me."

"Maybe. We'll see."

Five minutes later Mally kicked in the hastily applied plywood covering the doorway of the next building they came to, and they entered the darkened anteroom of what had looked like a medical office. The bell above the doorway that had announced patients rang when he kicked down the makeshift barrier. Looking through a broken interior window to a smaller room, there sat a mid-century dentist's chair. With a smirk and a slight shake of his head, he said, "This is appropriate."

All three entered the small room, standing newly acquired weapons in a corner. Aidan climbed into the oversized reclining chair, clutching the pliers. The room still carried a medicinal smell embedded in its wallpaper. Without asking, Mally took the pliers from Aidan, leaned over him and planted a huge meaty knee in his chest. A stunned look on his face and gasping from the weight on his body, Aidan said, "Wait a minute. Let me do this. You're going to crush me."

Mally backed off. To give himself a firm dry surface to grip, Aidan pulled a paper hand towel from a dispenser on the dentist's tray and, on front and back, wrapped the ailing top right canine. Jeanette angled a mirror on a swivel above him so he could see what he was doing even in the dark of the small space. She covered his body with a large apron like a barber's cape, popping it as she did.

Aidan spread his maw as wide as he could. He stared into the polished mirror and a gaping mask of terror stared back at him. The pliers in his hand seemed to rise on their own into the flinching hole in his face, the excess hand towel hanging from where it wrapped the troubled tooth. He positioned the pliers' serrated claw on the offending upper bicuspid and clamped down as hard as he could stand it. He nearly passed out from the pain, but somehow managed to hold on and gave it a hard yank.

Blood poured from the gaping hole onto the large cloth Jeanette had strategically placed in the perfect position to catch the torrent. Then he screamed and wished he had had some Novocain. He recognized the salty metallic taste of his own blood and was unsure if he was going to pass out from the sight of the blood; or the pain, probably from the pain.

The pliers and tooth fell into his lap.

They had to wait until Aidan came to before they could leave. After a few minutes Mally slapped his face to encourage his waking. Jeanette went to the loo. Even in the dimness of the maze of small rooms she located the door marked washroom. She knew the plumbing wouldn't work, but at least she would feel more human using a proper toilet instead of squatting like an animal in the woods. She hadn't gotten used to that. After she returned, Aidan came to sputtering and spewing more blood.

"That was a piss poor idea," he said, rubbing his face regretfully. Jeanette handed him a bottled water to rinse with.

He flashed a painful insincere grin at the mirror, unable to even notice the blonde hair women admired, or the strong chin or elegant cheekbones; all he could see was the gaping hole where a tooth should have been, had always been before. He flinched at his returned visage. He picked up the offending ivory from where it fell, opened a flap pocket on his vest and dropped it in. A souvenir of Armageddon.

"It makes you look tough," said Mally.

"I'd rather have all my teeth," Aidan said, honestly.

Mally said, "Well, at least if the world is about to end you won't have to live without it for long."

Jeanette gave her husband a dirty look, not believing he'd actually said that.

"Leave it to you to make a bad situation worse. I didn't think that possible. You need to work on your bedside manner, mate," Aidan said.

Σ Chapter Fifty-Six

Virginia Backwoods:
Destination — Georgia Guidestones

Put It Behind Them

With all the blood and body parts, the small patch of dirt had the look of a well-used slaughter yard. Their captors punished for their sins, Strange and Fleetwood grabbed the dead men's' shotguns; now they had three weapons. All four made their way to the Toyota SUV.

"Do we need to look for your keys?" asked Fleetwood.

"If they're not in the ignition I have a spare in a magnetic case under the front left wheel well." The keys weren't in the ignition, so Strange located the extra in its hiding spot. He then pulled the SUV alongside the ancient pickup. "Go to the barn. Find some tubing. There's got to be some."

The others walked off less than enthusiastically on the necessary scavenger hunt. Lace came back about a minute later. "Will this do?"

"Absofuckinlutely."

Strange took the gas caps off both vehicles and ran one end of the ten foot coil into the gas tank of the pickup. Putting the other end into his mouth, gave it a hard suck.

Orange pungent liquid spurted into his mouth. Coughing, he spat it out, inserting that end into his own gas vent. A short time later they had a full tank.

"There. That ought to get us to Georgia," he said, with a little too much enthusiasm. His adrenaline was still spiked from what he'd done to their captors. "Now let's see what kind of food they have," he said, striding toward the back door of the shack. They all dropped their bags by the Toyota.

Strange tore open the old ripped and squeaking screen door barely hanging on by its hinges. The tiny, turn of the previous century, barely usable kitchen, had ugly, cracked yellow-patterned linoleum covering the small space. A Formica-topped puke-green kitchen table could seat four in red vinyl upholstered chairs. Partially-filled unmatched coffee cups sat on all sides but one.

A cupboard, not large enough to be called a pantry, was the most likely place to contain foodstuffs. A gallon-sized plastic bag of what looked like homemade beef jerky would make an easy-to-eat driving snack. The worrisome thing about that, though, was who knew if it was even beef or any other edible protein? A horrifying thought no one wanted to ponder. And an unopened, new, according to the date on the package, bag of fried pork skins — none of them had ever eaten those before — and a trio of cans of beef stew would be filling if they built a fire, or even unheated right out of the can.

Done with their scavenging, they stormed back to Strange's tired but welcome vehicle. An ugly, hungry, tan-and-white mongrel cur, thus far an Armageddon survivor, appeared head down and crouching, and growled at them diffidently as they jumped in. Dust flew as they tore out of the dirty barnyard and raced down the rutted two-track. They each allowed themselves to breathe a momentary sigh of relief as they leaned back in the well-worn seats.

"I hope I never have to do that again," said Strange, after pondering what he'd done and touching the shotgun, not with a caress, but with appreciative respect.

"I never even want to see that again," Lace said.

» Chapter Fifty-Seven

Sawnee Mountain, Georgia:
Evil Dwellers 'HQ

Taking Matters Into Their Own Hands

Although Queen Gertrude told her sycophants they were ahead of schedule, she was antsy. She wanted more people to die faster. She felt the need to hurry it along. She'd tasked Bad Penny and Drummond with taking the point in leading hit squads out to kill anyone they encountered. But they decided Drummond should stay back to guard her; Bad Penny alone would lead a squad; a hand-picked follower would lead a second platoon.

Boasting one of the country's largest metropolitan areas a mere twenty-five miles south, and Bad Penny's former stomping grounds, Atlanta would be an easy place for them to begin their mission. A no-brainer.

"I know exactly where we'll go first," Bad Penny thalked to his squad of six Dwellers.

They piled into a generic, rusted-brown American-made mid-size pickup. They wouldn't have to worry about police stopping them for having passengers riding in the back. Three rode in the cab; three in the open bed. The vehicle was similar to the one he'd used in his previous life to disappear after a kill when his goal was to be America's most prolific killer of all time. A lofty ambition considering Samuel Little's claim of at least ninety, and the FBI's verified total of sixty victims.

Peachtree Street, known as Atlanta's Broadway, ran several miles from the city's entertainment district in Midtown/Buckhead south to Downtown Atlanta's business district. If anyone was out and about, it would be on the broad avenue that was known the world over. And since Bad Penny had called his home the penthouse of a Buckhead high rise, that's where he led them first. It had only been a few months since he'd seen his building and a couple of weeks since The Plague had been set off, but already it looked like it had been long-deserted. The kind of desecrated structure one would see in a wore-torn Middle East country.

"Damn," he thalked.

Bad Penny had never made many friends in his building, sometimes not even wanting to speak to others when he walked through the large lobby. That attitude did nothing to endear him to them, yet in his classically narcissistic way he didn't care about what happened to most of them. He did, however, wonder if Young, the kind Chinese woman who ran the dry cleaners in the building, and Abby, her sweet dog she brought to work with her every day, might somehow still be alive. He loved dogs and it still upset him when he recalled running over a poor mutt and accidentally killing it when he was in the pickup he drove on his murderous rampage.

"Go south," he instructed the driver, a wolf-like creature.

It was fortunate the pickup was an automatic, because without opposing thumbs, the creature would have found it difficult to shift gears. Penny had to admit it was a little unsettling to be consorting with all the varied types of creatures that were part of the Dwellers family. One, a large, long-armed orangutan, a member of the species famous for being the killer in the famous Edgar Allen Poe classic, *Murder In The Rue Morgue*. Another, a creature that could only be described as a possible bandersnatch, a mythical creature primarily in British lore.

A couple of miles south where Peachtree Street pierced the Midtown area, they came upon an obvious gang numbering around a dozen, breaking in stores, restaurants, and the occasional home in an effort to acquire food and supplies. As they drove slowly along the vast artery the gang started to chase them.

"Stop the fucking truck, Bad Penny thalked. "

It's on."

The wolf pulled into a shopping center parking lot. The gang rushed them. The three in the back of the truck, including the orangutan and spotted leopard, piled out before the truck had even stopped. Bad Penny, the wolf, and a creature whose origin he didn't know, stormed out of the cab. The wolf tore out throats of five in less than half a minute. The other creature sprouted evil, black wings and swooped into the group with talons ripping and tearing all exposed flesh. Bad Penny himself grabbed a gang member the size of a nose tackle by the throat and choked him until breath terminated.

"That'll teach those sons of a bitches."

The gang dispatched, the Dwellers, spent and a little bloody, climbed back into the truck, pulled out of the parking lot onto Peachtree Street, and continued south toward Downtown ATL.

Z Chapter Fifty-Eight

Unknown Shires of England:
Destination — Stonehenge

Sojourning South

Since they were already ensconced and dark was approaching, they decided to bed down in the dental office. Warmer than out in the open, the dentist's chair and two hygienists' chairs would make for comfortable sleep.

Before they settled down Mally secured the boarded up door to the office to discourage anyone that might have bad intentions. Although he looked down the street each way before he did, the look in his warm brown eyes was confrontational. They were already adjusting to life without creature comforts. No conditioned air, warm or cold; no plumbed fresh water; or Jeanette's most missed — indoor, properly working loos.

For their dinner, Jeanette heated the last of their canned vegetables over a fire she laid in a stainless steel sink. Aidan, however, sore-mouthed, could only risk eating two small cups of yogurt she'd found in a sealed fridge that, though not cold, had nevertheless been unopened and cool since Armageddon began. He decided he would take his chances with e-coli.

Jeanette found a couple of sample packages of painkillers, names she recognized just in case the pain from his mouth became too unbearable.

***

When he woke, Aidan's jaw ached, but he knew it would feel better soon. Coffee heated over a hot fire would be a great start. After searching the cabinets in the small break room and finding a jar of instant coffee and somebody's cup reading *Walt Disney World* in large red script, he started toward the sink where Jeanette had cooked the previous night's dinner and began to reignite a fire.

"Let me do that. You men don't know your way around a fire, or a proper kitchen." Jeanette had snuck up on him and he was grateful for her help.

It wasn't long before Mally joined them. Fascinating how just the aroma of hot coffee — even if it was cheap instant — could make life a wee bit better even during the most troubling times of all. Jeanette began to tear up.

"What's wrong, luv?" Mally asked of his wife.

"Just look at us. Huddled around a sink in an abandoned dentist's office, happy to be drinking terrible coffee. Do you think things will ever be normal again?"

He gave her a strong hug and said, "I don't know, luv. But I do know as long as we're together, life's worth living."

"You always know what to say." She even felt like the sweet wan smile she gave him was honest.

"That's my girl," he said.

They filled two thermoses with coffee for the road. Even if it didn't stay warm, at least it was caffeine and hopefully would supply them with the energy they needed for walking.

Σ Chapter Fifty-Nine

Virginia Backwoods:
Destination — Georgia Guidestones

The Guidestones Call

The SUV's worn tires squealed shrilly when Strange made a ninety degree turn out of the dirt two-track onto the two-lane mountain highway pointing south at a speed higher than was smart. In the backseat, and trembling like a pair of hummingbird's wings, Lace and Cody held each other.

"Fuck," muttered Fleetwood, shaking his head and running his hand over his hair pushing it back.

"You can say that again," said Strange.

"Fuck," he said again, just because he could and because it made him feel better after what he'd just seen.

"We need to make up time while we can," Strange said, putting the pedal to the metal.

"Just get us away from here as fast as you can," said Lace. No matter how long she lived she would never be able to unsee what she'd just witnessed.

Cody said, "Shouldn't we try and report it to the authorities?"

"Well, number one, we probably couldn't find any. Number two, it's the end of the world. This is going to be commonplace. Number three, that old geezer said he was law enforcement. And if that's true we probably don't want to let anybody know."

"So, on top of everything else, now we're wanted felons," said Lace, starting to cry again.

"No, we're not," said Fleetwood. "We only did what we had to do."

Strange adjusted the rear view mirror so he could see her sobbing face. "Fleet's right. We're not like them. We would never do what they did. We were saving ourselves. Okay?"

She snorted in reply, which made him chuckle, and even caused him to smile sadly. But while he drove, Strange battled with his conscience and questioned himself in silence. How could he do the horrific things he'd done? Killing three people in such a callous manner as he had and without hesitation. It seemed like Fleetwood had been right when he said only the strong would survive. He just hoped the end justified the measures he'd had to take.

« Chapter Sixty

Cumming, Georgia:
The Good Guys 'HQ

Memories Get In The Way

While leaving Bill to plan, and Jeff to get a quick nap, Patrick went out to the terrace to get in a workout. His workouts were very important for Patrick. Some years ago, having suffered a stroke during a karate tournament, he worked hard to come back from that. He still has a residual limp and his workouts help to reduce the doubt in his ability to perform if push came to shove. Pushups, jumping-jacks, mountain climbers, and chin-ups from a portable bar hanging in a doorway. Counting reps, his mind wandered to his time married to Trudy. Meeting her when he was scuba diving at Lake Lanier and she was a Park Ranger. His black standard poodle, Hawk, had been his wingman, meeting her first and roping her in. Patrick still missed her and Hawk desperately. The beautiful dog had died, broken-hearted, not long after she disappeared from his life.

Tears streamed down his face as he counted jumping-jacks. Hot salty tears that burned twin tracks down his cheeks. He tried to use them to steel his resolve. To help him do what he would have to do if it came to that. His workout done, he rejoined Bill in the study. Jeff walked in, wiping crusty slumber from his eyes.

Patrick said, "I could use a stiff drink. Could anybody else go for a small batch bourbon?"

Bill said, "You know me."

"I knew I could count on you. Jeff?"

"It's not my usual, but I'll give it the old college try," he said.

"Good man."

Jeff, a fairly disciplined All-American football player, probably tried quite a few things in his halcyon days of college. But what happened in college, stayed in college.

›› Chapter Sixty-One

Atlanta, Georgia:
Evil Dwellers

Close Encounters

Bad Penny's band of Dwellers continued south on Peachtree Street. The broad avenue was not completely blocked with automotive coffins, but there were many. Next would come Midtown Atlanta. Not as trendy as Buckhead, but nevertheless it had once had good restaurants, clubs, and bars. In his completely human days Bad Penny had closed many of them down at three on many mornings.

He thought it unlikely they would encounter many more survivors, but nevertheless, he would follow the Queen's orders to a tee. As an unproven follower, he was still feeling his way in the Queen's dimension. He had the uneasy feeling she was waiting for him to fuck up.

And his intuitions were not usually wrong.

Z Chapter Sixty-Two

Unknown Shires of England:
Destination — Stonehenge

Picking Up The Pace

Aidan finished his cup of coffee and splashed the remains in the sink to douse the remaining hot coals. "Let's move. We should probably try to pick up our pace today."

Jeanette pouted. Mally looked sadly at his love. They collected their weapons and bags filled with belongings and canned goods from the examination room.

"How's the mouth feel, by-the-by?" asked Mally.

"I've felt worse," said Aidan.

They didn't bother to secure the door behind them.

"How long can the skies stay so grey? I'm sick of it," lamented Jeanette.

The greyness was more than a color. It was something tangible. The shroud of death had become something one could touch, something one could feel. And it felt permanent. The fog was as dense as it was in the early morning hours not far away in London almost one-hundred-thirty years before when Jack the Ripper butchered his first two victims.

"Winter is on its way, too," said Mally.

Looking at the date on his watch, Aidan said, "And if my watch is still accurate, tomorrow is Halloween."

"I still have some treats," said Mally. From his pocket he pulled a handful of colorful cellophane-wrapped hard candies he'd filched from the lonely jar on the duty sergeant's desk. Aidan shifted the carbine to his opposite hand. He and Jeanette each took one of the offered candies.

They dropped wrappers in the gutter of the narrow cobblestone lane. Mally hacked and spit in the street. They trudged south, around disabled vehicles and corpses. The smell of death permeating all, even the very clothes they wore. Heeding Aidan's admonition not to dawdle, Mally grabbed Jeanette's hand and pulled her not gently forward, at his quicker pace. "Don't dilly-dally," he said to her, then more animatedly, "Whoa! Gimme a minute."

"What is it?" He'd gotten Aidan's attention with the intensity of his voice.

"Only a proper packy. Just stay right there." He ran to a boarded up spirits store.

Aidan looked in the direction he was running and saw what had gained his attention. "There won't be anything left. Looters will have already gotten all of it," he hollered.

"You never know. It's worth checking," he yelled over his shoulder. Mally was a man on a mission, ripping the shattered glass door from its hinges and flinging it aside.

Indeed, once inside, the shelves were empty, the air thick and sour. But he didn't stop at the shelves. He searched under the counter where the ransacked old-style cash register once collected the community's quid. Unsuccessful in the shelf search, his head popped up, and rotated on a pivot. He located a closed door. Mally rushed to the unopened door, barely slowing down to shove it open. Jeanette and Aidan were fast on his heels. A few unsullied bottles were in open cardboard boxes. He tossed those aside until he found what he was looking for. An eighteen-year-old Macallan Fine Oak Scotch. As a Scot, Mally called it whisky. He lifted it upward and kissed the label.

Jeanette feigned a pout. "You never kiss me like that."

He winked at his wife. "We bevvy some ay thes tonecht an' Ah shaa. It pleases me lips, it diz, but nae as much as yer sweit kiss."

Σ Chapter Sixty-Three

**Rural Virginia:
Destination — Georgia Guidestones**

From Bad To Worse

"We need to find somewhere to bed down," said Fleetwood.

"Plenty of barns around," said Strange.

"I'm afraid to go to sleep," said Lace. "I just know I'll have nightmares."

"Well, we need to get some sleep," said Strange.

"And I'll hold you while you sleep. I won't go to sleep all night if you don't want me to," Cody said comfortingly, yet not thinking only of her lover.

Appearing ahead was a dark barn constructed at least four decades before and sited close to the road. Strange slowed and turned into the short dirt road as quickly as he could. To lessen the chance of being noticed, he pulled to a stop behind the old building.

"What do you think?" he asked.

"Let's do it," Fleetwood said.

"What about you guys?" he asked of the back seat.

"It's not the Ritz," said Cody, "but it looks better than our last digs."

Lace nodded pathetically. Strange turned off the engine. They climbed out painfully. It was probably more psychological than physical pain. The pain of stress. The dark was all enveloping in the remote mountains and underneath the veil of dismal low clouds. One could smell and feel the darkness, and it smelled and felt like death. The planet wore the dark like a shroud of death, an eternal Stygian night.

"I've got to pee," said Lace, as she started to walk away.

"Me, too," Cody agreed.

"Y'all stay together and don't stray too far," said Strange. The further south he went, the more his Tennessee accent and vernacular came out. Maybe it had to do with crossing the Mason-Dixon Line.

"Don't worry," said Cody.

"No way," said Lace.

Inside, the barn looked like it had been abandoned for at least half a century. Dust and cobwebs were everywhere enhanced by the odor of old age and mildew.

***

"There's a small stream just inside those trees," Cody said, pointing over her shoulder through the barn door at the copse across the turnaround.

"Cool, maybe we can wash up before we leave in the morning. Unless Strange wants us to get an early start."

"That would be wonderful," said Cody, "I've never felt this dirty."

"Me either," agreed Lace. In truth, lying on the floor of a chicken coop pretending to be deathly ill would make one dirty.

"Then maybe we can wash each other," Cody said with a hopeful gleam in her eyes.

"That would be nice."

Having just peed against the outside barn wall, Strange and Fleetwood heard another stream and headed toward it, toothbrushes and toothpaste in hand. They could be taking a chance cleaning their teeth in the possibly tainted water, but Strange carried the bottle of Irish whiskey, prepared to gargle with it. Fleetwood said, "That stuff will clean anything it doesn't kill." They hoped it would kill any resident microbes in dirty water.

Strange carried the shotgun, just in case they encountered anything that needed killing.

By the time they returned, Cody and Lace had already laid out their bedding and were sleeping the sleep of the dead. So much for Lace saying she wouldn't be able to sleep. They were curled up tight, trying to battle the cold with mutual body heat.

Looking at them, Fleetwood said, "I'm not going to let you cuddle me, Strange."

"Promise?"

"Smartass."

"Me?"

» Chapter Sixty-Four

Atlanta, Georgia:
Evil Dwellers

Reminiscing

As the wolf drove, Bad Penny gazed and remembered. Like parents trying to decide which of their children is their favorite, or a writer his favorite book, he fondly recalled the murders he committed. Two particularly heartwarming ones were at two of The ATL's best dance clubs — Tongue & Groove and Rain.

After passing those nightspots, further south on Peachtree Street they approached the Catholic Cathedral of Christ the King where Bad Penny caved in the skull of a monsignor with a jewel encrusted chalice he stole from the altar. The high priest was left lying in a pool of blood in a confessional. That one actually gave him pause since, as a practicing Catholic, he was worried about his eternal soul and damnation. Even so, seeing the cathedral flooded him with good memories of better times. He recalled sprinting across the large church's vast grounds to elude capture and his heart raced with the recollection.

A small white poodle bounded across a Peachtree mansion's once beautiful lawn. Probably wondering where everybody had gone and looking frantically for its family. The wolf slammed on the brakes.

Bad Penny thalked a scream. *"What are you doing?"*

The wolf pointed at the poodle and thalked, *"This one's just for me; it's been awhile since I've had the taste, and just because I want it."*

Bad Penny recalled sitting on the side of a road and sobbing after he'd run over a mutt with his truck and killing it. It still tore him up inside. He thalked sternly. *"No. Not on my watch. That will not happen. We're under strict orders from the queen to kill any Earthwalkers we encounter. Not helpless puppies."*

Properly chastised, the wolf backed down, and even had an obedient look on his face, but Bad Penny had read the wolf's thoughts before he shut them down. *"Fine, but this isn't over — not by a longshot."*

Σ Chapter Sixty-Five

Rural Virginia:
Destination — Georgia Guidestones

A New Day Dawns Still

Strange stirred as the dark of the nighttime sky gave way to early morning velvet gray. If there were anyone worth shaving for he would have, but now it would be a waste of time. He went to the stream again, toothbrush in hand, carrying a bundle of fresh clothing. After brushing his teeth, he stripped off his filthy clothes and eased into the icy stream. The clear, frigid mountain runoff was not only cleansing but cathartic after the trauma of killing three people. After bathing, he washed his dirty clothes ceremoniously in the crystal waters. His Heavenward hope was that he'd be able to wash away the pox he was sure inhabited them.

Shivering, Strange dressed in dry, fresh clothes and walked back to the barn, passing Lace and Cody on their way to freshen. Thinking like a woman, Lace had the forethought to abscond with individual-sized bottles of soaps and shampoo from a previous night's stay in the abandoned hotel so that, given the opportunity, they could have a soothing bath.

"We may be a few minutes," Cody said with a twinkle in her eye. She hoped that bathing each other with the sweet smelling products might lead to other more interesting activities. Of course, being the more physically demonstrative of the two, Cody was always hopeful an opportunity might present itself, even though she had to admit after the events of the past couple of days she might need to leave well enough alone and just hope for comforting each other.

"Well, don't be too long," Strange said with a mischievous wink.

At water's edge, Cody examined the products Lace carried. "What, no hair conditioner?"

Z Chapter Sixty-Six

Unknown Shires of England:
Destination — Stonehenge

Momentum

Looking forward to the vespers with a few glasses of the Macallan Fine Oak Scotch he'd picked up at the packy earlier that day, Mally walked with renewed vigor. They'd barely reached the outskirts of town when they approached the hamlet's lone cemetery. No more than four acres with a white two-story arch standing sentinel above the entrance.

"What the hell is that?" asked Mally pointing to the far side of the plot.

He pointed to what amounted to a foot-high cage of steel bars, embedded in the dirt over the length of a marked grave. To get a closer look, they entered the gates and crossed the grounds, dodging mud puddles all the while. They passed gravestones from at least five centuries before as well as a mix of eras between two fresh mounds of dirt.

They stopped next to the cage and set down their bags. The cage stretched a little longer than a full-size casket's length and a wee bit wider than its width. Mally and Aidan shouldered the weapon's they'd borrowed from the bobbies.

"I've never seen one before, but I've read about them. Four or five centuries ago, if a family was concerned about their loved one rising from the grave and becoming a member of the undead — a zombie, as we know them now — they would cover the grave with the iron bars to keep them from escaping the tomb."

Jeanette shivered and said, "That's spooky, so let's keep moving."

"Yeah, we've come a long way since then."

"I'll say."

They picked up their bags of essentials and retraced their steps, exiting through the burial ground's main gate, then turned south to continue their route. They walked alongside ancient railroad tracks. A locomotive's long bellowing whistle fractured the land. Aidan looked to the horizon, but it had been his imagination. He shook his head, trying to will the image from his mind. Wishful thinking, that a train full of living, breathing people filling its hard frozen seats would come barreling down the track, rescuing them from the loneliness of the end of the world. Of course, the way things were going it would have probably been an ancient steam engine from an Agatha Christie novel filled with apparitions and nebulated by an ethereal fog.

It was odd not to hear the sound of a train anywhere he'd been in almost two weeks. Or to hear or see an airliner high above. London's Heathrow is one of the world's busiest airports and normally jets, landing or departing, filled the sky all hours of the day. A few kilometers down the two-lane road and there were no signs whatsoever of civilization. Never would there have been many folk; seeing none at all, though, was quite disconcerting. Just greyness abounding. Sky, trees, ground, the dark ribbon of macadam.

The wilderness of old-growth, grey-barked-trees encroached both sides of the two-lane byway. Barely enough room for two cars to pass before the sides of the road were lost in the dark of the primeval forest. Black limbs like spindly arthritic fingers spidered outward from each side, meeting in the middle over the backwoods road. While continuing their path, a stentorian other-worldly roar pierced the stillness chilling them to their souls.

"Sounded like a lion," said Mally.

"Sure did," said Aidan, "but —"

"But there aren't any lions in this part of the world, except in the London Zoo, and it has to be at least a hundred kilometers from here. I know their roars are loud, but they couldn't carry that far, not on a dead wind. Eight to ten kilometers is about as far as their roars can carry."

Receiving astonished looks from the others, Mally continued, "When I was a wee lad, the King of Beasts was my favorite. I studied them all the time. I was sort of a lion geek. Back before Google we had to use encyclopedias. Britannica. The best there were back in the day. Although I'm sure they have a website now. Anyway, a lion can travel from ten to fifty kilometers a day when searching for food. And if that big boy got away at the beginning of Armageddon, he could easily have made it this far. So keep a weather eye, me mate."

He and Aidan unshouldered the carbines. "Do you know to handle the semi-automatic?" Mally asked Aidan.

"I think I've got it. Just pull the trigger, right?"

"Close enough." Mally slammed the magazine home and worked the slide slowly, showing Aidan how to do it, injecting a shell into the chamber. "Try it."

'Really?" The look on Aidan's face was skeptical.

"Like I said, we need to know. Here," he said, handing the weapon back to him. "Put your left foot forward, most of your weight on it, right cheek on the stock, and shut your left eye, or leave them both open. That's personal preference.

Jeanette, quietly getting more scared at their cavalier attitude, said, "Hello, there's a hungry lion."

Aidan took his time lining up the barrel on a single old tree in the distance and squeezed. The weapon fired and the crack echoed off a dying world, even more deafening than the lion's roar. But bark and grey dust flew from the huge tree's trunk.

"Splendid," said Mally.

"Good job, guv," said Jeanette, still frustrated at their lack of urgency. The look Aidan gave her could only be described as stern. He wouldn't brook passive aggressive respect. Properly chastised by Aidan without him uttering a sound, she said, "Sorry. Old habits die hard."

Aidan, said, "Alright then, let's keep moving, but eyes open."

It was well nigh mid morning when the sound of a roar was even louder.

"We must be getting closer to him," said Aidan.

"I hope so," said Mally.

"What do you mean 'you hope so'?"

"What I mean is, I hope he's not getting closer to us. I hope he's not stalking us."

"I agree. In the words of the immortal Shakespeare, that would sucketh."

They couldn't believe Aidan was trying to be clever at a time like this. And besides, it was common knowledge that math professors weren't known for their keen senses of humor. The trees on each side of the rural pathway gave way to fallow farmland, still in tidy rows. Had probably been a sugar beet field.

"There's the big fellow," said Mally, pointing across the field, as excited as the ten-year-old boy that fell in love with the second largest cat in the world.

"See that long mane and how dark it is? That tells you he's old and why females would want to mate with him — you know, to pass those good long-life genes on to their young. No doubt, at home on the Serengeti, he would be the leader of the pride. Those healthy genes, in fact, are probably the reason he hasn't succumbed to The Plague; at least thus far."

The lion held still and proudly lifted his regal head. No question that he picked up their scent on the wind. The lion turned its massively maned head toward them, lifted it heavenward, and roared a call of the wild.

"He's got us in his sights," said Mally, unshouldering the high-powered rifle.

The beautiful but deadly animal loped toward the threesome.

As the proud animal closed the distance between them, Aidan asked nervously, "Aren't you going to shoot him?"

"I don't trust myself not to miss at this distance. I need to draw him closer."

"Draw him in closer?" Aidan said, quietly frantic, as the beast picked up speed. "For Christ sake, are you quite mad?"

"Just a wee bit closer, and he'll be right where I want him." Mally hadn't even raised the rifle yet.

"A wee bit closer?" Aidan said, incredulously.

At one hundred meters, Aidan shouldered the rifle and put the sight on the unsuspecting courageous animal's massive chest to watch what unfolded. Closing his left eye and holding his breath, the loud crack from Mally's trigger pull caused him to jump nervously, like a soldier suffering from a severe case of PTSD.

After the shock of the gunshot, Aidan relocated the animal through the sightline of his gun and continued to watch, as it kept running toward them until a large circle of dead red spread dark on its broad chest and then the noble beast fell in its tracks. He hadn't known he was dead until the moment he fell.

Aidan was sweating and Mally exhaled his held breath. Jeanette collapsed to her knees in cold relief. After the sound of the blast and the release of the breath that followed, all that could be heard was the disquieting silence of the forest surrounding the open field. Mally helped Jeanette to her feet comfortingly, and they walked toward the fallen lion. Mally crouched on one knee and thought he saw the animal's chest move. Thought he breathed. It was wishful thinking, though. There had been no breath. He made the sign of the cross. The King of Beasts smelt of hot blood and wild earthiness. He truly regretted having to kill his favorite animal. It wasn't the creature's fault the zoo's doors had opened setting him free.

And the truth was, right up until the second he'd had to kill the beautiful beast, he'd been excited because most of the time when he'd seen them at the London Zoo they'd been asleep. To see one charging them like that had been horrifyingly exciting. It had long been a dream of his to go on a safari and see them in the wild. He had no idea he'd encounter one in the wilds of England instead of it's natural habitat, the wilds of Africa.

« Chapter Sixty-Seven

Cumming, Georgia:
The Good Guys 'HQ

Preparing For War

Patrick, Bill, and Jeff stepped up their preparations and pace of their training for an attack on the Dwellers compound. Running. Shooting. Working out. But they thought even during an Apocalypse it would probably be a little much to practice with the rocket launchers.

"Dude, we're shooting up quite a bit of the 9mm ammo. You sure there's plenty more?" Patrick asked.

"Yeah, no problemo. As mucho as we need." Jeff's Spanish sucked, but fortunately he had access to a large supply of ammunition at his former employer's HQ, the now derelict Forsyth County Sheriff's department.

"Awesome."

"Yeah, we can shoot our asses off. Not literally, though."

Patrick and Bill both gave him a "I can't believe you said that" look. After an afternoon session of working out on the terrace, Patrick heard from Duncan. *"Hey, Cuz, what's up?"*

"Not much, just getting ready. What are our friends up to?"

"Apparently, Trudy — excuse me, Queen Gertrude — wants things to move along faster than they are and she's sent out hit squads to track down and kill any Earthwalkers they encounter."

Patrick shook his head. *"Shit, they're killing ninety-nine per cent of the people on the planet and that's not good enough for her? Not the Trudy I remember."*

There was nothing about Queen Gertrude he would recognize. If indeed he met her again, neither would be capable of remembering the other fondly.

» Chapter Sixty-Eight

Atlanta, Georgia:
Evil Dwellers

An Uneasy Détente

Although Bad Penny wouldn't have wanted to take on the wolf one-on-one, he had the power and authority of the queen behind him; there was no way the wolf wanted to go cross with Queen Gertrude. So, they basically came to a gentleman's agreement to stand down. Although the wolf, with his mangy gray coat, not-of-this-world three-inch fangs, foul breath, and worse demeanor, was no gentleman and never would be.

Σ Chapter Sixty-Nine

Rural Virginia:
Destination — Georgia Guidestones

The Gray Day Dawns Brighter

On his way to bathe in the stream, Fleetwood passed Lace and Cody returning. They held hands. Smiles on their faces were proof of what they were feeling, showing that a satisfying physical relationship could make life worth living even at the end of the world. The sun rose, but the world was still gray. Although thrilled to be alive, the four were happier than they were when the sun set on the murderously berserk night before.

Dressed in their autumn colors, the mountains of The Blue Ridge Parkway would have been beautiful had it not been for the permanence of death's evil gray enveloping all. Underway and continuing toward Georgia, the going wasn't as tedious as it would have been on the congested interstate, but nevertheless, the roadway was still slow-going due to the dead vehicles.

"Unless we can get more speed, it's still going to take us too long to get to the Guidestones," said Strange.

"Even inching around all these cars is still better than walking," Fleetwood said gazing out the window at the expanding death around them.

"Amen," said Cody, even though she wasn't religious.

Lace made the sign of the cross.

Z Chapter Seventy

Unknown Shires of England:
Destination — Stonehenge

Persevering

Rain began to fall as they restarted their flight to save the world. They wore the only jackets they had, not heavy, and too light for this weather. Certainly not warm enough if their trek lasted into winter. Not long after, Jeanette began to limp and cry.

"What's the matter, luv?" Mally asked of his wife.

"I have a rock in my shoe and it hurts."

"And that's why you're crying? Why didn't you say something? Sit down. I'll get it out for you."

"Seriously? Are you quite daft? No. That's not the only reason I'm crying. I have a rock in my shoe. My foot hurts. It's raining. We're trying to walk hundreds of kilometers in the rain and cold to stop the end of the world from becoming reality. If. It. Hasn't. Already! I can't walk that far. I don't know what I'm doing. I don't know what anybody's doing. I don't know why this is happening. You just killed a lion. In England! To keep it from eating us. Do I need to keep going?"

She flopped herself to the cold damp ground, quite hysterical now. Mally bent and unlaced the offending shoe and slipped it off. Her sock came with the boot. He shook the rock out and handed it and her sock back to her.

"Just keep crying. It will be good for you," he said. He bent down, kissed her dirty foot, swept away her tears with a stubby thumb, and then wiped her nose using the same appendage. He wished he could make everything alright for her. But that was beyond his powers.

Underway again, using the sleeve of his jacket, Aidan wiped raindrops from the crystal and glanced at the date on his watch and said, "Six weeks at the rate we're going. If we step up our pace a wee bit, we might can make it in five."

"Beg your pardon," said Mally.

Aidan spoke louder. "I said at the rate we're going it will take us five or six weeks to get to Stonehenge, depending."

But they were yet to find out what they'd encounter along the way. With his tongue, Aidan explored the crater of the missing canine. Psychologically the space felt much larger than the size of the missing tooth. Eating no more than one less-than-hearty meal a day, combined with all the walking, each of them were already beginning to lose weight. Mally's huge muscles were even more defined. Already the physique of a lean triathlete, Aidan was getting skinny. Jeanette was losing middle-aged woman's fat. If she were trying to look for a flicker of good in all this, she didn't mind that.

"And bye the bye, are you guys still having dreams about the Stones? Hearing voices?"

Mally shook his head angrily. "Every goddamn time I close my eyes. And I'm about to get good-and-damn tired of it. Pardon my language, luv," he said, casting a sheepish sideways glance at his wife, "I just have a piss poor attitude from having to kill that lion."

"Me, too," said Jeanette, though not nearly so colorfully.

"Do you think they're just oneiric or do you believe someone or something is actually speaking to us?"

"I'm leaning toward them being real," said Mally."

"I agree. Why don't you guys tell me about them while we walk?" Aidan suggested.

>> Chapter Seventy-One

Atlanta, Georgia:
Evil Dwellers

A Change Of Direction

"We should move out of Atlanta proper," Bad Penny thalked to the wolf.

"You're in charge," said the wolf, almost choking over his thoughts.

"It's settled then. And you're my second-in-command," answered Bad. It couldn't hurt to extend an olive branch to the killer wolf. The wolf started the truck again and dodged disabled cars. *"See that huge granite-topped hill?"* Bad Penny pointed toward Stone Mountain about twenty-five miles to the east. The animal had a good innate sense of direction.

"Yeah."

"Just keep driving 'til you run into it." The others in the truck thought it was funny, even if the wolf didn't. Trying to make small talk, Bad Penny thought of the wizards who could change into animals in the Harry Potter books. *"By the way, are you an Animagus?"*

"Nyet. I'm not protean. I'm a wolf. Just a wolf. Always been a wolf." He didn't seem to be amused by the question.

"Okay, okay. Just asking."

"Well shit, don't ask. And just when we were starting to get along."

Bad Penny lowered the window on his side. The wolf's foul aroma was beginning to turn his stomach. Then he pinched a flea on his arm. He didn't have to wonder where that came from. But at least it wasn't as bad as a huge gray-blue cow tick would be. Bad wondered if fleas were something akin to cockroaches or bacteria with the ability to survive nuclear war or an evolutionary virus-based apocalypse.

❮❮ Chapter Seventy-Two
Cumming, Georgia:
The Good Guys 'HQ

Remembrances

Patrick reminisced about his and Trudy's first Christmas together. They were so in love. She adored the beautiful cream-colored standard poodle he gave her for a gift. He could almost hear the long-ago conversation —

"Thank you, darling. She's beautiful!" Trudy had said.

"What will you call her?"

"She's pearl-colored, so I think I'll call her Pearl."

Pearl became the sister of Hawk, the black standard who acted as his wingman and helped him woo Trudy. Now, all were gone and he missed them terribly. He actually hoped he would die soon. That would be better than living with this psychological and emotional torture. Die in battle with the Dwellers or by the hands of The Plague.

It really didn't matter which it was.

Σ Chapter Seventy-Three

Rural Virginia:
Destination — Georgia Guidestones

Hope For The Future

Still on the Blue Ridge Parkway, they came to a two-lane crossroads, made up of a general store, service station, and undefiled dry cleaners. With the same coil of rubber tubing they used the night before they were able to siphon some gasoline to top off the tank. With any luck at all they'd be able to make it to Georgia on the full tank and worry about finding more down there. At the dry cleaners were found some cold weather apparel.

Entering the small store for provisions, the sound of a baby's cry was both startling and comforting to them. A bone-thin young woman, her face pinched like a sickly sparrow, sat on a bench cradling a baby in a filthy blanket. She was in her early twenties at the most. The baby had the solemn look of a vagrant but beamed a beatific wan smile their way.

"Hello, sweetheart," said Lace, using her best bedside-manner voice. The young woman, startled by the stranger speaking to her, turned away quickly. "It's okay. I want to help you."

The young woman, really nothing more than a girl, mewled softly as if in pain.

"We have to help her," said Lace.

"We'll do whatever we can," Fleetwood said.

Strange flashed him a stern look. They were on a mission and didn't have time to waste.

"Why are you here?" asked Lace.

"My boyfriend died. My parents died. River's only two months old. Isn't she just beautiful. We're all alone. I'm Emily. We don't have nowhere else to go."

"She is so beautiful," said Lace, "and it's so nice to meet you, Emily. I'm Lace and this is Cody." The baby, apparently getting enough to eat probably at the mother's expense, was still fat and cherubic, with a full head of mocha-colored hair turning to a rich dark auburn.

"Can we take you anywhere?" asked Fleetwood.

"We've been sleepin' here, in the store. We ain't got nowhere else we can go. And there's still food, as long as I'm creative. I keep hoping this will end and people will come back. What do you think? I don't know what I'll do if they don't. I'm not going to let her starve."

"It's obvious you're a good mom. I don't think you have to worry about that. I think you'll figure it out." Lace still had images of the woman who jumped off the skyscraper in Philadelphia with her baby, crashing into the car's hood. She didn't want to think about this girl doing something similar.

"I try to be a good momma, but it's hard without any help and with everybody dying. Do y'all know what's going on?"

"You don't know?" asked Fleetwood.

"Well, the TV ain't working, and the newspapers are from before it started. Besides, I might not coulda read them real good anyways. I only graduated eighth grade, and I never have been any great shakes at readin'."

It seems she was resigned to her fate.

Z Chapter Seventy-Four

Unknown Shires of England:
Destination — Stonehenge

Truth or Misdirection

The road they walked paralleled the meandering southward path of a languid grey river, itself a funnel that would disembogue into the English Channel near the Isle of Wight. At the base of the low but substantial mountains to the west, a heavy mist hid its silent sloping banks, swollen from the ever-constant cold tears from the abundant clouds.

Mally scratched his chin where the wiry hairs of his coarse grey beard were getting longer. He was thinking about the dreams he'd been having. "Well, this one, he says his name is Bad. I don't understand that. All of them keep saying we should speed up, get to the Henge faster. But for some reason, I can't quite put my finger on it, it feels like they are trying to mislead us." It was obvious Mally'd put a lot of thought into it.

"Well, I think the bigger concern is, if you think that," Aidan tried to draw it out of him, at the same time not wanting to lead him, "do you think it's someone really talking to us and not just nightmares?"

"I haven't thought about that, but yeah, I guess that's what I'm saying."

"Me, too. What about you, Jeanette?"

Easy to go along, Jeanette said, "I agree with you guys. By the way, how's your mouth?"

Aidan said, "It doesn't hurt as much as it did, but I still couldn't eat a steak. And I don't know what else to do except keep going. And I still believe I'm right about the Stones having a role in this."

"I'm in," said Mally, "even though I'm getting more knackered with every step. You, on the other hand, are used to this with all your running, cycling, and swimming."

"I don't know about that. This is different from what I'm accustomed to. And I'm not used to running, or walking even, in heavy lace-up boots. My feet are killing me."

"As they say in America, 'Don't feel like the Lone Ranger.'" Mally clapped his hands together to cast off the cold and return them to sensation. "So, let's pick up the pace." Instead of tootling, they strode with a purpose in the direction of the equator.

"You really think this will work?" Jeanette asked.

Aidan nodded. "I do. I still believe Earth has pissed off some minor deity, and if we go to Stonehenge and pay proper respect and pray, hopefully it will have pity on us and call an end to it. I have to believe that. I don't believe for a second this is an Anthropocene event."

"Ahthropo-what?" Malley said.

"Anthropocene. Caused by man," Aidan explained.

"Well, I certainly hope you're right," Jeanette said. The wet and mind-numbing cold was making it next to impossible for her to keep a positive attitude.

"Me, too," Aidan said under his breath. He wasn't as confident as he tried to project, but he didn't want Jeanette and Mally to suspect the truth.

» Chapter Seventy-Five

Stone Mountain, Georgia:
Evil Dwellers

Pleasant Memories

While technically a quartz monzonite monolith, most locals called it granite. Its name was Stone Mountain in any case. It rose up before them on the landscape like a huge swollen bruise. Just seeing it brought back warm memories to Bad Penny of one of his most satisfying kills. The vision he recalled was of being on top of the mountain, seeing a cute Asian girl wandering alone. He had punched her in the mouth, breaking perfect white teeth and knocking her unconscious before throwing her small form over the safety fence around the mountain's face. News reports said her name was Tess, a computer science major at Georgia Tech. She bounced off the massive back of Robert E. Lee's horse, Traveler, part of the largest bas relief sculpture in the world. CSI found her face and half her brain in an angry wash of blood and gray matter. Her corpse landed in a boscage of pines more than eight hundred feet below.

Bad Penny was jostled from his soul-warming reverie when the wolf crashed the pickup through the inert arm that was previously an active entry gate.

"Been driving long?" He chuckled to himself. *"Don't worry about it. Follow the road around to the right. There'll be a rear gate from the park that will exit onto Main Street and we'll see what we find there."*

"On it," replied the wolf.

"Do you have a name?" Bad Penny was still trying to connect with him.

"Not particularly original, but it's Wolf."

"You need a better one, then. Good thing I'm fairly clever," Penny said with a self-satisfied grin, *"I'm going to call you Fleatus. No offense."*

Wolf snarled without looking at him and tightened his grip on the wheel.

"By the way, Fleatus, how did you get here?" Penny knew he was pushing the envelope but he couldn't help himself. Living on the edge was just his way.

Wolf wasn't happy with the sobriquet, but he begrudgingly answered. *"You mean with the Dwellers?"*

"Yeah."

"Well, strange as it may seem, my ancestors, my grandparents, were unfortunate participants in the Chernobyl disaster. The reactor's actual name was the Vladimir I. Lenin Nuclear Reactor. In the Ukraine. You wouldn't want to go there. Terrible snow. Near the town of Pripyat. The reactor had a core meltdown about one o'clock in the morning causing a massive blaze visible for hundreds of miles. And since nearly every able-bodied man in the town worked there, every house and apartment's lights were soon on when everyone should have been asleep. Lighting up the city like Christmas. The fire department's vehicles raced to the site to try and control it."

Although Bad Penny was but a mere baby at the time it occurred, from history classes at Georgia Tech he knew Chernobyl had been the site of the world's worst nuclear disaster of all time. The April 25/26, 1986, accident released over four hundred times the amount of radiation as the bomb dropped on Hiroshima at the end of World War II. Wolf continued.

"Well, anyways, to make a long story short, the Soviet government relocated all the people from the affected area around Pripyat — about a thousand square miles. No one can ever live there again — well, maybe in a thousand years. But now, it's a vast desolate snowy wasteland of abandoned apartment buildings, factories and even a giant Ferris wheel in the once lively village."

The affected area was about the size of the entire state of Rhode Island, but mostly undeveloped. *"But as usual, they didn't concern themselves with the animals."* Wolf slammed his huge balled up paw against the steering wheel at the thought that still pissed him off.

"And a bunch of wolves, my ancestors, were exposed to radiation and started mutating. Bigger, stronger, faster, smarter. And more aggressive. The rest of the story I've only heard from others. But according to the ones I've thalked with, when Queen Gertrude remembered the event and about us, she thought we might be a good addition to her cause. But to try on a limited basis, if you know what I mean. She sent a team to the region and they brought me back. I'm kind

of an experiment. If I work out well, I assume they'll go back for more. Or, I was told, they may want me to spread my superior radiation-charged DNA to other species. Since we wolves have already spread it among other animals in the old Soviet bloc."

Wolf liked the idea of spreading his DNA. He finished his long tale just as they reached the rear gate exiting to Main Street in the little village of Stone Mountain.

That was more information than Bad Penny expected…or wanted. *"So, you're what? Some kind of lycanthrope?"*

"Hell no. Do I look like a goddamn wolfman? I'm all wolf. Just mutated. Evolved, if you will."

"An interrogative, if you will," Bad Penny thalked. *"Why do you stay?"*

"Why do I stay?" Wolf reflected on the question. *"The same reason you stay. The same reason we all stay. She saved my life. She saved all of our lives."*

Bad Penny knew he meant Queen Gertrude.

Wolf continued. *"I mean, I'm under no illusions that I'll live much longer. I'm sure I won't. I'm sure none of us will. But every day has been a gift, and we owe her for that. We owe her fealty. We owe her our allegiance. But that's just me."*

They reached the gate that opened onto Main Street of the quaint eighteenth century village of Stone Mountain. Wolf crashed through it just like he did the entry gate. Just in time to see two young men throw a cinderblock through an as yet undamaged store window. Bad Penny recognized them for what they were — their next quarry. He gave Wolf and the rest of the unit the go-ahead to take them down. For multiple millennia this was what wolves had been made for. At first he raced on all fours for maximum speed. When he drew close he raised up on his hind legs like a human and leapt. His front paw talons, magnificently long exposed fangs crowding his mouth, and long red tongue in an angry snout, all flashed and hung dramatically. His lips turned up, uncloaking angry blue-tinged gums snarling viciously. He ripped at one young man's exposed throat until the unsuspecting victim succumbed to the violence. Before the other could react, Wolf attacked him.

The others in the crew, the orangutan and leopard, didn't even have time to get involved. That was a helluva display, Bad thought to himself. But he forgot to use the thought blocker he was taught and Wolf heard him.

"Thanks. I guess this means we can work together."

"Maybe so. Maybe so." But Bad Penny still wasn't sure things wouldn't turn Batman, one of the terms he knew kids use for a fight today.

"Let's call it a day," thalked Bad Penny, *"but first..."* He grabbed a large black-handled fixed-blade buck knife from the broken glove box and hopped out of the truck. He walked toward the front fender thalking with a maniacal grin, *"By my count, I think that was fourteen. Of course, math was always less than my best subject."*

Figuring he'd get less respect if he were thought of as too smart, Bad always tried to downplay how smart he was. He bent over the truck's fading surface like an artist toiling delicately on an intricate canvas. He scraped stick figures into the faded green paint. Diagonal slashes were over two sets of four vertical lines, plus four more vertical scrapes to keep a visual record of the number of kills for the day.

"I think I'll drive," thalked Bad Penny.

Wolf exhaled a grim, low growl and looked unwilling to give up the wheel. Bad Penny grinned as if it were his hoped for reaction.

The orangutan, bored with their posturing and macho display of testosterone, thalked, *"I'm tired of y'all's bullshit. Why don't y'all just settle this like men...errrr...or like I don't know what, but just settle it. Damn."*

He didn't understand how funny that sounded. Everyone was aware of the notion orangutans didn't have a well developed sense of humor, unless it came to the elementary act of shitting in their hands and throwing it at people. They were low on the primate totem pole.

"You know what? Just drive. It's good for you. Keep you out of trouble."

Bad Penny was throwing shade at Wolf, trying to get under his skin. Of course if he were successful he didn't know what he'd do. Hoped maybe the orangutan would side with him. Then he might have a little bit, if not much more, of a snowball's chance in Hades.

Σ Chapter Seventy-Six

Rural Virginia:
Destination — Georgia Guidestones

No Reason To Be Optimistic

Cody gave Emily a clean blanket that she and River could use together. They'd be warmer sharing body heat. Unfortunately, it was dark blue and not pink, but hopefully neither of them would mind. Strange was impatiently tapping his watch trying to get Cody and Lace to hurry. Back in the SUV, he said, "It's not that I'm unsympathetic, but I don't know what else we could do. I don't want to see her baby die. But you tell me: What could we do?"

Fleetwood spoke first. "Couldn't we have taken them with us?"

Strange said, "And do what with her and the baby? Besides, she would not have come with us. That store is her comfort zone. Where she feels safe. That's where she belongs."

Cody harrumphed and Lace crossed her arms over her chest and stuck out her lower lip, but they all knew he was right.

"Next stop, North Carolina," he said.

They continued south on the Blue Ridge Parkway. Riding along the mountaintop, seeing the autumn colors and view to both the east and west, would have been spectacular if not for the gray dread tinging the atypically dismal reds, oranges, and yellow. Continuing south they skirted just to the east of the small and formerly vibrant city of Roanoke, now barely visible.

"You know, this area is where some of the greatest civil war movies ever made have been filmed," said Strange. Even though he'd been away for close to two decades, he still enjoyed and studied the history of the area. Indeed, he thought himself a Civil War expert. Something of an anomaly in New York. And he was still a Volunteer fan.

"Even though that's not my genre, I would love for them to make more in the future," Lace said. "That would mean there is a future."

"Amen," said Cody.

Z Chapter Seventy-Seven

Unknown Shires of England:
Destination — Stonehenge

One Foot After The Other

Mally took Jeanette's load from her. Threw it awkwardly over the shoulder with the carbine. He could handle two loads easier than she could one. Even though it was cold, when he swung the bag up he revealed the sweat stains soaking through the layers of both shirt and jacket.

"Thank you, luv. Let's get moving. I'm ready to go now."

"That's my girl," Mally said, with a grin.

Her burden eased, she was able to walk considerably faster and her mood even improved; even carrying the increased load, that made Mally feel much better. She was his life.

"I still miss the birds singing," she said. It seems her attitude wasn't quite as good as she wanted Mally to think.

"I know, luv. But at least I still have the beautiful sound of your voice."

"Charmer."

"Okay, you two. That's enough of the mushy stuff. Concentrate."

In all honesty, Aidan didn't really mind. He liked to see them happy under their dire circumstances. At the same time they had to maintain forward progress. A dead fat black raven, on the wing no more, fell at their feet. Probably succumbed to The Plague after feeding on dead animal...or human...carcasses. That was his last supper.

"A bird falling dead out of the sky. Well, bullocks, never seen that before."

"There's a lot going on that we haven't seen before," said Aidan.

Mally nodded in agreement. But he didn't want to slow down and anxiously tapped his foot, ready to go. He shouldered his packs again, gazed into the grey, and shuffled off south following his busted nose. A monumental step if there ever had been one. Dogged determination his driving force.

« Chapter Seventy-Eight

Cumming, Georgia:
The Good Guys 'HQ

Almost Ready

"I'm ready," Jeff said, to Patrick. "I'm tired of working out, target shooting, and running. I'm over this. And Bill is a slave driver."

"Sorry, but it comes with the rank." Bill grinned. "Speaking of that, let's do some more pushups."

"I've already done five hundred today. How many more do we need to do?"

Bill wrote in the air a one and three zeros and gave an evil grin as he said it. "I think five hundred more for a nice round thousand would be good."

Jeff just shook his head. Patrick said, "Come on Big Byrd, you can do it." Calling him Big Byrd would piss him off and hopefully serve to motivate him.

» Chapter Seventy-Nine

Greater Atlanta, Georgia:
Evil Dwellers

Tension Builds

"You know what? Fuck you," thalked Wolf. *"Just fuck you, and fuck Queen Gertrude too, if she doesn't like it."*

"You better hope she wasn't eavesdropping on us," thalked Bad Penny. *"You'll be up a shit creek if she was."*

"I'm sick of you both," thalked the orangutan. *"You're both goddamn morons."*

Wolf turned around and gave him a blue gums-bearing angry snarl.

Σ Chapter Eighty

Southern Virginia:
Destination — Georgia Guidestones

Better Accommodations

Slow going. The Blue Ridge Parkway continued to be choked by car coffins. It kept them from doing anything more than maintaining a speed at which they could walk faster. But at least they weren't walking. After a full day of creeping slowly southward, Strange said, "That looks like where we'll stay tonight."

Without flicking on the less than necessary turn signal, he made a last-minute hard left off the highway into the parking lot of a once elegant antebellum mansion. A hundred years before it had been a beautiful plantation home, but more recently a bed and breakfast, and had been in want of paint long before the Apocalypse began. It now had an even more bereaved look. They parked between two dirty, dust-covered cars, windows broken and doors open. A silver late model Nissan mid-sized SUV, the license plate showed it to be from Virginia, a local car. The other, a decades-old blue Volvo sedan, bore an Alabama tag. That had to be a guest. Spray painted in white on one side were the words "It was inevitable".

Maybe we'll get lucky, thought Strange. If the folks from Alabama had succumbed to The Plague before they could leave, it might be that they could scavenge some clothes or other items needed. Across the highway was an aged, dirty-white, low, rambling, concrete block building. A dive bar wearing rusted aluminum signs advertising nationally recognized and regional brews. The usually bright neon ones were dead. The bar shared the structure with a pawn shop that had once had a working doorbell.

Cody gazed longingly at the bar and said, "I sure could use a frozen Margarita."

Knowing how much her partner liked them, Lace grinned, "There's no way that dump would have a frozen Margarita machine. Costs way too many pesos."

"Besides the fact there's no electricity."

"And there's that."

"I so like Margarita brain freeze. It lets me know I'm alive."

"You're weird," Lace said.

"Maybe, but you love me."

"Yes, I do."

Thunder rolled low and threatening. The already thick humidity was soupy and clung heavy on the skin; the gray ash of death was still heavy on the air. After gathering everything they would need to spend the night, they exited the SUV. Lace watched Strange and Fleetwood gather weapons. With palpable fear in her querulous voice, she said, "Do you think we'll need those?"

Strange said, "Better to have it and not need it, than to need it and not have it."

A capricious wind blew through the tops of the towering paternal pines. They walked up a stone sidewalk passing through a trellised archway. Like the inn itself, it could use a coat of paint. Yet it still had the charming allure of a previous time. Stepping onto the shaded broad wooden front porch, Strange thought it would have been the perfect place to enjoy the prototypical Southern Gentleman's favorite afternoon cocktail, the mint julep, in a stainless steel cup polished to a high sheen, mixed with the perfect genuine Kentucky bourbon. It was the only drink that might cause him to forgo his beloved Irish whiskey.

The double front doors moaned loudly when they pulled them open. The ripe smell of old age and mustiness greeted them. Fleetwood dead-bolted the doors behind them. An ancient wooden valet stand with real brass room keys hanging on matching hooks, standing testament to a different era, greeted them. Strange scooped up the eight room keys that started with the numeral two. They trudged up the broad staircase carpeted in a green and gold design of large magnolias, dragging their rollers, their carry bags slung over their shoulders.

Fleetwood thought it reminiscent of the hotel in the great Stephen King book and movie, "The Shining". He regretted thinking it. Upon reaching the second floor landing, Strange glanced around and divided the keys equally between them.

"Y'all go that way," he said to Cody and Lace.

"I've never heard you say y'all before, Strange," said Fleetwood.

"I try not to, but I guess being south of the Mason-Dixon Line has brought it back," he said with a diffident shrug.

They walked off in opposite directions. The first room Cody and Lace tried had not been cleaned since the last guests checked out, most likely in a rush; so they checked room 204 and found the bed made and fresh towels. Fleetwood and Strange took rooms 206 and 207. A few minutes later Strange and Fleetwood knocked on the women's door. Not sure what to expect, Lace opened the door cautiously and peeked out.

"Want to see if we can find something to eat? Save what we have left?" Strange asked.

"Sure, we're pretty hungry."

"Come on, babe," she said to Cody. "Going to find something to eat."

"I don't want anything," Lace moaned. "This bed feels so good."

"Get that sweet ass of yours up. You need to keep up your strength."

"Okay, but only because you asked so sweetly."

Back downstairs they found the bodies of an elderly couple in the office area. They closed the door behind them to squelch the angry stench of death's bloat before locating the house's kitchen. It had been expanded and modernized to commercial size with the accompanying commercial grade appliances.

"I bet we can find something to eat," said Fleetwood.

Right then Cody spotted a row of large boxes of Raisin Bran cereal on the top shelf of a wire rack. "Bingo," she said, as she hopped up and poked a finger through the wire rack's bottom, punching the box to knock it out. Lace caught it when it fell.

"Nice catch," said Cody. "Now to find out if it's fresh."

Taking it from Lace, she ran her thumb under the seam at the top. The cereal was still enclosed in the sealed plastic bag so she popped a handful in her mouth, crunching it happily before handing the open box to Lace. Fleetwood found bowls and silverware, then grabbed another box. Finding a carton of Dasani bottles of water, he poured a third of a bottle over the dry flakes, digging in with a large spoon with the others looking at him like he was crazy.

Fleet stopped mid-chew. "What? We used to do it all the time in college. Healthy fiber and the water keeps you hydrated." He swallowed. "The only problem is they give me gas."

"I swear to God, you're the whitest black guy I've ever known, but I'm glad you have your own room," Strange said.

They collected all the boxes of cereal, then found large bags of corn chips apparently used for making cheese nachos. Two flashlights stored in a cardboard box in a corner might come in handy. Twin boxes of dry oatmeal and wild rice were healthy. They could add water and cook these over a fire. Those would stave off hunger at least for awhile. They felt good about their impromptu scavenging. Outside, even though it was obscured by gray, the sun was setting. They knew it would be best to be in their rooms before it was full dark.

"I brought cards. Feel like a game of Hearts?" Fleetwood asked Strange.

"Sure. What about you guys?"

"We have other plans," said Cody, winking at Lace. "I mean we'd love to watch Game of Thrones reruns on TV, but without electricity this is the next best thing."

"Next best thing?" said Lace like she couldn't believe Cody said that.

"Thanks, anyway," said Lace to Strange, with a sweet wan smile.

"Come on down if you change your mind. We'll be in my room. 206. It'll be cleaner than Fleet's — and smell better."

"Hey now."

"I'm just sayin'."

Z Chapter Eighty-One

Unknown Shires of England:
Destination — Stonehenge

One Foot in Front of the Other

Rain was falling again, but this time with pellets of sleet looking like bits of shiny shattered glass bouncing off the shoulders of their jackets. Mally and Jeanette put up their hoods and pulled the drawstring ties, fixing the toggles. Aidan pulled down his deerstalker's ear flaps and secured them. Jeanette didn't mind the rain since it kept Mally from seeing her tears. He would worry about her even more if he did. And she didn't like it when he worried about her. She wanted to protect him any way she could.

"Damn, just when I was getting use to the cold the goddamn rain starts again," Aidan said.

"And sleet," said Jeanette. She could hear it bouncing off the nylon shoulders of her parka.

"Thanks for reminding me."

"Anything for you, boss."

He gave her a dirty look.

"Just keep moving," Mally said, "and you'll be fine."

After spending most of the day walking in rain and listening to pinging sleet, they came upon a farmhouse and barn.

Jeanette said, "I think we should stay in the house tonight and sleep in proper beds."

"I think that's a positively brilliant idea," said Aidan. "And since this hole in my mouth is hurting I'd like to climb in bed early with a wee dram of Mally's whisky."

"Mayhap that's the best idea I've ever heard," said Mally, agreeing with Aidan. Of course he was buttering up his wife just because he wanted to get her in bed with the bottle of Scotch. "And I got the whisky for all of us."

Like the cottages from the previous nights, there was no candlelight, indicating the residents were most likely dead. They approached their target as fast as they were able to move with no plan other than to knock on the door and hope no one answered. A dog barked in the distance, and in the deathly silence it startled them. It was a frightened bark, yet at the same time lonely and angry.

Jeanette said, "I don't know, but I think maybe the world has already ended and we're still passing through on the way to the end. I mean what kind of capricious and arbitrary God would let this happen?"

"You already know what I think," said Aidan. Doubtless, tired as they were, he was more committed than ever to get to Stonehenge and kneel before the gods. In reality it consumed him.

» Chapter Eighty-Two

Georgia:
Evil Dwellers

Expanding Their Reach

Since they were already east of Atlanta in Stone Mountain, Bad Penny made an executive decision that they would continue driving east about another hour toward Athens, home of the University of Georgia. In his serial killer days he'd had good luck with college coeds and thought lightning might strike twice or who knew, even more. Bad Penny had taken over driving and his adversary, Wolf, seethed. The truck had developed an earthy smell from the scents of wolf, orangutan, and Bad Penny's own sour sweat.

Cars filled with bodies blocked their way and the one hour turned into two before he finally turned onto Broad Street, the darkened main thoroughfare through the college town. Like most university towns, Athens was crowded with bars, restaurants with patios, and clubs catering to the college-age set. On a normal Thursday evening in early November the town would have been packed with students succumbing to the beckoning call of happy hour.

An unsavory-looking young man scavenged through a corral full of trash cans looking for his supper. He was digging directly under a sign on a masonry wall reading 'No Trespassing'.

Bad Penny pulled to a stop, pointed, and thalked, *"Fleatus, sic em'."* He used language that would probably piss off Wolf, but he didn't care; he couldn't back off now or the others in the truck would perceive him as weak.

The strong stench of rotting garbage from the cans carried into the truck. Although it wouldn't be an impressive kill, Wolf couldn't turn down an easy score presented to him as a challenge. He leaped through the open passenger window. He would have leaped through the window even if the glass had been closed. Talons and teeth, growling and snarling, he tore into the young man's pink flesh. Thankfully for the young man, Wolf made it quick and the attack was over in but a few sanguinary seconds. Knowing the quick kill wasn't up to the proud creature's lofty standards or worthy of his heritage and provenance, Wolf self-consciously moped back to the truck.

Trying not to throw too much shade or call too much attention to the sad act, Bad Penny thalked, *"Good job. I could use a beer. How about you guys?"* Then turning to Wolf he said, *"I forgot, Fleatus. You don't have opposable thumbs,"* he thalked, slapping a hand on his knee. *"But that's okay. I'll pour your beer in a bowl."* Unable to help himself, he giggled at what he thought was a clever line.

It sent Wolf over the edge. *"I'll show you opposable thumbs, mudak,"* he thalked, taking a swipe with his left paw and anointing Bad Penny with four razor-thin horizontal threads of deep-red blood across the delicate white skin of his throat.

Bad Penny didn't know the meaning of the Russian word Wolf had used, but he was pretty sure he'd been insulted. He immediately realized he'd crossed over an unknown line. His eyes grew as large as saucers and in them the others could see that he knew how close he came to being royally fucked. He examined the wound in the truck's rear view mirror, gently touched it with the fingers of his right hand and touched fingers to his tongue. He felt an electric surge, besides thinking it a cool and tough-looking gesture in front of the others. He'd forgotten how warm and salty his own blood tasted. It made him more appreciative of life. His own, anyway. Kind of like watching your own heartbeat in an MRI. Life affirming but a tad spooky. Hoping it doesn't stop.

Bad Penny hopped out of the truck and went around to the huge rusty toolbox in the rear that spanned from side to side behind the cab. He shooed away the two creatures sitting on it, popped the top, and pulled out a large Styrofoam ice chest he had loaded down with beer before they left the estate. Told the two creatures in the back to help themselves before withdrawing a six pack of Dos Equis and returning to the cab.

Inside, he pulled off two for himself and gave Wolf and the orangutan two each. He couldn't resist and winked at Wolf. *"Don't hurt yourself, Fleatus."*

Unworried about seeing law enforcement while drinking as he drove, Bad Penny continued on Broad to the east side of Athens where he pulled into a small, ten room motor inn. A low, fifties-era motor court, the Travel Lodge probably wouldn't have been busy even if they weren't in the middle of an Apocalypse. Looming two-stories high, a neon sign with moving arrows pointing toward the motel leading weary travelers to its door was big enough to see even without lights. The flashing Vacancy-No Vacancy sign probably hadn't worked even before the electricity went off.

Bad Penny retrieved another six pack from the ice chest before they walked to the rank of rooms. Making it seem colder than it was, rain splashed in the asphalt parking lot, its spaces marked with faded yellow paint. There was no sound from the splashing, absorbed as it was by the heavy unjust clouds.

They were sure to get rooms. Doors were ajar and beds made. They secured five of the small rooms with old school double beds atop worn green shag carpeting that looked like sparse grass. Which was at least an indication that it had been remodeled in the seventies after being constructed in the fifties. The rooms smelled of bleach coalescing with the staleness of the old age of the rooms or just as likely from the age of the people that had been its usual guests.

Bad Penny let the others choose their rooms first and then, opting to be the loner that came natural to him, walked down the sidewalk past them, to the last room in the motor court, to get some separation between him and the heathens that were literally animals. He wondered if Fleatus would sleep on a bed or curl up on the floor and chuckled at the notion. He hoped the animal wasn't reading his thoughts at that moment. He still didn't want to bite off more than he was capable of chewing.

He plopped down on the sixties-era double bed covered with a beige knitted spread camouflaging unthinkable stains. It squeaked noisily. He popped the top on a beer like he didn't have a care in the world. And as far as he knew, he didn't...yet.

After a rest and a couple of beers, as Queen Gertrude's appointed leader of the motley crew, he went and banged on the doors of the others, moving on to the next without waiting for the previous to appear, before rendezvousing in the parking lot as the rain eased.

Bad Penny wondered if it were raining all over the world. He knew there was a good chance the planet would never recover from the ecological trauma they'd set upon it. Fuck 'em. He figured if he survived the next few weeks he would consider himself lucky. Might as well enjoy himself while he could.

Σ Chapter Eighty-Three

Southwest Virginia:
Destination — Georgia Guidestones

More Relaxed

"Do the goddamn honors, Fleetwood."

Strange was getting a little annoyed listening to him shuffle and reshuffle and wanted him to just deal the damn cards. They'd set a flashlight on a high cabinet in the corner that cast a wide beam on the room in a feeble attempt to bathe it in what they'd hoped would be more than a fading dim light.

Over jeans, Fleetwood had changed into a white Snow Patrol tee with a sunshine yellow image on the front — one of the many shirts from his rock and roll tee shirt collection. He'd sleep in it tonight. At least he hadn't put on the black Ramones concert tee that everybody was tired of seeing.

Strange said, "Are you sure you're black? Wearing a goddamn Snow Patrol tee?" He shook his head. "Jesus H. Christ, you are so white."

"Cool your goddamn jets and give me a fuckin' second." Fleetwood shook his head. "No wonder you're wound so damn tight."

"You'd piss off the Pope."

"All right, all right, I'm dealing the goddamn cards." Truth was, the reality of the end of the world was getting to both of them.

After an hour of Hearts and each sipping a glass of Irish Whiskey, both were getting bored. There was a light rap on the open door. Lace and Cody stood to the side grinning.

Cody said, "As it turns out, didn't take long."

Lace punched her lovingly on her upper arm.

"TMI," said Fleetwood.

"How about a glass of Irish?" asked Strange.

"Sounds good," they said in unison.

Everybody thought alcohol might help. It certainly couldn't hurt. Strange topped off Fleetwood's glass, and poured one each for the women before adding two fingers to his own. Able to forget where they were for just a moment, a self-satisfied smile found itself at home on his face as he did.

Z Chapter Eighty-Four

Unknown Shires of England:
Destination — Stonehenge

Keep Moving

The door rattled loosely when Mally forced it open into a small parlour. The comfortable but tired room's ceiling was water-stained. The cottage was a sight. A mess that made it obvious to Jeanette, at least, that a middle-aged divorced male was the sole occupant. Women always connected the dots better than men. It wasn't that the house in itself was that terrible. It's just that the signs were clear.

No pictures on dingy beige walls that could use a coat of paint. Unwashed dishes holding pizza bones. Coffee mugs in the sink. Empty pizza boxes and Chinese takee-outee cartons on the parlor coffee table. And several empty ale bottles in the overflowing plastic but unlined trash can. The walls and floor were imbued with a permanent stagnant smell of weed, old pepperoni, MSG, and stale ale. The owner had probably succumbed to The Plague somewhere else, work or the pub, maybe.

Looking around at the detritus-filled cottage, Jeanette said, "We should have picked one of the other houses to sleep in, instead of this one."

"It's better than sleeping in a barn, luv."

"I'm not so sure about that."

"Well, let's take a turn around and see if it gets any better," said Aidan.

He guessed the small house to be built right after World War II, when England was safe from the blitzkrieg, and soldiers returning home needing affordable housing. Many had participated in D-Day, along with American and Canadian soldiers in neighboring Normandy, France. Hard to believe to most Brits, now almost three quarters of a century removed.

Typical of small town cottages in rural England with its ubiquitous high-pitched wood shingled roof weathering grievously to grey. The tired shingles wore a sheen from a coating of frost. It had probably been a pleasant small cottage for starting a new family once upon a time, and if only for a moment the joyful sounds of children's voices replaced the bitter coldness of death. Passing through a small hallway, the owner's bedroom was as bad as the rest of the house with separate piles of dirty and clean clothes, one on the huge four poster oak bed and one in a corner of the worn wood floor. A small crucifix was hung gracefully on the wall above the bed's headboard. It brought back memories for Aidan of a wooden reliquary crucifix he'd had as a wee lad with a small niche in the back of the cross for the keeping of two paltry candles. The cross was incongruous with a small stack of light porn magazines on a nightstand, proof the cottage belonged to a single man. If he'd taken part in the sacrament they'd have been hidden away and not in the open. And if he were in a relationship he'd probably keep them in the boot of his car.

Most likely because it was rarely if ever used, the only room that wasn't a mess was the guest room, or if there never were guests, the vacant spare bedroom. Aidan said, "So, that's your room for the night." Mally smiled broadly about the prospect of privacy. The structure sagging with age, its floor sloped to the rear of the house just enough to notice.

"I can sleep on the settee," Jeanette said, gesturing from the small hallway through the open doorway to the humble green corduroy thing in the parlour. Once upon a time it had probably matched the forlorn rug on which it sat. A tan threadbare wool blanket was folded over the back. Used to cover up on a chilly night, before going to bed. It faced a huge flatscreen television, most likely in perfect working order; another sign of a single man living alone. For watching his favorite team of the United Football League. Probably worth more than the house it inhabited. But it was silent; silent and as dark as the night.

"I can set a blaze in the fireplace and it will be lovely," she tried again, not really convincing herself or Mally, who cringed at her offhanded comments.

"I insist that you two take the spare bedroom," said Aidan, "I trust you're fine with that, Mally." He looked like he wanted to kiss Aidan.

Jeanette went to the main bedroom and after searching through the bathroom cabinets and under the sink, returned with a bar of soap still in the wrapper. "I don't particularly like this brand, but it smells better than you right now, so if you want to sleep with me, go take a shower."

"Where?" asked Mally, unbelieving.

"Outside."

"Outside?"

"Don't tell me you've never taken a cold shower before."

"Oh, I've taken plenty of cold showers before, just not outside in the cold rain and sleet and snow."

"Well, just keep your mind on climbing in bed and getting under those warm clean covers with me after you do," she winked.

"'at warms th' cockles ay me heart, it diz," he said, enthusiastically taking the soap from her.

"That's mah big cheil."

Mally broke into a hopeful grin at the prospect of making love to his wife for the first time since before The Plague began. He headed toward the rear of the house where a door in the kitchen would take him outside. On the broad porch, he sat down to undress on a brown wooden preacher's bench, a work of art that appeared to have been handmade from a door. Even he had to admit that the odor he was giving off wasn't pleasant. Proof that Jeanette did indeed love him.

The interminable greyness was bound for wintriness. The scent of the coldest season carried on the still air. Everyone knows shadows can conceal evil, but when the whole of the planet is draped in shadow, they can't all cloak evil. Or can they?

Mally stepped behind the shadow of high bushes to shower, sure that no one would spy him by chance. While he soaped up, a bright red cardinal, startled by his presence, skittered from twig to twig in the top of the small tree next to his head. He hoped it was a sign from God of better things to come. After finishing his washing in the mixture of rain, sleet, and light snow, shivering and turning blue, he all but hopped onto the porch and dried off with a cheery clean yellow towel Jeanette had laid out for him along with clean underwear, new chinos, and a beige heavyweight cotton long-sleeve Henley he could sleep in. He'd lost so much weight on their journey that the chinos wouldn't stay up without a belt.

Mally entered the house, locking the door behind him. Inside, Jeanette had lighted some used candles she had found while searching for the soap. The dark cottage looked positively cheerful. Even as manly as Mally was, he liked it. Of course, Jeanette had been doing her best to help him get in touch with his feminine side for years, or so she would say, knowing it to be an untruth. He joined her in the bedroom before she said "My turn" with a grin and spun on the ball of her foot to go outside.

Mally said, "Well, hurry up and get back in here and get your hot buns in the bed."

"Don't be so cheeky," she said, turning again to leave, "No pun intended."

"Stay right by the porch. Don't wander off. We still don't know what might be out there."

He punched the pillow with a meaty fist then plopped down on his back, hands under his head, and watched the candles' flickering shadows dance on the ceiling of the inky dark room.

Until Jeanette returned, Mally lit a cigarette, thinking it might help him sleep, then counted sheep. That made him think of the great Phillip K. Dick novel "Do Androids Dream Of Electric Sheep", which had been made into the popular movie "Bladerunner" starring Harrison Ford. He shook his head to get that image out of his mind and thought of something more pleasant: The sight of Jeanette in a tiny, lace, something-something.

The door cracked open.

He was right about the tiny lace something-something. "That was worth waiting for. I'm glad you thought to bring it." Truth; she'd lost too much weight in his eyes. Probably only five kilos, but he liked her a little curvier. If he had wanted a skinny woman he would have married one.

"I knew it would make you happy."

The sheets were warm from Mally's body heat when she slipped into bed. And he still had enough meat on his bones to keep the both of them warm.

Mally had what remained of the bottle of whisky and poured a single tall glass. Jeanette was a lightweight; he would give her a wee sip and that would be enough to satisfy her…well, partially satisfy her anyway. He grinned in the candlelight.

Meanwhile, in the other room, Aidan took off his boots and set them side-by-side to dry on the wide stone hearth where a fire had been set. He went to bed all alone except with two fingers of fine Scotch, his old leather journal, a platinum Mont Blanc Meisterstück rollerball pen, and a sore mouth. As part of a community that uses computers for all communication, he knew his chirography could use the work. Thus the pen and paper. Even when going to bed alone at the end of the world he did it with panache.

He could have gone outside to scrape some ice off the front walk of stone, but he preferred his whisky neat. The strong warm alcohol immediately hit the angry gaping hole on the left side of his upper gum like a mollifying balm. But before turning in, he made the decision to get up and write for awhile at the old scarred claw-footed desk standing ready to work beside the bed. Aidan hoped writing could brighten his mood dark as the room.

He pulled a chair up to the desk, pushed his knees into the kneehole, and lighted a Lambert and Butler. The British-made cigarette wasn't well known anywhere but in the U.K., but Aidan thought it perfectly proper as a prop for writing. He didn't often smoke, but he envisioned Hemingway, or the famous cartoon of Henry James chained to his desk, writing while plumes of white smoke curled around their heads. The image suited him. It also helped him to stave off the cold in the unheated house, but the nicotine burnt the tip of his tongue. On the scarred surface of the ancient writing desk sat an old oil lamp. He turned the key to raise the charred wick and lighted it. Before even writing a word, he considered that his technique of writing would be dadaistic rather than realistic, which in itself would be in the stylings of Haruki Murakami, or if he were going to dream, Umberto Eco, himself a professor. In the dark of the room like a tomb, the lamp's flame reflected in the prism of his reading glasses' lenses. Aidan had always believed if one were going to dream, one should dream big.

A white cloud of warm breath in the cold room engaged with the smoke from the cigarette before inflating above the candlelight. He pondered his reflection in a glass-covered painting on the wall above the desk and his blood ran cold. In the gloominess of the room and with his pallor turning as grey as the universe, while getting thinner with every step and unable to maintain his grooming, he thought his visage ghostlike. The crater where the missing tooth had been was bothersome to his eye. With his tongue he explored the pit in his gum. It felt the size of a canyon.

Still, he could hardly believe he'd extracted his own tooth. The physical agony of that act was easing even if the psychological suffering wasn't.

The greying stubble on his jaw was growing longer. He thought it an apt look for a brilliant writer. He put the last pain pill from the dentist's office in his mouth, took a swallow of whisky, snapped his head back, and swallowed. He hoped it would ameliorate the hurt. In his journal he intended to record his thoughts about the world's end. In the dark lighted only by dim candlelight, he was soothed by the scritch-scritch of the pen on the rough sheepskin paper.

The Real History of The End Of the World
by Professor Aidan Walker

What can one say about the end of the world? Or even think about it? Alas, it has begun.

If you're reading this, it must mean I was successful in saving the planet. God knows it wasn't going to save itself. But, now that I think it through, if I'm going to muse by putting pen to paper, I'm part of the world, so maybe the world did save itself. And I was just the instrument. Yes, let us go with that. But this is no apologia. I will do my ablest to humbly accept my role of saviour. Nothing more than any god would do.

You're probably going to think this is a novel, a work of fiction, but believe me, it's all true. This is the way it used to be. I hope future generations — if indeed, there are any — will consider me like the Physics concept, a direct human wormhole to the end of mankind, and this book an epistolary. A letter between old friends.

So, we must go back to when it started. To begin at the beginning. But it's ironic that

the end is also the beginning. So, I shall start
where I shall start.

He twirled the tumbler on the desk and raked a hand through his long blonde hair getting longer. Not in an attempt to encourage the words to appear on paper, but to imagine. He pushed his reading spectacles to the end of his still-perfect nose and read the dim words before ripping the lonely page loudly from his journal and spewed the words "That's crap." He wadded it and threw it on the floor and started again. He rewrote the entire passage. Upon reading that, he only marked out the 'To', in the eleventh line. Nodding satisfactorily at the negligible variant, he muttered, "Now, it's perfectly concinnated. Full of verve and a splendidly luxuriant start to my story."

This was not to be a palimpsest however, he thought, so for that reason and it alone, it had to be perfect. And doubtless without containing a single meaningless trope. Indeed his goal was to keep the last days of the current world from becoming antediluvian. He hoped his book would be an organon for future generations...if indeed there were any.

It seems he thought he had the makings of a real author. If only he didn't sound too Murakami-like. God knows he wouldn't want to do that, even if he were capable of achieving that lofty status. Aidan thought writing by candlelight in longhand script, in a battered old leather journal was positively Hemingwayesque or, more apropos in England, Anthony Burgess-like. If his wildest dreams came true, then Kafkaesque.

He had penned twenty pages in the fading worn ledger when, glancing at the luminescent dial of his watch, saw it was after two in the wee hours of the morning, and so he set the daybook aside, stubbed out his third cigarette in an empty candy dish and snuffed out the candles Jeanette had so thoughtfully lighted. He wasn't quite sure why he cared about the time, unsure if time even mattered during an apocalypse. Why must they hurry? Why must they worry; about such things?

He felt surely that people who'd lived their lives by the clock — rushing to the office, scrambling to conferences, getting kids to school on time, racing to breakfast meetings to arrive before the eggs got cold — he hoped those people, if they were still alive, were allowing themselves to slow down. Because the end of the world would wait for them like a clown waiting in a sewer when they got there.

Before he fell asleep, he sensed a visitation from Burgess. Pissing off the erudite revenant, he'd probably summoned the great literary apparition himself by overestimating the heights of his writing prowess. And he reminded himself that if someone were imposing their thoughts on them, encouraging them to reach Stonehenge as some sort of red herring, what if those same beings could read his thoughts. Could they nick the manuscript he worked on? He'd have to push the words out of his mind.

***

Adhering to the habit that had become ritual, they all awoke with the light of dawn. Aidan met the other two in the kitchen.

"I just don't think I can walk even a single step more. Could we possibly rest for a day?" Jeanette asked of their de facto leader.

"I don't see how we can," Aidan said, "But how about we walk three more days and then we shall take extra rest after?"

"You're as tough a leader as you are a department head."

"Thank you," he said with a wink.

"And besides, your surname is Walker. I hadn't thought of that until just now."

"I hadn't either. Fitting, I guess."

After making love the night before, Mally thought the coffee had even better flavor than usual. Even if it had been cooked in an old pot over flames in the fireplace. It made Jeanette happy that Mally was happy, and that they could find some physical pleasure in the vast emptiness around them.

After coffee and collecting their gear, they rendezvoused on the front porch. In dramatic contrast to the dark grey firmament, the landscape was covered by white virgin snow. The white almost too intense for eyes desensitized by the interminable grey. The winter was wretched even though it had yet to begin. The aging blotchy white picket fence looked older compared to the brilliant frozen white. Even after sleeping in the cold house overnight, the outside chill stung one's skin. Especially on the face. Oddly enough, however, the cold dulled the pain of the cavernous void in Aidan's mouth.

They exited through the creaky fence gate, loud in the muffled quiet of the snow, and headed south through the undisturbed heavy white powder. Their boots shuffling through the frozen landscape sounded cold. The cold of the landscape matched the cold in their bones. Unsure as they were be it physical or metaphysical.

The snowy scene looked like a Christmas card and would have been pretty if it weren't for the reality of the end of the world.

» Chapter Eighty-Five

Athens, Georgia:
Evil Dwellers

Back To School

"I think we should reconnoiter, see if we can find any other opportunities, before we bed down for the night," thalked Bad Penny.

"Not a bad idea," agreed Wolf. Truth was that an impressive kill or a larger number at one time would make him feel better about himself and hopefully help him to look better in the eyes of the others after the shameful display of his earlier solitary kill.

The orangutan shook his head sadly at Wolf's thought. He wanted to see them, Wolf and Bad Penny, settle their differences once and for all. He thought he would be given more responsibility, no matter which way it went, no matter who survived. Thought he should be given more responsibility, since everyone knew primates were the smartest of all land animals. He wanted it only to curry favor in the eyes of the queen. Otherwise, he didn't give a shit. He didn't like either one of them. Believed they were both assholes.

The six Dwellers walked to the truck in the dumpy motel's parking lot, Bad Penny slapping the fender where he'd scratched the number of kills into its rusting paint.

On the east edge of Athens was an icehouse of the type that produced five and ten pound bags of cubes sold in large freezer boxes in front of convenience stores. Next door to it and across the gravel parking lot sat a service station that looked looted of its tools, oil, gasoline — things that could be useful. But if they got lucky, maybe people wouldn't have thought of beer in a cooler in the adjoining convenience store.

Unfortunately people had broken the glass doors of the refrigerated units, and the beer, sodas, and all foods of any kind were gone. But they hadn't thought of the stacks of cases of beer in the establishment's storage room. All they could find were a couple of mass-produced, American lagers brewed in the Midwest. Not one decent microbrew to be had. As the strongest of the crew, the orangutan waddled off toward the truck with three cases under each arm. With two each carried by Bad Penny and Wolf, they figured they'd be set for a few days.

Next, to the icehouse to see what they could find.

"Score," thalked Bad Penny.

Enough ice to last them for a month, if they had a way to carve manageable pieces off the what was probably more than thousand pound blocks even after slowly melting since the electricity went off. Hefting the sledgehammer they'd used as a weapon high over his head, in one powerful swing the orangutan broke the slab into three smaller suitcase-sized rectangles before proceeding to smash one of those into multiple pieces ranging in size from egg to football. Then, it was up to him to carry the larger blocks and the others the smaller ones, back to the truck. The larger two were clunked loudly into the black plastic-lined pickup bed. As large as the slabs were, and with the weather so cold, they wouldn't soon melt. Then they dumped the smaller pieces into Bad Penny's ice chest.

Back at the motel, Bad Penny stepped onto the sidewalk and thalked, *"Y'all come on in and we'll have a few and thalk about tomorrow."* He set the big ice chest down on the old carpet with a thump. *"Help yourselves."*

He went first, pulling out a Miller Lite and thalking, *"I haven't had one of these since high school."* He took a hearty swig. *"Fuck, shit tastes like dog piss."* Then looking at Wolf, he said, *"No offense, Fleatus."*

"I'm not a goddamn poodle," Wolf proudly thalked in return.

Bad Penny couldn't help it, even if he was digging himself in deeper. He guzzled another swallow, hacked up a mouthful of sickly yellow phlegm and spit it onto the filthy green shag carpet. *"So, I'm guessing probably nobody should curl up on the floor tonight,"* he went on, not easing up on Wolf.

The orangutan smiled sardonically and shook his head. His mouth alone smiled; his large somber eyes were emotionless. He couldn't believe Bad Penny said that. Seemed a little too much even for him. After finishing two beers the orangutan said good night and left to go to his own room.

Wolf agreed. *"Good idea."* Then turning to Bad, *"Dasvidaniya, asshole."*

The ape couldn't wait until it came to a head between those two. He looked forward to what he was certain would be a battle royal.

Σ Chapter Eighty-Six

Southwest Virginia:
Destination — Georgia Guidestones

A Replay In The Woods

Having polished off the bottle of Irish whiskey, Strange said, "That's a dead soldier. And we should probably call it a night. Nothing's changed. We still need to get moving early."

"Slave driver," said Lace, with a fake put-out grin.

She took Cody by the hand and said, "Take me to bed or lose me forever."

Cody said, "That line is getting so old and tired. It was even old and tired when Meg Ryan said it to Anthony Edwards in *Top Gun*."

Said, Lace, "Yeah, but you love it when I say it to you."

"I do."

"Okay, you two. TMI," said Strange. "Dawn's first light."

The flashlight was growing dim. Strange lit a candle they found in the large kitchen. He picked up one of the three shotguns and offered it to them with one hand grasping the barrel and holding it vertically. "Why don't you guys take one?"

He should have known what the answer would be even before Lace recoiled in repulsion and made a sour expression. She said, "Just come running with one if you hear us scream."

Cody said, "I'm not sure about that. I hope to be screaming."

Strange said, "So I'm supposed to distinguish between screams of ecstasy and screams of terror?"

"You got it," Cody said, winking at Lace.

The women padded softly off toward their room. Tilting the bottle of whiskey, Fleetwood shrugged happily and said, "Since I'm not driving."

Strange matched his shrug with one of his own and said, "Well, I can't let you drink alone."

"I knew I could count on you."

They sipped the warm liquid slowly, neither admitting they didn't want to be alone with their thoughts, and both enjoying the distraction from the night by the other's company. A half-hour later, just after the bewitching hour, Fleetwood stood, placed the glass in the small kitchenette sink, and said, "Okay, that's enough for me."

Strange stood and fist-bumped Fleet. Selecting one of the shotguns in the corner, Fleetwood crossed to the door and closed it softly before walking off to his room. Strange brushed his teeth, flossed, and literally fell onto the bed's springy mattress. Fleetwood did the same next door. Not a quarter of an hour later Strange was snoring like a foghorn.

Three a.m., a herd of motorcycles pulled into the inn's parking lot. A moment later came the sound of glass breaking. Strange recognized the achingly eerie creak of the Inn's old wooden front doors. Deep voices that weren't even making an attempt to be quiet.

This didn't sound good.

Wearing the sweats he slept in, Strange grabbed one of the remaining shotguns, crept to Fleetwood's room and rapped lightly on the door. Strange knew his friend was a deep sleeper, but he didn't think it would be possible he could sleep through the sound of a half dozen thundering motorcycles arriving, the shattering glass, and gruff voices. Turns out he couldn't. Fleetwood, more alert than Strange expected, answered the door holding the shotgun he'd taken to bed with him.

"What the fuck is that?" Fleetwood whispered.

"Not sure, but I'm guessing it's not the welcome wagon."

Almost at the other end of the hall, Lace and Cody stepped out of their room in their astonishingly tiny sleepwear. Strange raised his arm chest high, palm out and thumb down, and swung it violently to the right, parallel to the ground, trying to force them back in the door through sheer will alone. With them unseeing in the lifeless dark, he said in a stage whisper, "Back, get back."

Recognizing the urgency in his tone, if not the volume, they did as he said and hastily retreated to the room and shut the heavy door. The heavy lock clicked loudly when it turned.

The intruders sounded like they were checking things out just like Strange and crew had done a few hours earlier. Doors opening, closing, cabinets banging. Strange and Fleetwood hoped they would think the old Toyota SUV was derelict and leave without coming up.

Hoping for the best, but preparing for the worst, Strange and Fleetwood took up positions on each side of the broad staircase, shielded by walls with only the long dark barrels of the weapons exposed in the dark. Both were aware they couldn't shoot unsuspecting men without them proving to be a threat, which climbing stairs was not.

That would be the classic definition of murder.

In cold blood.

≪ Chapter Eighty-Seven

Cumming, Georgia:
The Good Guys 'HQ

Getting Bored

With nothing to do but work out, do a little shooting, and prepare mentally for their mission, Patrick, Jeff, and Bill were losing their collective minds. None of them were ones to sit around waiting.

Pacing on his terrace overlooking the shooting range Bill had designed, Patrick said, "I know we're ready, but, I'm sorry: Something just doesn't feel right, yet."

Colonel Bill Crain said, "We aren't in a hurry. Trust your gut."

"Thank you for the vote of confidence, my friend. But it won't be long now."

Z Chapter Eighty-Eight

Unknown Shires of England:
Destination — Stonehenge

New Transportation

They slogged through the heavy wet snow until the grey day began to turn black. The good news was every cottage they saw was dark, without so much as candlelight. They neared one that looked inviting, with a fine barn. Deciding they got lucky with the cottage the night before, this evening they opted once again for the barn.

Theirs were the only tracks in the heavy snow, boot or tire, leading up the long drive. Opening the double barn doors, the fresh smells of hay and horse greeted them. Disturbed by the intruders' presence, a whinny and snort surprised the group.

Aidan said, "Jeanette, I think we're in luck. We just may have found some reliable transportation."

The four horses had plenty of fresh hay to eat and a large trough of water and appeared to be in relatively good spirits and good health. Jeanette approached the smallest one softly, gently caressing her neck and nuzzling her nose. She was a beautiful chestnut with a small diamond-shaped patch of white between her eyes. The sweet mare seemed happy with unexpected human attention and gurgled a satisfied quiet neigh.

The rain, sleet, and snow had waned, so there would be no cold outdoor showers tonight.

And again they built a fire on a concrete-floored stall with the abundance of clean hay and a pile of fresh-sawn planks they found in a corner.

Mally said, "Let's have something different tonight. Instead of having Lima beans, corn and green beans, let's have green beans, Lima beans, and corn."

"You're such a goof," said Jeanette, "but I love you anyway."

"And I'm happy you do, I am."

After getting a healthy fire started, Jeanette opened the tins and placed the victuals in the blaze. She watched labels curl up and burn off in blue flames. The sheltered setting and warm food were nourishing to both body and soul, but try as they may, they couldn't forget where they were and what they hoped to accomplish. Lighthearted conversation didn't come easy. Aidan withdrew the old journal from his overnight bag and began to write by the dying firelight. That caused Jeanette to say it was time to brush her teeth and Mally went with her.

When they returned, Jeanette said, "I'm going to check on my horse."

It was funny to Aidan and Mally that the sweet mare had already become her horse. After too long, and Jeanette still hadn't returned, Mally went to check on her. He found the object of his love blithely curled up in the hay wrapped in the horse's loving, if bony, embrace. Each snoring contentedly, he needn't have worried if they would bond. The thought crossed his mind, what she would do if she had to answer the call of nature with the horse wrapped around her the way she was? Mally shook his head with a smile as he turned away. He found some horse blankets then draped her and the horse.

No beasts of burdens, these; they'd been somebody's pets.

Aidan decided they should sleep in. At least until it was full grey outside and not just a wee bit of lightness tinging the sky. Awhile later, Aidan was awakened by the vibration of air from movement through the barn. With barely enough light to see by he could make out Jeanette's form, dressed and wide-eyed, walking her horse toward the barn door dressed in a well-worn leather saddle and bridle.

» Chapter Eighty-Nine

Georgia:
Evil Dwellers

Return To The Fold

Early morning. The number one Dwellers hit squad, led by Bad Penny, made the decision to start back to the Sawnee Mountain stronghold of Queen Gertrude. One of the advantages to nearing the end of the world was one didn't have to check out of a motel; didn't even need to present a credit card.

The tension between Bad Penny and Wolf that had seemed to abate the previous night, was palpable and could have been cut with a knife or…perhaps wolf claws. But probably no one would want to see that.

Each seemed individually to block their thoughts from the other — the same as not speaking among the less evolved mouth talkers — and suffered in silence. The trip back to Sawnee Mountain from Athens, Georgia, typically two-and-a-half hours, would most likely take double that. Nobody was clearing vehicles from the roads.

And the tension would cause it to feel even longer.

Σ Chapter Ninety

Southwest Virginia:
Destination — Georgia Guidestones

A Close Encounter

Three tired large men trudged up the broad stairs. Each dressed in black leather biker boots — most likely steel-toed — heavy denim jeans and black leather jackets. One still wore his Nazi-style helmet. Probably to keep his ears warm even inside.

Using his deepest, whiskey-stained deejay voice, Strange threatened, "That's far enough," and ratcheted a shell into the shotgun's breech. He knew he should have had it locked and loaded, but he wanted the sound of it going home to welcome the intruders. Even louder in the dark quiet.

"Be cool. Be cool," said the biggest of the bunch.

"We'll be cool if you will," said Strange, as Fleetwood injected a shell into the breech of his weapon, even if it were not as smooth as when Strange did it. Perfect timing on his part, though it was unintentional.

Even the two carrying their helmets raised their hands placatingly, palms down at first, as if calming the angry seven seas.

"We're just looking for a place to bed down for the night."

"It's all full," said Strange, "Try the next place."

"Come on man. Give us a break. We're tired, too. We're just like you."

"I don't think so."

"What're you saying? You some sort of badasses?"
"How many people did you kill yesterday?"

"What're you sayin'? You killed somebody?"

"Three   somebodies."

They couldn't see him do it, but Fleetwood nodded, confirming it.

"Get the fuck outta here."

"I shit you not. I've had a piss poor week. And I don't need you to piss me off more."

"Okay, okay, we're leaving. Just don't shoot us."

"So leave now and I won't shoot you. But I can't speak for him," Strange said, gesturing toward Fleetwood with the shotgun.

The three exhaled a collective sigh of frustration and relief, not sure if they were yet free of the confrontation but started backing down the staircase anyway, not wanting to turn their backs on Strange and Fleetwood. Losing his balance, one tripped and almost fell.

Listening for the doors to the inn to open and close in the quiet, Strange went to the nearest upstairs window overlooking the parking lot to make sure they left without messing with his vehicle.

Z Chapter Ninety-One

Unknown Shires of England:
Destination — Stonehenge

Forgetting

Mally and Aidan chose and saddled horses that suited them. They noticed that for the first time in days Jeanette was enthusiastic about getting started. She and the loving mare had formed a tight bond. They made sure the horses had blankets on them, too. It took a little while to figure out how to attach their packs including extra horse blankets, but they got it done. They mounted and walked slowly through the heavy snow toward the road. The horses stepped gingerly. Jeanette's cheerful grin was infectious. She beamed even brighter at Mally's attention.

"'at smile warms me heart, it diz," said Mally.

Aidan felt as if Stonehenge was calling him to a place he'd never known. And to a belief that their mission was noble, above any others of their lives. "Alright, then, let's see if we can maintain a steady pace today. We might even make it to the stones quicker than I thought with our new friends."

"Brill," said Mally.

Jeanette asked, "You know how I always tell you I look forward to autumn and the return of cool weather?"

"Certainly I do. Ye drive me bonkers, all the time wishing your life away," Mally said.

"You shall be happy then. I think I have finally had enough of the cold and shan't find myself saying it ever again."

» Chapter Ninety-Two

Sawnee Mountain, Georgia:
Evil Dwellers 'HQ

End of the Beginning of the End

The hit squad drove up the narrow road leading to the mountaintop mansion. It was Bad Penny's intent to avoid the queen for as long as he was able. It wasn't as long as he'd have liked. She summoned him forty-five minutes after they arrived.

He replied, *"How about thirty minutes? Give me time to freshen up?"*

"Fifteen," she snapped.

She was conflicted about the meeting. She wanted him to know she controlled his literal existence. But she also had no desire to smell him or have him defile her private quarters after two days cooped up in that truck with those filthy animals. So she'd compromised by choosing the time of the meeting, just to be sure he knew she was always in charge. Fifteen minutes later, on the dot, came a timid knock on the large double doors to her suite.

"Enter," she thalked.

"Thank you, Your Majesty."

"Have a seat." She gestured to one of two sumptuously upholstered wing chairs in the sitting room, looking out at the fifty mile view.

"Thank you, and an interrogative, if I may?"

"Certainly."

"Since you and I can talk, why don't we?"

"Because, dear Pennington, it would be an evolutionary step backward. We are evolved."

"Okay, I can respect that."

"And if I may be so bold, I don't give a fuck what you respect. Are we clear?"

"Yes, Your Majesty. What can I do for you?"

"How did your trip go?"

"Effective. I think it was fifteen kills over a little more than a day."

"Is that all?" She paused with a finger in the air to shut him up.
"Moving on. How did you and the others get along?"

Bad Penny glanced away before answering. An obvious, to Queen Gertrude anyway, disturbing tell. *"Just fine."*

"Are you being honest with me? Remember, I can read your thoughts when you aren't expecting it."

"Well, to be honest, Fleatus — that's the nickname I gave Wolf — had some problems with my authority, but I think we settled it."

"You do, do you?"

"Yes, Your Majesty."

"Fine. I'll find out what he thinks."

He shrugged as if to say suit yourself. An unwise decision on his part.

Σ Chapter Ninety-Three

Southwest Virginia:
Destination — Georgia Guidestones

Georgia Dead Ahead

"What was that all about?" Lace asked after letting Strange and Fleetwood in.

"You heard the motorcycles, didn't you?"

"Of course, the whole East Coast probably heard them at three o'clock in the morning."

"Well, they looked like they could be dangerous and we dissuaded them from deciding to stay here."

"It was all Strange," said Fleetwood. "He was a real badass."

Strange looked at the floor sheepishly, but with a sort of self-satisfied smirk.

"You should have heard him," Fleetwood kept on.

Strange gave him a look that even in the candlelit darkness stopped him from continuing.

"Let's try and get a few hours of sleep before daylight. I don't think they'll be coming back," he said with confidence...at least he hoped so.

***

When morning came it looked the same as the previous ones from the past three weeks.

Gray and deathly dismal. But they weren't. Dead, that is. So they must carry on. Laden with bags, extra food and shotguns, they looked like tired pack animals trudging to the truck.

In their usual seats and settled, as Strange started the vehicle Cody said, "I, for one, think we've had enough excitement."

Lace said, "I agree. How about just a nice, quiet end of the world?"

"Look who's making jokes now," said Fleetwood.

"I can't let you guys have all the fun."

Z Chapter Ninety-Four

Unknown Shires of England:
Destination — Stonehenge

An Easier Trek

The horses were more surefooted in the snow than their riders would have been. And they made carrying the bags full of gear effortless.

Even though he'd lost weight, Mally was still heavier than Jeanette and Aidan. So he thought he should ride the bigger horse. He chose him for his size; it had been a splendid choice. Mally was growing fond of the large black stallion. Aidan's mount, however, had a bit of attitude and he struggled to keep him under control. His soft snort sounded like he was happy with himself and was enjoying being difficult. The fresh smell of clean snow was in stark contrast to the natural equine smell.

"This certainly is better than walking," Jeanette said, "although it doesn't help with the cold."

Mally said, "But they're faster than we are, which means we won't be in the cold for as long."

"Good point, mate," Aidan agreed. Jeanette had been his admin for six years, and he liked her, but he was beginning to tire of her whining. As glad as he was to have them along, a man could only take so much. She should have known it wasn't going to be easy, he thought. At least she had only been his work-wife and not his real wife. If he were married to her, she would drive him crazy with that carrying on she did.

An hour of slow but steady riding through the vast snowy wasteland and they approached the outskirts of a small town. Two-story high Golden Arches were the first thing they noticed. Alas, like everything else they were dark. Much of the golden glass was broken by rocks.

"What I would give for a Big Mac," wished Mally.

"I'm with you, mate," agreed Aidan, "and I usually don't even eat those things."

"I think we could all do with one," said Jeanette. Indeed, they had all lost weight. Perhaps riding the horses instead of walking would keep them from declining as fast.

It was hard to imagine, but the skies grew even darker and snow began to fall again. Aidan wondered how the great City Of Light in France looked in the dark. Approaching the outskirts of a town with civilization and possible living beings, Aidan said, "Mally, weapons at the ready."

With that, Mally pulled out the rifle he'd pinned between his left leg and the horse's huge body and lay it on the saddle across his legs. "Done, mate." Although probably unnecessary with the high-powered rifle, he also readied his old Webley revolver, eying the loads in the chamber, as well, before lighting a cigarette. The nicotine helped to relax him.

Aidan readied his weapon. He thought it surprising how accustomed one could grow to the feel, the weight, the uncharacteristic appendage of a weapon in one's hand. So much so that one wouldn't dream of taking a step without it. Jeanette simply hoped they would see no one, but especially no one with bad intent. Aidan couldn't know what it would be, but a sixth sense he didn't have a name for told him trouble was imminent.

They entered the town at a slow pace while a group of dirty individuals, male and female, hiding in the dark of alleyways and abandoned storefronts stared intently as they rode past. The lurking observers thought the horses would be good to eat. Edible, even if an uncommon source of protein, and filling to their bloated empty bellies.

"Mally." The leader had said nothing but his compatriot's name, but that was all it had taken, along with registering the look of heightened awareness in Aidan's eyes, for Mally to fasten his steel vise-like grip on his rifle and raise his alertness to a higher level.

» Chapter Ninety-Five

Sawnee Mountain, Georgia:
Evil Dwellers 'HQ

Truth Will Out

"I thalked with Wolf," Queen Gertrude smiled cunningly. Bad Penny didn't respond. He wasn't going to make it easy for her. *"He's of the opinion the problems between you two are anything but worked out. In fact, I think the word he used was…insurmountable."*

Bad Penny appeared bored by the scene, shrugging his shoulders as if he simply could not give a shit. She continued, *"But I think I've come up with a solution to the problem. Oh, I finally have your attention, do I? Well, I can't have one of my protectors, and another I have big plans for, at odds with each other, so I think you should fight it out."*

Bad Penny's canny eyes flashed with wary excitement. He attempted to interrupt. She held up a hand. *"Let me finish. A fight to the death. May the best man live. Or best sentient being, since our friend Wolf isn't technically a man. Although he is a male of his genus."* She paused to take a sip from a delicate ceramic teacup sitting on a matching tray placed in front of her. *"You may speak now."*

Bad Penny cleared his throat to buy a moment's relief even though he didn't need his voice to thalk back. But it was his habit. *"So you want me to go up against a killer wolf empty-handed?"*

"You're right. That probably wouldn't be much of a contest. You can have a weapon of your choice. Only, not a firearm…or explosive, just so you don't get any ideas."

Bad Penny grinned. He didn't think it would be much of a contest with his intelligence and cunning against a stupid animal. He'd just need to be smart in his choice of a weapon. He was already thinking about a medieval-style axe, or maybe a mace — a spiked steel ball and chain attached to a handle for swinging. He thought he remembered seeing one in the former owner's collection of historical artifacts on a wall in the lower level. And he wouldn't feel badly about filching it since it wasn't possible anyone else would need it more than he.

« Chapter Ninety-Six

Cumming, Georgia:
The Good Guys 'HQ

The Time Draws Near

Patrick concentrated. *"Cuz, are you around? Duncan? We need you."*

"I'm here. What's up?"

"I need you to check on the bad guys and see what's happening with them."

"Can do. Thalk soon."

"Thanks. Sounds good."

The dread Patrick felt about attacking Trudy's compound was almost more than he could bear. Although he guessed it would be unlikely, especially so if he came face to face with her. He wondered how they both would act, what they would say, if indeed there would be anything to say. It wasn't long before he heard back from Duncan.

"That was fast," he thought to his cousin.

"What can I say? I'm good."

"Yeah, yeah, okay. Give."

"Bottom line, something big is happening."

"Bigger than the end of the world?"

"No, not that big, but big. Apparently, they're having some sort of internal power struggle and they're going to fight it out. That's all I can discern."

"So, how does that affect our plans?" Patrick was already calculating.

"I'm not saying it does, except that they might be distracted during the big event they're hinting at."

"Okay, see if you can find out anymore — when, where, what, etc., and we can plan accordingly."

"Will do. Keep you posted, Cuz."

Σ Chapter Ninety-Seven

North Carolina:
Destination — Georgia Guidestones

Carolina on My Mind

They felt safer and more comfortable once back in the old SUV and on the move again. It had been nice to sleep in a bed, but with the darkness of night came too much fear.

"By the way, have any of you guys been to North Carolina?" asked Fleetwood.

"Not me," said Cody.

"Nor me," Lace said.

"When I was a kid in Tennessee," said Strange, "They're next door neighbors, you know. And its mountains might even be prettier than Tennessee's."

"Charlotte's a real cool city, from what I hear," Cody said.

"Not to change the subject, but I've been thinking," Strange said.

"Do tell," said Fleetwood.

"I think we've been looking at this the wrong way. I think we're some of the lucky few."

"How so," asked Cody.

"Think about it. We're still alive. That's a big one. We haven't gotten The Plague, knock on wood," he said. "And if we had died last year or even last spring, we wouldn't have even been here for the end of the world. I think that's amazing. We're living it. Think about all the previous generations that have missed it."

"Always the philosopher, huh, Strange?" said Fleetwood "But I have to admit, that's pretty deep."

Strange exhaled a huff of breath on his fingernails and buffed them on the chest of his shirt.

"Probably a little too deep for you," Fleetwood continued, throwing a little shade toward his friend.

"Yeah, right."

Z Chapter Ninety-Eight

Unknown Shires of England:
Destination — Stonehenge

Discovering The Past

A cobblestone brick sailed past Aidan's head even though he didn't notice it until it bounced off its brethren under the snowy street.

"Mally," he shouted. All three whipped the horses to go faster in the frozen precipitation. It distressed Jeanette to no end to take the crop to the sweet animal she sat astride. More bricks followed the first, but the horses were able to get them quickly out of the danger zone.

They made it out of town without further incident. It wasn't long until they made it to one of the many newly abandoned castles, like could be found all over the U.K. This one, a mirthless stone grey, rose up before them with glorious dignity. Like a great hall of Valhalla offering itself to be used as a stronghold. No Potemkin village this, but a Brobdingnagian redoubt. They hoped it would enable them to breathe easy, at least for a time. To the logy wayfarers, it was welcoming.

The ancient stone edifice had four turrets, six cylindrical towers higher than the battlements, and thick rampart defenses topped with crenelations from where archers would defend the castle's integrity. From the castle's highest point, a vertigo-inducing keep looked like those of the late medieval period from the fourteenth century. A time when British society was faced with the twin challenges of the Black Death and the Great Famine, along with many other feudal disputes.

An august castle in every classical sense of the word, although the original owners most likely referred to it as their summer estate. Older than America, itself; but anything but banal. And as grand as the Royal Opera House in London. But the stouthearted stone had thus far withstood more than six hundred years of the United Kingdom's bitterest winters with little adversity to show from the pounding of rain, sleet, snow, and wintertide wind. A wee bit plumbeous in appearance, it could heighten one's fears; nevertheless the need for temporary shelter and the hope of found food and water far outweighed their trepidation.

The low depression of stone surrounding the fortification had most likely been a deep defensive moat, but now waterless allowed the sure-footed equines to descend stealthily into the rocky near side declivity and rise up on the other with the slow graceful movement of an adagio of human and horse. They crowned their achievement with proud snorts of accomplishment.

Mally patted his huge mount on the side of its strong neck and said, "Good boy."

They reached the massive wooden entry, where Aidan, like a pro, dismounted the chestnut-colored steed with the blonde mane. The horse looked as if it could've fit the setting anytime during the last several hundred years. The others descended their mounts, though not nearly as elegantly.

They tied the horses to receptacles that had held fiery torches. Mally banged fiercely with a large brass knocker on the broad arched-top solid mahogany door. When no one responded, Jeanette pulled the heavy woven hemp cordage as thick as her wrist that hung next to the opening. If it were in order, most likely a bell would ring in a housekeeper's vestibule. Indeed, they heard no tintinnabulation at all. When no response was returned, they attempted to open the creaking ancient door. They succeeded with the simplest option: A push.

They did not want to leave the horses tied out where predators could get them, so they brought them into the great hall. Gingerly entering the shadowy maw of the bilious aperture, their weary shuffling steps and the clomp-clomp of the horses hooves echoed on the dark stone floor of the vast empty hall. It smelt of damp mineral and mould, but also, surprisingly, of being. Mally went back to the door and dropped a massive timber into place locking the door behind them. Wouldn't want anyone...or anything, surprising them. They unloaded their gear from the horses, and set it all in a corner opposite of the entry where the hallway narrowed.

As they continued their ingress deep into the castle's elegiac interior, they reached a center rotunda covered by a circular worn rug of dull red wool and a faded gilded edging. Like spokes from an aged wheel, passages led off in different directions.

Jeanette asked, "What are we doing?"

"Let's look for the kitchen," said Mally.

"Let's do it," said Aidan. "It appears abandoned now, though someone has lived here recently."

"And we need to find the horses something to eat. They'll be getting hungry," said Jeanette, always the worrisome mum to all living things no matter the number of legs.

While they tried to make a decision, a family of black rats skittered across the rug.

"Looks like we disturbed those guys," Aidan said.

"I'm not worried about them. Which way?" Mally said.

Aidan deferred. "Your guess is as good as mine."

"I'm glad you aren't worried about them," said Jeanette, proving her love of animals has its limits.

"Let's try this way," Mally said pointing down one of the passageways.

"Wait a sec," said Aidan. Shifting the shotgun to his other hand, from a wall sconce he withdrew a sheave of sticks the size of a bundle of arrows, and lighted them for a proper torch in an attempt to overcome the increasingly oppressive darkness.

"That's better," he said.

"A banging idea, mate," said Mally.

The dim corridor reflected the warm glow of the flame. The fire helped to overcome the ill smell of the dank mould making bolder the scent of a living castle in response to beings and warmth from the fire. The castle had a living sound of its own. Hollow but with the sound of what seemed like breathing, or maybe a heartbeat. It sounded and felt like a barely alive but comprehending organism.

Truly, the castle bore its age proudly.

They walked down the seemingly endless moldering stone hallway, its middle settling with age, past gold-framed oil paintings of landscapes, portraits, and botanicals from different eras by English artists, and on to where a pair of dark knights attempted to persuade them from their mission.

Glancing around, Mally said, "I should have been born to royalty. I could stand living in a wee castle, I could." Funny because he knew he didn't have a regal bone in his body, plebeian to his core as he was.

Jeanette and Aidan didn't laugh, but none knew if that was because they didn't think Mally's joke funny or if they thought there was nothing worth laughing about while facing what was the possible, if not yet probable, end of humanity, in this grey castle.

A regal banner of red and silver, bearing the castle's crest of crossed swords embraced by a protective serpent, reminiscent of the four house flags at Hogwarts, hung from the hall's ceiling between the two suits of armor shiny in the reflected light of the flame.

"I've seen that flag before," said Aidan.

"Where?" asked Jeanette.

He hesitated, a confounded look on his face. "I can't remember. It almost seems like a dream...or worse," he said with a frown, "a nightmare."

Jeanette left that answer to hang on the stale air without response, not desirous of an elaborative explanation. One of the suits of armor posed on high alert on a plinth with an approximately four meter long battle lance of ash wood tipped with iron. The lance was decorated with a streamer in the same red and silver as the estate's labarum. Moving closer and squinting to study the lance, Mally concluded, "They could have just as well used a good-sized narwhal tusk."

Aidan thought that a splendidly simple yet brilliant observation.

A fine German-made grandfather clock, even though the craftsman who made it probably called it a horologium, tolled three times in a sign of insouciant concordance, though probably to toll little longer, due to age and lack of the diligent upkeep required to keep one working precisely. Admiring the other museum-quality knight's armor that held the antique axe in its grasp, Mally said, "That would make a fine weapon, it would. Not as fine as the blade with which to cross swords, but nevertheless, mayhap I shall have to decamp with it in my possession when we take our leave."

Aidan shook his head disbelievingly, then with the palm of his empty hand at his waist, and a slight bow, said, "I admire your command of the King's English when you so choose. Positively grandiloquent and just irreverently Ciceronian enough and worthy of the theatre when you do."

"He just doesn't so choose very often," said Jeanette, teasing her husband sweetly.

They continued their trek down the long drafty corridor, past a receiving parlor. Aidan thought he detected the telling aroma of fine brandy and expensive pipe tobacco. A huge room with a high timbered ceiling, it had a fireplace possessing a firebox large enough for a tall man to stand in without bending. A large porcelain crucible, most likely containing the ashes of the Lord of the manor, or his faithful dog, had been carefully placed on the mantle. The dining room boasted an equally large fireplace. Revealing the vastness of the castle, a huge wooden table that could seat sixty in gilded-back chairs sat on a massive fringed Persian rug that covered the entire stone floor of the room except for a one-foot strip in front of each of the four walls. Next came a minstrel room that would have been used to entertain royal guests with the lovely sounds of a string quartet. Aidan could almost hear the strains of Gerald Raphael Finzi's epic "Dies natalis" for soprano or tenor and string orchestra. The room continued the regal theme of gold, surely a constant throughout the mammoth old world residence.

Built on low valley land and luxuriously appointed, one would find no troglodyte rooms here. The spaces had the surprisingly comforting grace of charred oak. The nearer they drew to the end of the passageway however, the more their senses were assaulted by the putrid stench of decaying flesh.

Indeed, when the hall opened onto a large kitchen of near commercial-size, the bodies of a man and woman, the uniforms they wore those of handyman and housekeeper, were in the depths of decomposition and being feasted upon by more and even fatter black rats. That made the prospect of any found food somewhat less than a wee bit appetizing.

"That's disgusting, but I still think we're bound to find something suitable for us and the horses to eat," said Jeanette, still motivated by finding nourishment for the noble animals.

"Aye, I hope you're right," said Mally, "especially the part about finding food for us. But you can take solace in knowing those shameless vermin shan't be alive much longer. Not after feasting on those unfortunate souls. The Plague will surely put an to end their miserable existence."

"Oh you," Jeanette said, slapping him playfully.

"Okay, that's enough daffing," Aidan said. "Concentrate. See what you can find that we can take with us. Not too large and non-perishable, if possible."

"Slave-driver. We're not at work anymore, remember."

"I think you enjoy reminding me of that."

They saw a huge decades-old scarred farmhouse kitchen table with room enough for eight and frayed yet proudly upholstered chairs wore their sullied age proudly. High open shelves held ale steins the size of a large man's neck next to unopened bottles of whisky.

"I could drink me fill in one of those," said Mally, looking upward at one of the steins. Doubtless, one would fit well in his massive workman's hands.

A double-doored pantry might hold the answer for them as Jeanette opened the portal slowly, both hopeful and fearful at what she might find.

"Carrots. Horses love raw carrots. They last for weeks, and these still look fresh." Jeanette was truly enthused as she examined the find of homegrown produce.

"Rabbit food," Mally sulked.

"Relax. You'll like them." She held up a bunch by their leafy green stems, "And they're good for your eyes." She didn't think that would work to convince him with the end of the world looming before them.

"I'm a meat-eater," he said, "A real man needs a proper shepherd's pie. And it would have carrots and peas besides, and mashed potatoes. I'd still be getting me veggies." He was enjoying give her a wee bit of a hard time just a little too much.

Aidan held up a basket laden with fresh laid goodness in whites and browns. "Can you eat your protein in the form of farm-fresh eggs?"

"Indubitably. Probably laid right here by their own hens. Nothing finer."

Jeanette said, "We can fry them up in an iron skillet."

"Or boil them in a pot of hot water over a proper campfire. We could easily take boiled eggs with us," said Mally excitedly.

"However you'd like, luv," said Jeanette adoringly.

"That's my girl."

A case of Diet Pepsi and a box of cigars rounded out their find.

"Nothing better than a proper stogie while sipping a wee glass of Scotch," said Mally.

《 Chapter Ninety-Nine
Cumming, Georgia:
The Good Guys 'HQ

Imminent War

"Dude, I got some news for you," Duncan thalked.

"Spill," Patrick thought his response.

"Well, they're going to have a battle royal, between — now get this — a Chernobyl wolf and a dude who was a serial killer."

"Get the fuck outta here."

"I'm not kidding."

"When is this happening?"

"That's a good question. It's going to be awhile. Queen Gertrude, er, Trudy, has her sycophants constructing an arena to serve as a battleground for them. Imagine the colosseum in Rome, but on a smaller, wooden scale. I would guess a few weeks at least, perhaps a season. But I'll keep checking on them and let you know."

"Sounds good."

» Chapter One Hundred

Sawnee Mountain, Georgia:
Evil Dwellers 'HQ

Preparing for Battle...or Death

Bad Penny began prepping for the upcoming clash by starting a workout. He figured it couldn't hurt to help him win...or if he was killed, at least he'd leave a good looking corpse.

He found a bench and a cheap, old, one-hundred-ten pound vinyl-covered Sears weight set in the mansion's dark, dank undercroft. Weight training and running up and down the stairs to the crypt to strengthen his legs and help with his cardio, all would help. Then a prison memory came to him. His mentor had taught him karate and boxing. He would work some of that into his training, too.

The subbasement's walls were carved into the stone of Sawnee Mountain and the floor was unfinished concrete. It smelled like his grandmother's basement and looked like how he imagined the Batcave would look minus all the electronics and expensive Batman shit.

Σ Chapter One Hundred One

North Carolina:
Destination — Georgia Guidestones

The Reality of Reality

Without fanfare, they passed into North Carolina on the mountaintop parkway with nothing but a small rusted signpost to notify them of their entry. Might as well be a signpost to the world. The trek for the sojourners from the Big Apple, got no easier as corpse-filled abandoned vehicles made speeds above fifteen miles per hour near impossible. At highway speeds, they could make the trek in eight hours. But it would take a week of eight hour days to complete at their present rate of progress.

"We need to start looking for more gas," said Strange. "Can't wait 'til the last minute."

"Yeah, running out of gas during an apocalypse would suck big time," said Fleetwood.

"I'll say. Don't even think about it," said Strange.

Z Chapter One Hundred Two

Unknown Shires of England:
Destination — Stonehenge

Keep Moving

Gazing around at the castle, Aidan said, "Even though it's early, since we're making better time on the horses, I think we should stay here tonight. The day isn't long from waning."

Indeed, if there had been a sun to be seen it would have been setting to the west, over the blue mountains in the south of Wales.

"That's a grand idea," said Jeanette.

"Mally?"

"I'm with you guys," said Mally then, gazing westward, he sniffed. "It's possible I smell Wales, however, and if there's one thing l loathe more than a goddamn Irishman, it's a goddamn Welshman. Mayhap, we should keep moving."

Joining Mally in his westward gaze, Jeanette said placatingly, "Now, now, don't go getting yourself worked up. That's probably only the salty aroma of the Irish Sea that you smell just beyond. Besides, I can think of an Irishman you like."

"And who's that?"

"Van Morrison."

"Aye, I do like me some Van."

"And he's an Irishman."

"Yeah. Well, he shouldn't be. He's from Northern Ireland and that's practically Scotland." Mally thought his logic irrefutably brilliant.

"And you like Hozier, and he's another Irish singer."

"Okay, that's enough from you."

"Ah, Ah tooched a wee nerve, Ah did?" She shook her head. Rather than needle him any further, no equerry she, she nevertheless took it upon herself to feed carrots to the horses.

"Don't tarry," Mally said to her back as she waved him off.

"You know I can't stand to be away from you any longer than I absolutely must," she said, teasing him. "I shan't linger a moment longer than it takes."

"How are my babies," Jeanette asked as she nuzzled them, breathing in the pleasing smell of horse that was so cleansing to her. She caressed each one's necks and manes and gave them carrots to munch on. They snuffled appreciatively, making her sad to leave them again.

Rejoining Aidan and her husband, they determined to set up their bedding in the receiving parlor they'd passed. It was probably one of several. They'd set a fire in the large stone box and with several plush velvet settees and sofas of various colors to push together they could create a large sleeping surface with more body heat between them. Large aged paintings of the castle's previous owners watched over them from the walls on which they hung, either protectively or with worry as if to make sure they did no wrong. Residing on a dark wall among the paintings of landed folks, as if it belonged, an ancient triptych of questionable provenance was decorated with unicorns and narwhals, each of both species bearing knurled tusks of brightest gold. The room had the look of a spartan museum, comfortable with but a few well-selected *objets d'art*.

But before creating their sleeping area, they would take a turn around the castle's perimeter just to make sure they were safe, at least as safe as one could be when one was at the front in a battle for the survival of the world. An evil, yet at the same time, sacred battle. In fact, as a man who'd always been a believer, but was never really interested in putting his beliefs into practice, Aidan would face the end of the world not hagridden but hopeful. His wish being that saving the world might rescue him from perdition, salvage his mortal soul. Even sanctify it in God's judgmental eye. Which raised a question in his mind. Did a minor deity need sanctification from The God of Man? Not that he considered himself a minor deity — no more than others, anyway. He knew he was flawed, but in a mathematician's language, that was a plus and not a minus. All minor gods were flawed before they reached their greatness and claimed their destiny. Were the flawed Alexander the Great and Dionysus and the centaurs deities? And if indeed they were, it begged the same question. Would their souls need to be saved by The God of Christianity?

And although they weren't exactly at the edge of the sphere, they weren't far from it, and he would ponder those weighty questions as they continued their walk through the world.

» Chapter One Hundred Three

Sawnee Mountain, Georgia:
Evil Dwellers 'HQ

Construction

"Professor, I need you to find out if any of my followers have building experience. Draftsmen, architects, contractors, laborers. I need an arena built posthaste."

"Yes, you're highness."

She continued. *"If Wolf and Bad Penny are going to fight to the death they need a suitable setting. Something like the Colosseum, in Rome, only not quite as grand. It would be disrespectful to both and to the memory of the non-survivor, not to give them something so noble."*

"I'll get right on it."

"Splendid. And while we're on the subject. If Bad Penny doesn't survive, is it going to affect you? Considering he was your mentor?"

"No more than if he were a cur in the street."

She smiled an evil grin and thalked, *"That's what I thought. Happy to hear it."*

I'll have to keep an eye on this one, he's despicable. She blocked the thought from him.

« Chapter One Hundred Four
Cumming, Georgia:
The Good Guys 'HQ

Coming To A Head

"Cuz, I've got some more info." Duncan projected his thoughts into Patrick's brain.

"Whatcha got?"

"A serial killer, some dude they call Bad Penny, is fighting, now get this, he's fighting a Chernobyl wolf. Can you believe that shit?"

"That's some pretty crazy shit, alright."

"I'll say, and Trudy, er, Queen Gertrude, has her people building a colosseum-like arena for them to fight in."

"Trudy always did appreciate grandeur. Any word on when yet?"

"She wants it fast, but I'm sure it will take them awhile."

"Okay, cool, keep a weather eye."

"Will do."

Σ Chapter One Hundred Five

North Carolina:
Destination — Georgia Guidestones

Nearing the End?

Built in the previous century, a no-name service station and market was on the right hand side near the corner of the intersection they approached. A gasoline tanker truck sat in the parking lot. Worth finding out if the driver was dead and if the truck held any gas. Like everywhere else, the store and station were bereft and dark. Strange pulled up next to the tanker and yanked up the parking brake. He grabbed a shotgun before hopping out; then banged on the metal side of its tank with the weapon's butt and said, "Sounds like there's gas in there. Grab those two plastic jugs out of the back, will ya, Fleet."

"Got it."

Lace and Cody rushed across the parking lot to the store in search of sustenance. Fleetwood met Strange at the back of the truck. and said, "Well, we can't suck the gas out of this one. So, you know how to get gas out of one of these things?"

"You're the engineer. I figured you did, or at least you could figure it out."

"What? I'm a recording engineer," Fleetwood said.

"Okay, we'll figure it out."

After looking around and studying the truck and, feeling the pressure Strange had put on him, a few minutes later Fleetwood said, " I think I've got it. The only problem is the nozzle on that rubber hose is too big for our jugs and we'll waste a lot of gas. Kind of like drinking water from a firehose."

"Don't worry about it. It doesn't matter if any spills. As long as we get what we need. Just make sure to fill the jugs all the way…to the top. We have to take advantage of this."

Fleetwood turned a flywheel-like device on the rear of the truck and heard gas begin to flow. He hopped off the truck bed with the hose in hand and began filling the two red plastic jugs sitting side-by-side on the pavement, spilling more than he was filling. The women returned laden like packhorses with all the snacks and drinks one could hope for.

"Looks like the shelves were full," said Fleetwood.

"Not exactly, but there was a full delivery truck around back," said Cody.

"Cool. That was good thinking to check out there," Strange said.

"Thanks, but it was Lace's idea. I was just following her."

Lace said, "Just keep doing that and you'll be fine."

"Oh, you," said Cody.

Z Chapter One Hundred Six

Unknown Shires of England:
Destination — Stonehenge

Another Century, Another War

With shotguns at the ready, Mally and Aidan, with Jeanette in tow, toured the exterior of the castle. Late in the afternoon, the grey was turning to dark and the temperature was beginning to drop, even though the wind was less than slight, almost nonexistent. As the castle faced east they walked north on its front before turning left to go along the west curtain to continue its circumference as large as a city block. Walking briskly to get out of the biting cold and back to the shelter of the castle's interior, they made the eastward left turn to return to the front.

"That doesn't look good, it doesn't," said Mally, gesturing with his chin across a disturbed field of milo toward the dark tree line of now-grey conifers. They saw the blaze of a campfire to the southeast. Mally's biggest problem was controlling his natural and innate desire to attack first and ask questions later.

Although it was possible the people gathered 'round the warm fire were like themselves, just trying to survive by avoiding contact with civilization, it was just as likely they had nefarious intentions. And so it was best not to draw their attention.

Aidan agreed. "Let's get back in quick. Hopefully they haven't already seen us."

"Maybe they're friendly," said Jeanette, hopefully.

"Maybe," said Mally, not wanting to upset his sensitive wife anymore than she already was. "But Aidan's right. Shake a leg." They crouched and ran, trying to draw as little attention as possible. Fortunately they were dark shadows against the dark-stained walls of the centuries-old castle.

Safely inside, Aidan said, "I think we should set up a watch from the top, from the watchtowers, just in the case they did see us and decide to try something."

"I think you're right, mate," said Mally.

"What about me," Jeanette asked.

"You'll be nice and warm inside, except for when you'll be keeping us supplied with whisky."

"I was hoping I could be more useful," she complained.

"I assure you, my luv, that is the most important duty of all."

» Chapter One Hundred Seven

Sawnee Mountain, Georgia:
Evil Dwellers 'HQ

Raising the Past

Professor Drummond located an architect, a former contractor, and a construction project manager among Queen Gertrude's followers. With plenty of sycophants to enlist as common laborers, he felt good about their ability to build a suitable mountaintop arena in the time she ordered. Still, Trudy was no little pleased with his results. What she had thalked was, "What took you so fucking long?" Even though it had been less than forty-eight hours since she'd given him his marching orders. Her comment didn't faze him, though, since he'd become accustomed to her less than thoughtful outbursts. Anger overused became less than somewhat effective and threatening.

She thalked, *"Professor. It is November 10th. I want it completed by Christmas Eve. And it better look good. A Christmas battle will be infinitely appropriate."*

"You can count on me, Your Majesty. It will not be a problem."

"It better not."

« Chapter One Hundred Eight

Cumming, Georgia:
The Good Guys 'HQ

Imminent War

Patrick said, "Trudy loved Christmas, so either something big will happen then or nothing will. I think that will be a good time for us to go."

Colonel Bill Crain said, "Big, or nothing. That's a big difference."

Jeff Byrd said, "And don't forget, Thanksgiving is in a couple of weeks. Are we going to celebrate?"

They didn't know if he was serious, but considering how much he liked to eat, he might have been.

"I don't know. Where will we find a turkey?" Patrick wondered.

"Besides, I have a feeling your stuffing wouldn't be that good," said Bill, throwing a little shade in Jeff's direction.

Jeff feigned hurt feelings.

Σ Chapter One Hundred Nine

North Carolina:
Destination — Georgia Guidestones

Last Leg

With the two plastic cans of gas filled and stocked up on snacks, they were on their way again. Strange said, "Unless we encounter more disruptions than we're seeing, I think we can be there by tomorrow evening."

"We can't make it today?" asked Cody.

"Not unless all these cars suddenly disappear."

"I guess we can always hope," said Lace.

Z Chapter One Hundred Ten

**Unknown Shires of England:
Destination — Stonehenge**

In Defence of the Castle

Mally, Aidan, and Jeanette stumbled upon a narrow, winding, hidden stairway to the castle's uppermost reaches. Jeanette going along just so she'd know where they positioned themselves so she could keep them hydrated.

Once on the roof, Mally, being larger, decided he preferred the openness under the menacing dark sky instead of the narrow stairs. They passed a long-idle centuries old catapult of timber and iron behind the crenelated battlement and between two pediments. Although they hadn't walked the circumference, there were probably catapults on the other side's battlements as well. Aidan chose the interior of a tower with a port the shape of a two foot tall and wide cross through which he could aim and fire a rifle. Though designed for the bow, Aidan would remain fully protected. If lucky, they might not even notice him until they were fired upon. Aidan pulled out his binoculars to keep watch.

"I'll be back in an hour with the whisky," she said to them both.

"An hour? A man could die of thirst he could in an hour. Before the end of the world even arrives. And that would be a shame, indeed, it would." Mally was incredulous at the thought.

"Just you mind your manners and I'll tend to you. " Jeanette wouldn't put up with his shenanigans, even if she truly enjoyed the *prévenance* of her husband.

"Aye, you always do, my luv. And might you find a snack when you do? I'm quite sure I'll be feeling a mite peckish by then."

"I hardly know of a time when you're not feeling peckish," she said, using his words against him. She disappeared through the doorway to make her return trip down the concealed stairway, then through the hallway back to the kitchen where they'd spied the bottles of whisky.

A moment later, Aidan called out in a loud whisper, "Mally, look."

"Aye, I'm looking. It looks like their campfire is moving."

"I think they're lighting torches."

It appeared that several people were bent over the fire, lighting bundles of wood.

"Keep a keen eye," said Aidan, "I'm afraid they might be coming our way."

They had waited until full dark, but with the fire, they could easily be seen. Aidan and Mally, on the other hand, were unobservable on the castle wall.

A moment later, without counting, Aidan quickly saw in his mathematicians eye a dozen torches strung out in a long serpentine line make their way through the milo field toward the castle. A living, breathing, fiery twelve-headed snake moving between rows of crops toward the ancient acropolis. The one in the lead puffed on a glowing cigarette. They obviously were unconcerned about the bright flames from the torches warning the castle's occupants of their advance. In fact there was no way to know if the purpose was to instill fear in or to immolate their quarry. Or both.

Mally said, "They're on us, mate." Though his normal state was stolid, the sight of the fiery group with unknown intentions stirred something primeval in the typically unperturbed man. "And if they continue I'll give them their comeuppance, I will."

Aidan was a little concerned that Mally appeared to be looking forward to the possibility of butchery a wee bit much. In any case, they made ready to receive them.

» Chapter One Hundred Eleven

Sawnee Mountain, Georgia:
Evil Dwellers 'HQ

An Arena To Die For

After locating the needed leadership for the project, Drummond sat down with them and discussed what the Queen wanted. The former architect said he'd have plans for Drummond's review within forty-eight hours. *"Better make it, twenty-four,"* Drummond thalked, recalling how pissed the Queen was at him for taking forty-eight to find the people they needed.

Then they would sit down again to review the drawings as a group so he could present the plan to Queen Gertrude.

***

When they regrouped, the architect showed them all a drawing of a small all-wood arena.

He explained to the group, *"Even using manual tools, hand saws, and hammers instead of electric saws and nail guns, if we work three shifts a day, we should be able to knock it out by the time the Queen wants it."* What had been left unsaid was that without electricity they would be reduced to using tools dating almost back to the stone age. At least they had plenty of trees for wood on top of Sawnee Mountain.

The next day, Drummond got the plans approved by Queen Gertrude after, of course, a couple of changes that she had. Mostly involving her royal box, which simply had to have the best seats in the bowl.

Σ Chapter One Hundred Twelve

North Georgia:
Destination — Georgia Guidestones

Georgia, the Whole Night Through

The highway congestion didn't get any better, but it didn't get any worse.

Strange said, "I think I'm going to keep driving. You all can sleep, though. I think we'll be just as safe in a moving vehicle as we would be in a barn or an abandoned inn. And it will get us there sooner."

"We're all for getting there sooner, but it's up to you," said Lace. "As long as you stop to let us heed the call of nature."

"All you have to do is let me know."

"Believe me, we girls will let you know when we have to go."

"That's what I understand," said Strange.

They continued driving south throughout the day. If there had been a visible sun they would have watched it set, but since there was only gray, all they saw was it going grayer before turning to the looming dark of night.

Z Chapter One Hundred Thirteen

Unknown Shires of England:
Destination — Stonehenge

Break The Walls

One of Aidan's senses, though not one he could ever remember using before, a primordial one more primeval than the others, told him a crossing of the Rubicon, a point of no return, was about to begin. Indeed, as if they read his mind, one by one, the torches went dark.

"Ready yourself, mate," Aidan called out to Mally, as he looked down the fixed sight of the rifle, although dark as it was, unseeing.

Mally said, "Where is that woman with our whisky? A man can't be expected to do battle without a proper drink of Scotch." It was in fact true. He'd gotten in most of the fights in his younger days while imbibing. His intemperateness was not on display but if you knew what to look for you knew it was there, roiling just below the surface.

"Calm yourself, mate. I'd rather you have your wits about you," said Aidan, always the clearer thinking one.

And almost as if she heard them talking about her, Jeanette appeared with an unopened bottle of twenty-five year old Dalmore single malt she'd found and two small glasses. She offered Aidan a wee glass. He carried it back to his post. He took a small sip; the smoky sweet whisky soothing the still tender gaping hole in his upper jaw.

She guessed that Mally would want a drink of the ridiculously expensive whisky directly from the bottle. She had guessed right since as she offered her husband a glass she saw him reaching for the bottle in her other hand. He inhaled a huge gulp before mopping the excess dripping from his mouth on the sleeve of his coat.

"Why did you hide from me?" she asked.

"We didn't hide from you, luv," her husband said, wondering what she meant by the odd question. And it dawning on him just how much weight she'd lost. He'd have to start insisting she start eating before looking after him. "Thank you, luv, and by the bye, I've been thinking; I can't wait 'til spring arrives." Indeed Mally hoped they'd survive until spring.

"Spring?" She said, with a confused look on her face.

"Yes, luv, and all the joy it brings; the flowers, the green trees and especially being warm, everything you like. You know how much you love the flowers in our front garden in the spring. Those halcyon days are your favorites."

Still looking confused, Jeanette dolefully cheerful said, "Spring? What's spring? What's flowers? What's green? And I've never been warm. All I've ever known is cold and grey." Her typically gentle voice had turned strident reflecting how upset she was.

"Aidan," Mally shouted. "Come quick. Something's wrong with me Jeanette."

But a flaming arrow sailed overhead, lighting up their position for the gang of twelve. At the same time, four of the largest ones were running with a huge tree trunk, using it as a makeshift battering ram pounding the large wooden door below. The crashing frightened the horses. Aidan thought the intruders looked like they were continuing to eat well and shuddered at the thought of what they could be eating.

An older one stood to the side. He was shaped like a cob of corn...without the kernels. With his hoary look and matted beard, long hair, and face covered in dirt and ash, he could have been anywhere between forty and seventy. He urged them in a loud discordant voice, "Pummel it harder, lads." The four grunted and cursed loudly with each strike, much to the chagrin of the horses.

Aidan would rather do battle with an abstract like The Plague than these animals pounding the door. Mally, on the other hand, had real experience fighting bad men and was more at home fighting the corporeal. Aidan fired down on them with the rifle but, lucky for the unwanted invaders, it was dark and he was somewhat little less than a skilled marksman. The worse that could happen is he might frighten them to death. Although he couldn't see them in the dark, he could smell them. The foul stench of sweat, filth, and the rancid odor of death. Probably from the rotting meat they had eaten. It smelled like wild animal, or worse...human. He didn't know it was possible for anything to smell that disgusting and still be living.

And those actions proved to Aidan that he, and Mally and Jeanette were still the good ones. That they hadn't lost their humanity and was confident they never would no matter what happened, no matter how bad, or indifferent, or hungry they became.

Watching the men and imagining their depravity, what they'd already done, all Aidan could think of was the concept attributed to Plato, though he couldn't remember it verbatim. "That the human animal must be trained to feel pleasure, liking, disgust, and hatred at those things which are pleasant, likeable, disgusting, and hateful." He could tell that, at worst, these men had lost their training and their way. At best, decided to embrace nihilism as a philosophy and depravity as a way of existence. Perhaps it was a root result of being hungry.

He wished they had a vat of boiling oil they could pour down on them like they would have done three centuries before. That would certainly mess up their day and possibly encourage them to change their wicked ways. Mally was too upset over Jeanette's condition to contribute much in the way of aid to the skirmish, especially after she asked him, "Where's Mum?"

She didn't remember her mother had died almost a dozen years before, and Mally didn't have the heart to tell her. She was traumatized enough. And since his parents married relatively late in life, they had been gone longer than that.

《 Chapter One Hundred Fourteen

Cumming, Georgia:
The Good Guys 'HQ

Coming Down to the Wire

Duncan thalked to his cousin, *"It's on."*

"Talk to me," Patrick thought back.

"Christmas Eve. It's a hard line in the sand. Basically, what Trudy said was, heads would role if the stadium isn't ready on time. Sorry, I still can't call her Queen Gertrude."

"Good to know. And don't worry about it. I'm not going to call her that either. Especially if I come face to face with her. I guess we'll find out for sure if that ever happens."

» Chapter One Hundred Fifteen

Sawnee Mountain, Georgia:
Evil Dwellers 'HQ

Under Construction

To make room for the arena, the first thing that had to be done was clearing the trees from part of the mountain next to the mansion. A group of four was appointed to drive a pickup pulling a trailer to a nearby highway site where road construction had been underway before The Plague began. They were to procure a small bulldozer to clear the land. If no one could drive a dozer they were shit outta luck. There would be hell to pay with the queen. The nearest site didn't have what they required. So on to the next, and ten miles later, they found what they wanted. A front-blade dirt-mover coated in red Georgia clay.

Back on the mansion grounds, a stuttering, middle-aged, sunburned, male Caucasian was able to make someone understand that he possessed the skills to operate the machinery. Then he only had to put his money where his stu-stu-stuttering mouth was. With no one else offering, they figured what the hell. Indeed the man could pull wheelies and spin donuts. But they needed him to uproot trees. He could do that as well.

Two days of work in the cool early November weather, and the crest of the formerly evergreen-covered mountain was cleared and ready for construction. The former contractor and builder combined forces to lay the groundwork of the architect's design. A day later, dozens of workers dressed in all manner of red-stained work clothes were crawling like enthusiastic ants all over the worksite.

"Things are moving along nicely with the construction," Drummond told the Queen.

"They damn well better be," she thalked back, *"or heads will roll."* No one doubted her veracity.

Σ Chapter One Hundred Sixteen

Georgia:

Arrived — Georgia Guidestones

Guided by the Stones

They arrived at the top of the bald-headed hill where the Georgia Guidestones were sited at what was formerly known as sunset. But since they hadn't seen the sun in weeks, it couldn't rightfully be called sunset though the day was changing from gray to black.

Rather than fumble around in the dark to find out what was what, they decided to sleep in the SUV and wait 'til morning to check things out.

***

They stirred with first light. Stiff, creaking, and cranky from the cold and cramped quarters. Strange and Fleetwood got out first. Strange pissed on the driver's side rear tire, Fleetwood on the passenger's side. Then, raising and reaching through the rear window into the storage compartment in the rear, Strange retrieved a plastic bottle of blue mouthwash from his overnight bag. Gargled and swished a generous mouthful, before spitting it in the brown grass. Returning to the SUV, trying not to wake the ones in the backseat with the car door, he eased in and shut it gently. Then, seeing they had awakened, passed the mouthwash to the others. They said they'd brush with water from the plastic bottles.

"Well, let's see what we've got," said Strange.

On the isolated chilly hilltop they needn't worry about encountering people even if it weren't during an apocalypse. They stepped into the cold wind in the early morning dim gray.

"So, what do they say, Strange?" asked Fleetwood.

Chuckling, he said, "Well, since my understanding of Spanish, Swahili, Hindi, Hebrew, Arabic, Traditional Chinese, and Russian are all fairly weak, I need to find the English carving. Well, actually my Spanish isn't bad," he corrected.

Locating the rules written in English on the structure that's almost fifty per cent taller than Stonehenge, Strange read aloud reverently, almost as if delivering a homily:

Maintain humanity under 500,000,000 in perpetual balance with nature.
Guide reproduction wisely — improving fitness and diversity.
Unite humanity with a living new language.
Rule passion — faith — tradition — and all things with tempered reason.
Protect people and nations with fair laws and just courts.
Let all nations rule internally resolving external disputes in a world court.
Avoid petty laws and useless officials.
Balance personal rights with social duties.
Prize truth — beauty — love — seeking harmony with the infinite.
Be not a cancer on the earth — Leave room for nature — Leave room for nature.

He finished reading and said, "Nice sentiments, but not realistic."

Fleetwood said, "Wow, that's scary. Although I do like the one about avoiding useless officials, of course. That's most of them, isn't it?"

"I think it's beautiful," said Cody.

Fleetwood said, "Yeah, well you've always been our most international and progressive one."

Lace, agreeing with Cody, said, "It sounds like Utopia to me."

Strange said, "That's ironic, marching as we are straight to Dystopia."

He dropped to his knees, shut his eyes and began solemnly to pray to gods unknown that they stop the evil of The Plague. Following his lead, the others did the same, unknowing what deity the others would beseech. Cody, deciding this place was as good as any to offer her plea to God, made the sign of the cross before she began and upon finishing.

As Strange finished his litany, a jarring detonation of thunder and a flash of lightning, brief but awesome, severed the dark sky as if it was too fearful to defy orders. It was the first natural light he'd seen in weeks. He thought, Is that the answer to my prayer?

All rising, Fleetwood said, "Look, it says there's a time capsule buried under this concrete slab." A weathered brass plaque gave no clue to what was it contained.

"I wonder what's in it," Strange said.

"Our secrets," someone…or something said. Unknown to him, he alone had heard it in the most primeval depths of his gray matter. He would have thought he was asleep and dreaming, but he was standing up and his friends were around him.

"What?" he said aloud, since he thought one of the others had spoken.

"What what?" asked Cody.

"Nothing. Sorry. I thought I was talking to myself."

The calm, but sinister voice continued in Strange's brain: *"The time capsule explains how we did it. How we started every major conflict; how we caused every natural disaster that's ever befallen earth. Vlad The Impaler, aka Dracula? Us. Genghis Khan? Us. Tamerlane the Great, his towers of rotting skulls? Us, my idea, by the way; Air disasters? Us; The ayatollahs? Chernobyl? The 1945 B25 bomber crash into the Empire State Building, blamed on dense fog, yeah, but who do you think caused that fog? Aleppo earthquake in 1137, the Antioch earthquake in 526, 1976 Tangshan earthquake? Us. Us. Us.*

"Yes, we control the weather. Why do you think its been gray for weeks now, without even the slightest hint of sun? We could make winter last for years if we wanted to, but to what end? That's a rhetorical question, by the way. You all will be dead in less than four weeks. And don't even think about comparing us to the Illuminati. Rank amateurs. Some even knew about us, back in the day, but they cast their lot with the wrong force. Their mistake. They've regretted it ever since.

"Since even before the time that Stonehenge was erected. That's the reason this monument resembles its ancient brother, by the way. All with one goal in mind. To either control the planet or end it, enlighten the masses or exterminate them. You people screwed it up so bad. In the bigger scheme of things, to the cosmos, what does this pissant little planet matter, anyway? That was a rhetorical question, too, by the way.

"And what did you think about that lightning bolt shit? That was just me fucking with you. Making you think for about half a second that you'd actually accomplished something. And you should be able to tell by now that we don't play by the rules. Not any rules you ever thought

were gentlemanly, anyway. Not the Marquess's; not Robert's; not the Golden one; and certainly not any of your gods'."

Rather than sounding Machiavellian, the voice was boastful, like it was somewhat more than a little proud of his claims. Strange was glad the voice couldn't see the scornful look on his face, for he'd never been one capable of controlling his expressions even if it got him in trouble.

"Anyway, back to the time capsule. The old man who contracted to have it constructed over forty years ago thought it was his idea. But what he didn't know was that it was us guiding him, just like we were leading you here.

"That's what we like about pasty-skinned old white men. They love their conspiracy theories, even if they manufacture them. So you can be proud of yourself in that you were right about the Guidestones having something to do with The Plague. But you were wrong in thinking you could do anything to change it. Even so, your little group of mouth talkers provided a nice distraction for me and my friends, so that's why I encouraged you to come here. Kept urging you on, leading you here. It was just because it amused us so."

"I don't believe any of this." All Strange did was think it. But he thought it with every fiber of his being. He did not believe what he was hearing. That this discarnate voice, from perhaps an unknown coterie of creatures, people even, more evolved than man, could control their lives, their futures, their existence, without him or anyone else able to do anything about it, unable to stop them.

"You damn well better believe it. Your life, nay, all living beings on earth, their lives depend on it. All extant creatures." The voice spoke without a doubt. Strange was taken aback that the voice in his head had heard him.

"Well, I need to see this for myself. We're going to dig up that fucking time capsule."

"Really? You sure you want to do that? And risk pissing us off even more? You've already seen what we can do. Most of the planet — over seven billion mouth talkers — dead or dying. I can end the planet or end it's suffering right now, with a mere snap of my fingers. Come on Strange…is that really your name? Strange? Maybe I'm giving you more credit than you deserve, but I think you're smarter than that. Or at least you should be. So please, don't disappoint me."

Discretion being the better part of valor, besides it being obvious that whoever or whatever it was could read his mind, Strange decided it best if they just leave well enough alone. However, he decided that they should wait awhile to see if their pleas for mercy would be answered soon. Before they could walk away, Cody said, "Lace and I have decided since who knows if we'll even survive this and might never get to be married, we want to recite our vows to each other, right now, here."

Indeed the bald-headed hill with the Georgia Guidestones was somebody's idea of paradise. "Anyway, you guys are our friends and we've had our vows written for a long time and would like to say them."

Strange said, "I think that's a great idea, and I for one am happy to be a part of it." He looked at Fleetwood questioningly.

"Me, too," said Fleetwood.

Cody said, "Let me get something from my bag." A moment later she returned with matching rings and the vows they'd written on a computer print out.

"Cool rings," Fleetwood said when she got the gunmetal gray-colored bands out of the double box.

"Thanks. We found them online. They're made out of meteorites and no two are exactly the same. Kind of like me and Lace," she said with a grin.

Z Chapter One Hundred Seventeen

Unknown Shires of England:
Destination — Stonehenge

Battle of Wills

"Mally, come quick," Aidan said, standing next to the catapult, centuries-old large stones of ammunition at rest in a pile next to it, "Help me lift one. If we can get it to one of the crenelations we can probably take out two or three by dropping it on the ones at the door."

"Brill," replied Mally in a no-nonsense manner that included a shrewd grin, "but I can lift this wee stone myself, I can. Just ye stand aside."

What he called a wee stone was a granite boulder that probably weighed seventy-five kilograms. *For the love of God, help me, after talking so big,* Mally thought as he squatted to lift it. Then grunting and straining, in anything but a torpid action, hoisted the boulder.

He stood and raised it and clutched it to his body, before taking three unwieldy steps toward the crenelation of the battlement. Aidan cocked an eyebrow and emitted a low whistle at what he'd just witnessed and thought Mally's confidence in his physical prowess both impressive and contagious. He was beginning to think the man could do anything he set his mind to.

He gave it a huge push outward toward the men wielding the heavy log at the door below.

After shoving the massive stone through the opening, they glanced to see it had taken out three of the invaders. They would literally sleep the sleep of the dead. "If we ever find our way out of this rabbit hole I may never leave Scotland again," said Mally.

"I still wonder how much of this is the ghost in the machine," said Aidan thinking of the great British philosopher Gilbert Ryle's introduction of the term in his 1949 book "The Concept of the Mind". "Or maybe *deus ex machina*, which, if my high school Latin serves me, translates to 'a god from the machine'."

« Chapter One Hundred Eighteen

Cumming, Georgia:
The Good Guys 'HQ

Maintaining

Duncan thalked to Patrick, *"They're stepping up their pace. They might be ready for the battle before Christmas."*

"And we are too. We'll be ready for them whenever it is."

Patrick and his two man crew had been continuing their training, shooting and preparing themselves mentally for whatever they would come up against. They knew they had kickass weaponry.

» Chapter One Hundred Nineteen

Sawnee Mountain, Georgia:
Evil Dwellers 'HQ

The Queen's Power

Apparently everyone had heeded Queen Gertrude's warning about heads rolling. The arena was quickly rising from the red clay and looked like a remote outpost of the Colosseum of Rome, hewed from wood instead of stone.

Still, she was less than pleased. *"Tell them to step it the hell up,"* she ordered Drummond.

"But they're ahead of schedule."

"I don't need any backtalk from you."

Even for her she seemed somewhat more than a little unhappy. There was no way to know what might bother her, real or imagined.

Z Chapter One Hundred Twenty

Unknown Shires of England:
Destination — Stonehenge

The Morning Still Dawns

Killing three of the intended invaders appeared to take the starch out of the rest as they turned and made their way back through the milo field. This time without their torches, which meant their intent had not been lighting their way, but to frighten the castle's occupants.

Mally and Aidan made their way back down the narrow cloistered stairway and met Jeanette in the long corridor to where they had decided to bed down for the night in the parlor. They gave the horses more carrots. Adrenalin still pumping from their brush with danger, all three found it hard to fall sleep, but once past the throes, they passed out.

Then voices were received by all. Unsure if by dream or communicant.

***

Feeling an overwhelming urge to piss, Mally rose early, while Jeanette snored delicately and Aidan snorted. He made his way to the huge kitchen, where he decided it would be more pleasant for the breakfast he had planned for the others and a nice thing to do, and so dragged the bodies of the castle staff out to an area close to the traditional formal British garden. It containing a tangle of unkempt rose bushes that, at this point, looked little different from a snarl of briars, thus proving this was no refugium. The once pretty patch had probably had an assortment of close-growing green flavorful herbs for cooking planted among the flowering plants during the summer. A proper British herbarium with basil, fennel, parsley, sage, rosemary, thyme, and marjoram, among others.

The earth was frozen and he couldn't dig it. So he covered them as best he could with what he could find. It was a somewhat less than proper burial for them newly-departed souls, but one still better than none. Finally done, the simple man said a simple prayer. Recalling what he'd been taught by the nuns in catechism classes what Jesus said on the mount of Calvary at the end of his own faithful life, he repeated, "It is finished." He made the sign of the cross.

Uncomplicated, but reverent.

Upon returning Mally washed his hands, found a spray cleaner in a cabinet below the deep sink and wiped down every inch of the kitchen counter and the huge country breakfast table. He laid a fire in the massive stone fireplace at the end of the large wood table in the large eating room. Now it was time to cook. He grabbed some of the eggs Jeanette had found, located a whisk, and beat the eggs. The whisk looked like a child's kitchen play toy in his powerful hand, scarred from inflicting beatdowns, yet he wielded the tool gently, almost delicately. He had found some still-fresh onions and peppers, and expertly diced them to sprinkle into the eggs.

Since they hadn't been eating enough, having somewhat little more than no protein at all, he decided three eggs for Jeanette and four apiece for he and Aidan would be a good start.

He found some oil and heated it in the heavy black cast-iron skillet. Onions and peppers went into the hot oil. After sizzling for a short time, he added the farm-raised golden-yolk treasures. With the aroma of the hot cooked eggs filling the room and the bodies now removed, the kitchen smelled cozy and warm.

Jeanette stirred to what her brain told her was the aroma of eggs cooking, not sure however, if it was her imagination or real. And wondering where Mally was.

"Professor? Professor? Do you smell anything?"

"Uhm what? What?"

"Do you smell anything?"

"Unless I'm crazy, I think I smell eggs frying."

"If you're crazy, then I am, too, because I smell eggs cooking, also. And they smell warm. I remember what Mally was talking about, now. I'm sorry I scared him so. But I'm okay now. He'll be positively chuffed."

Aidan said, "Well, I am, too. You're my right hand, you know."

"You mean, if we ever return to work again I will be?"

"Yes! So, let's follow our noses and see where they lead us."

Exhausted, the night previous they'd fallen asleep in the clothes they'd worn that day so, after a quick trip to a hallway bathroom, it didn't take them long to get moving. And their noses led them down the long dark corridor in the direction of the kitchen. They noticed the bodies were gone and their odor replaced by the aroma of strong hot coffee brewing as well. They entered the huge kitchen to find Mally laying a table, a satisfied smile on his face and humming to himself.

"About time you got up, sleeping beauty," he said to his wife.

"And what do you think you're doing?"

"You know how I enjoy cooking a wee breakfast for us on Saturday mornings when I don't have to leave early for work. And after last night's excitement and heavy lifting, I felt like cooking a proper breakfast. Protein makes me aggressive and you never know when we might need that."

Aidan said, "Well, I'm certainly glad you did."

"Well, belly up to the table, then." Always considerate about how he spoke to his wife, "Not you, luv. You don't have a belly."

The eating room would normally have been brightened from the large mullioned window that looked onto the estate's rear garden and agrarian land beyond. However the room was as grey as the outside, but the acoustics felt different. The feel of the usually comfortable room was divergent. It was amazing how the simple act of cooking a heartwarming breakfast with the rich aroma of good hot coffee could change the life of the kitchen from that of the rest of the massive residence. Jeanette walked an indirect path to the table to give Mally an appreciative caress along the way. He placed matching thick china mugs with the castle's crest before them on the sturdy wooden table for their coffee, before he returned with an ancient pot.

As he filled the cups with strong coffee, he said, "I wish I could offer you muffins, since I know you appreciate a quality blueberry muffin, I do. Or oh, oh—crumpets with fresh butter and jam," he said, eagerly.

"That would be lovely," Jeanette agreed, "but a wee bit much to ask under these circumstances, I'm afraid."

Aidan, curious about all Mally had found, said, "What else is out there?"

"We should probably check out the car park. You never know what we might find."

Mally stretched to reach a bottle of expensive Irish whiskey he'd spied on an upper shelf. Jeanette looked at Mally as if he was crazy. Noting the look he'd seen many times before, but was still less than accustomed to or happy with when he did, he said, "What? A wee cup of Irish Coffee before we continue our walk through the world will be brill."

"I didn't say anything," she said defensively.

"Aye, but you were thinking it."

"Just pour," said Aidan impatiently, holding out his cup. As he dug into the heaping plate of beautiful yellow eggs sprinkled with red and green peppers and onion, he said, "This is splendid. I didn't know you had it in you, Mally." Although truth be told, he thought there were a wee bit too many onions, but no need to hurt the man's feelings.

"My man's full of surprises, aren't you, luv?"

"Aye, to keep up with you I have to be."

All hungry, there was a pause in the chatting while they ate. Pushing his chair loudly away from the table a few minutes later, Aidan said, "Let's check out that car park."

"Let's do it."

"And I'll clean up the mess you made," said Jeanette. "It's comforting to know some thin's don't change even at the end of the world." She shooed him toward the door with a dish cloth.

A regular-size house door stood next to three discrete garage doors. The large ones were stained a medium brown with dark-stained horizontal and angled support slats.

Inside, a huge luxurious Bentley and a silver Mini Cooper Countryman sat side-by-side looking like parent and baby. Both autos backed in. The Bentley's famous winged capital B badge was shined to a high gloss even though the car was covered in a layer of dust. Checking the doors of each, they were unlocked and keys in the ignition; not unusual in rural England and in the protected grounds of the imposing castle and the car park.

"Jackpot," said Mally turning the key of the Mini and finding it had a near-full tank of petrol. The Bentley was almost on empty but they didn't want the attention that the expensive vehicle would have attracted anyway.

Aidan said, "Let's go collect Jeanette and our gear and, as those American cowboys would say, get the hell out of Dodge."

"What did that mean anyway?" asked Mally.

"Dodge City was a town in the American Old West and the saying was attributed to the bad guys when they needed to get out of town before the bobbies caught up to them."

"Brill. I didn't even know there was a Dodge City."

"When I was in undergrad before I decided on Math, I had to take some history tutorials. I guess I picked up a few things."

"Speaking of cowboys and the west, we'll have to set the horses free. Me Jeanette's not going to be happy about that." Aidan agreed with Mally about that.

While the men were in the garage, Jeanette had boiled a dozen of the treasures in their shells and put them in a plastic bag to take with them. They took care to load the hard-boiled eggs, the bottle of Irish whiskey with the broken seal they'd enjoyed in their morning coffee, and the whisky they'd begun the night before on the battlement.

Loaded and ready to go, their last good deed was to release the horses. Jeanette cried and hugged her little chestnut. Mally opened the main door and slapped his stallion's hindquarters. He took off with the other two following.

Aidan found a Queen anthology CD the owners had left in the glovebox and inserted it in the player. With him driving, they pulled out of the car park and pointed the small car south, continuing their journey on the snowy road. They passed the nearest point to where they first saw the campfire the night before and the intruders had lighted their torches. The branches of the trees were decorated with bones. And skulls. They were the remains of the unwanted visitors' meals. Obviously they'd devolved into something they hopefully could have never imagined themselves becoming.

It had the frightening appearance of an unholy priory's ossuary. Worse than anything ever performed at le Grand Guignol. The people who had caused it were unseen but were seeing.

Aidan swallowed a mouthful of bile as Queen sang 'Too Much Love Will Kill You'. Even from fifty yards away the stink from the trees invaded the small car's passenger compartment. Jeanette screamed horrifically. Aidan now knew he was right about why the intruders sweat and breath had smelled foul.

Mally said, "No matter how long I live, I will never forget that for the rest of me life."

Aidan said, "Well fortunately, that may not be much longer."

Nobody thought that fortunate.

Frantic and turning ashen, Jeanette yelled, "Let me out. Quick. Stop the goddamn car. I'm going to be sick."

Mally knew she was in a bad way since she'd never used foul language otherwise. Aidan yanked up on the parking brake forcing the Mini to an abrupt stop. Three soda cans rolled from where Mally had stowed them under his seat toward the front of the passenger footwell.

Jeanette flung open the door, leaving it open, and tore out of the car to where she vomited in the roadway. Condensation was forming on the inside of the windscreen from the outside cold meeting the warmth of the car. White steam rose on the cold air from the puddle of hot acidic remains from her stomach of the morning's breakfast. She climbed back into the comfort of the small, reliable car, shivering against the cold while daintily cleaning her mouth with a pale tissue. With three people in the tiny car's tight space a more than efficient heater, the warmth was only a wee bit less than oppressive.

Still shaken to their cores by the horrific scene they'd witnessed, none of them uttered a word for at least an hour. Aidan was glad to be moving again. He felt comfortable behind the wheel. Not that the small car was anything like driving his Range Rover, but it was better than walking. Driving, anytime, anywhere was therapeutic to him. He could be alone with his thoughts, to workout mathematical problems, or just be alone. But finally he spoke.

"I calculate that even if we're slowed by disabled vehicles, weather or other impediments, I feel sure we can make it to the Henge in most likely two days, certainly no more than three," said, Aidan.

"That would be nice," said Jeanette, still upset by what she'd seen.

"Brill," said Mally, though with less than his usual enthusiasm. "Speaking of that, tell me again why we decided on this wee car instead of the Bentley? It's kind of tight in here." He hadn't forgotten, he just wanted to make sure his discomfort was known.

"So we wouldn't attract as much unwanted attention. And besides, the Bentley was almost out of petrol."

"Aye, I remember now. Think it will work to keep us from attracting attention?"

"It can't hurt."

"It sure can hurt my back," Mally said, but he wasn't serious. Then he turned thoughtful, the sober look on his face betraying his intent. "What if it doesn't work?"

"What if what doesn't work?"

"Going to the Henge."

"In stopping The Plague?"

"Yeah, in stopping The Plague."

"I don't know. I guess we keep going."

"Going where?"

"South."

"If we keep going south, eventually we'll reach the sea. Then what?"

"I don't know. I suppose we'll build a boat."

"That will keep us busy for a while," Mally said chuckling softly.

"Or we could find one. I've always wanted to sail," said Aidan, thoughtfully.

Jeanette had fallen asleep in the backseat. Mally looked at her and said, "That's me wife. Put her in the car and she falls asleep. Just like a wee baby. Of course after last night's excitement and all the work I did this morning cleaning the kitchen, I'm feeling a wee bit logy, myself. And by the bye, where will we go on the boat?"

"Where everyone who sails goes," Aidan gazed to the south horizon. "Thither. To where the sea meets the sky. Greyness, giving in to all."

Mally gazed thoughtfully at the amorphous horizon through the windscreen, dusty from sitting in the car park, and nodded. He understood. It was an amazing incongruity how thoughtful and sensitive the usually brusque man could be.

Σ Chapter One Hundred Twenty-One

Georgia:
Arrived — Georgia Guidestones

A New Life Before Death

Lace and Cody recited their vows in a solemn, if somewhat less than legal ceremony. They exchanged the one of a kind rings, then kissed lovingly. The love and intent were real even if the rites weren't recognized by the state.

Fleetwood and Strange applauded softly, the sound lost on the ill wind on top of the bald hill, then hugged them sweetly. The men's beaming smiles conveyed their good wishes even without the sound of the disappearing applause.

Then, remembering the reality of the time and place, Lace said, "I only wish this were the beginning and not the end."

"Maybe it is. How do we know it's not? And when we get back we'll find someone to marry us for real."

« Chapter One Hundred Twenty Two
Cumming, Georgia:
The Good Guys 'HQ

Missing

"I miss normal things," said Patrick.

"I miss football," Jeff said.

"Figures. You're just a big athletic supporter. What about you, Bill? What do you miss?"

"Giving orders. Of course, I missed that before The Plague. I've been retired for awhile, you know."

"And Jeff and I don't follow orders very well, do we?"

"Not worth a damn if I'm going to be honest, and I've been meaning to talk to you guys about that, by the way."

» Chapter One Hundred Twenty-Three

Sawnee Mountain, Georgia:
Evil Dwellers 'HQ

Building Continues

All agreed that one good thing about being busy with the arena's construction was that it kept them out of Queen Gertrude's line of fire.

That was a place no one wanted to be.

Everyone believed she had lost sight of the end game. She'd wanted to punish Earth. Destroy it even, if needed. That was being accomplished even if she'd forgotten it. It had been set in motion and was now an unstoppable force, a fait accompli.

Z Chapter One Hundred Twenty-Four
Unknown Shires of England:
Destination — Stonehenge

The Road Wanders

There weren't as many disabled cars as before, but still too many to attain much speed on a regular basis. Experienced with a speedy small car due to a former girlfriend having one, Aidan would have loved to open it up. But, alas, that wasn't possible. He was still optimistic that they could make it to Stonehenge by the end of the next day. Assuming they didn't encounter anymore roving bands of cannibals. That could really mess up their day.

Snow again started to fall. Huge fluffy flakes landed on the windscreen. They would have been pretty at any other time. Aidan turned on the wipers and got nothing but a loud, angry scrape against the glass for his trouble as they smeared the dirt and damp into something the color and consistency of cheap brown gravy.

"I used to love the snow," said Jeanette. "But never again."

"I know, luv. I feel the same way," said Mally. "Of course, I've never loved it as much as you do," he said, twisting in his seat and reaching across his body with his right hand to give her knee a loving squeeze.

She looked at him wistfully, happy with the gentle touch from the strong man. Mally reached to pop open the glovebox and retrieved three of the candies he'd thought to hide away; one for himself and two to share.

The next hamlet to which they came had once been home to a vibrant, living Starbucks. Now, like everything else, it was derelict in less than a month. Right across the way from it had been a decades-old antique-junk store. Of course, it looked no worse for the wear from facing down the end of the world. Still full of worn out old crap generously called antiques. Stuff nobody wanted. Still had a black and orange sign with white letters reading OPEN hanging in the front door.

It was doubtful. The store's old glass windows were covered in a layer of dust. Had probably been there before The Plague began. Still, it had probably been the kind of place to which people flocked from all over the shire to fill their homes with more of the same sorts of treasures of which they already had many. The kind of place with overt banality but what had made it popular.

An old coin-operated music machine sat silent on the sagging wood porch that could use a coat of paint. From the car, even at the lethargically slow speed at which Aidan inched around abandoned vehicles, Mally couldn't read the name to make out if it were a Rock-Ola or a Wurlitzer. From his pub days he recalled they were similar in style. He remembered them as sensitive, comfortable machines, this one shiny red but covered in a layer of foul dust and similar in style to the ones he leaned against, pint in hand, head bobbing to the beat, during his pub days. Mostly music of The Police, Duran Duran and The Cure.

Bodies scattered to and fro, the village had probably been the same as most small towns. Full of gossips. Of course nobody really gossiped, or admitted to it anyway, only their friends or enemies did. People too nosy for their own good. People with secrets. All hid secrets. Those who thought they were too high and mighty for a place such as this. Know-it-alls. Now, all of them the same — dead and bloating. No difference in the cold vast permanence of death.

"A steaming hot, venti Starbucks Dark Roast to go with our Scotch sure would be good," said Mally.

"Indeed, it would be splendid," agreed Aidan.

"And a cigar, "added Mally, wishfully.

Aidan said, "If you say so. Runners don't typically smoke anything too much." Although as a college professor, which is akin to being a continuous student, he had been known to partake of the illegal variety of weed.

"Is whisky all you men think about?"

Aidan said, "I think about pints, too."

Mally said, "And food. I think about food. But I'm trying not to. No sense in torturing meself."

"I stand corrected. You do think of food. That's true," said Jeanette.

Aidan thought the closer they got to Stonehenge the angrier the ever-present clouds looked. Dark and grey scowling faces in the turmoil. Were spirits in the sky trying to deter them? But that wouldn't make sense if the voices they heard were encouraging them.

Unless they were in competition.

They drove slowly but steadily toward the end of the earth. Happy to be alive, but unsure and leery of what awaited them there.

« Chapter One Hundred Twenty-Five
Cumming, Georgia:
The Good Guys 'HQ

Getting Antsy

Sitting on the terrace, Jeff Byrd fired a flare gun at a medium-sized North Georgia mountain wildcat cautiously making his way across a detached stone patio below. A direct hit, dead center in the unsuspecting animal's side, it exploded in flames with a shriek of pain and was lifted into the opening of the outdoor fireplace. A good thing the animal had been on the patio when it was engulfed in flame, or the burning corpse would have set the ground around it afire.

"Hot damn. That's the shit," Jeff said, impressed with the weapon's effectiveness.

Watching from the gourmet kitchen that might never be used again, Patrick opened the door to the outside. "What in the hell are you doing?"

"Just having some fun. Besides, I need the practice. Make sure I'll be able to hit something with it when I need to. I guess we found out," he said proudly.

"Yeah, well I think you've had enough practice for one day." Patrick talked to his friend like a child, because in many ways, like many former athletes, he still was. They never grow up.

"Spoilsport."

"Don't despair. I have a feeling you'll get to shoot it all you want, real soon."

"Promise?"

"I think you can count on it. That poor animal. Geez, man."

≫ Chapter One Hundred Twenty-Six
Sawnee Mountain, Georgia:
Evil Dwellers 'HQ

Training Like There's No Tomorrow

Bad Penny rose early and went to the gym in the mansion's undercroft to get in a workout. Bench press. Shoulder press. Deadlifts and squats. And a karate kata to keep him fast and accurate.

He was almost as strong as he was when he'd been alive, that is, not undead. He'd never grow accustomed to being a part of the undead world; he still thought of himself as being alive. He thought it was probably a similar feeling to someone in their seventies still thinking they were in their twenties or thirties. Alas, he knew it was untrue and, although begrudgingly, he guessed he had Queen Gertrude to thank for that. For choosing him. Or he'd be fully dead — pushing up daisies, as people used to say. But she chose him because he'd been such a successful killer.

So again, that was on him.

Wolf had workouts consisting of chasing down other wild animals on the Sawnee mountaintop, rending them violently apart with his talons and fangs and eating the raw meat. Leaving nothing but a pile of mangy fur as evidence he'd been there. The fauna had fewer places to hide since the workers had been clearing the bald for an arena that would, most likely, only be used once. Cardio, strength building, and the best fresh protein one could ingest, all in one.

Wolf was ready, but he was of a mind he was always ready.

Z Chapter One Hundred Twenty-Seven

Unknown Shires of England:
Destination — Stonehenge

The Nearer You Get

They returned to their previous routine of seeking out abandoned cottages to stay the night. Aidan pulled up to one that looked functionable. Shut off the engine. Walked to the stoop. Forced the door. Then took a turn around the interior. Less disheveled than the bachelor's cottage, but not nearly as prim as the elderly woman's, they'd found the perfect compromise. Neat, well maintained, and only a little messy; one might even call it lived in.

They could easily spend the night or longer, if necessary, even though they hoped it wouldn't be. It was even conveniently sited next to what in summer would be described lyrically as a babbling brook but was now a grey glacial boulder-festooned icy-edged creek that would provide them with crystal clear fresh water for drinking and cleansing, if, frigid bathing.

"I need a bath," said Jeanette. "It seems like a week since I've been clean."

"And I'll go with you, I will," said Mally. He grinned, "For your protection, of course."

Indeed, they each wanted a bath to rid themselves of the stench of death they were afraid had permeated their very souls. Jeanette didn't think for a second that he was daft enough to think that she didn't know what he was up to. The almost unbearably frigid water and the nascent tree line smelled fresh and clean. At the stream's edge, Jeanette deliberately but quickly slipped out of the clothes she'd been wearing for two days. Had to do it as quickly as possible to get out of the cold dressed in nothing but her birthday suit. It would be even worse once she were wet.

Mally stood nearby guarding her as she eased into the frigid water holding a slippery bar of soap with both hands so as not to drop it in the icy, chest-deep water. To give the appearance of guarding her and not just watching over her, or looking her over, he carried with him one of the rifles they'd acquired from the local constabulary a few days before.

Meanwhile inside, Aidan searched the cupboards, and although he would have preferred coffee, he knew how much Jeanette liked her tea and he put a kettle on to boil. He thought it would be a nice treat for her and it would be ready before they returned.

"Oh my goodness," said Jeanette. "Is that tea boiling, I smell?"

"Just for you," said Aidan, "I thought you might like a wee spot of tea, even though I'm sure your husband would have preferred coffee."

"Yeah, what's up with that, mate?" said Mally.

Jeanette gave Mally the evil eye. "Earl Grey, or Harrod's?" she asked Aidan.

"Nothing as fancy as that. Just what I found in a cupboard."

Nevertheless, it's just what they needed.

《 Chapter One Hundred Twenty-Eight
Cumming, Georgia:
The Good Guys 'HQ

The Tension Builds

"Dude, I'm ready to kick some dwellers ass," said Jeff.

"You're always ready to kick somebody's ass. Is that the way you were before the William & Mary game?"

Jeff snorted. "Not for them, didn't need to. But Florida State or the Fighting Irish? Hell yeah."

"Good, I think we'll probably need you in that state of mind."

"You can count on me, brother."

» Chapter One Hundred Twenty-Nine

Sawnee Mountain, Georgia:
Evil Dwellers 'HQ

Checking on the World

Queen Gertrude was receiving reports from countries the world over. Almost precisely as they'd predicted. Russia, ninety-eight percent fatal; China, ninety-seven percent; Germany, as near as they could tell, one-hundred percent; all of the U.K., ninety-nine-plus percent; Middle East, ninety-plus percent. Only reason it wasn't higher there was because not as many people traveled to that part of the world for business; but give it time. All of South and Central America, roughly ninety-nine percent. North America, nearly one hundred.

Needless to say, Queen Gertrude was ecstatic. She only wished someone could record her accomplishment for posterity so she could take what she thought of as her rightful place among history's most prolific killers. Alas, as far as she knew there was no one to record it because most writers would have died also. Her lack of posterity was almost guaranteed.

Z Chapter One Hundred Thirty

Approaching The End:
Destination — Stonehenge

Somewhere Near Stonehenge

Aidan lighted a candle on a nightstand and again went to bed alone except for his journal. The light of a new day and a fresh look at the manuscript had not dampened his enthusiasm. He still thought his writing and story were brilliant. He wondered if anyone else would ever find out. What he couldn't know was all writers had doubts, and all wondered if anyone would ever read their words. But his concern was real since he was unsure of the world's future. Would there be any survivors — future generations — to even know his story?

The bed was layered with varicolored patchwork quilts but they offered little shield from the chill of the un-heated room. Aidan struggled to keep his hands under the covers while wishing to write. The shiny silver metal of the Mont Blanc Meisterstück was cold to his fingers.

Mally had bathed in the stream after Jeanette and she'd been amenable to sleeping with him again. He thought that even during Armageddon he might have to find a way to bathe more often if that was to be the happy result. He never had liked sleeping alone.

Morning came and both it and the wanderers were somewhat less than enthusiastic about its early arrival and continuing their journey to the end of the world. Doubtless, one must do what one must do. Even though it was too dark to see, snow and ice were omnipresent. But what could they say but "Bring it on, Morning. Let's do this."

Carrying one of the semi-automatic rifles, Aidan abandoned the chilly cottage for the extreme outside cold of the early morning. He slung the weapon over his shoulder and bent to select a stone from the many in the gravel drive that he could easily cup in the palm of his hand to scrape ice from the Countryman's windscreen. Uncaring if it scraped the glass since the owners were most certainly dead and would never need it. He examined tiny crystals on the rock's cold surface; might be sand. He wondered if a Roman centurion noticed the rock two millennia before. Long in the bleak ground for almost two thousand years. He was intrigued at the idea of a connection to an ancient army officer of the invading crusaders.

Finished with his cold weather chore, he got in the small car, started the engine and turned on the heat for a moment to warm up the cold leather seats. By the time he returned to the cottage's door, Mally and Jeanette were coming out, bundled up and looking like Sherpas dressed for an assault on Everest. They hadn't even talked about what time to leave. They were just doing it by feel, feel, and repetition. By this time they each knew the others' habits.

"Good morning, you two. Let's be on our way then," he said a little too enthusiastically.

Both wondered if he was holding out on them and had secreted away some coffee. Starbucks or any other kind, including instant. It wouldn't have mattered. They would have been unhappy with him either way. It seemed that the uneasiness that accompanied the end of the world might finally be affecting them.

Aidan and Mally tossed their bags into the back of the small SUV less delicately than they did the day before. The tiny car rocked and tilted on its axles when they all climbed in at once. Making their way through town at a snail's pace, it seemed to have more destruction than one might expect in such a small, unimportant burg. Doubtless, there was an unsavory element there as well and they were glad to be moving on from it.

To anyone paying attention it would have appeared they were drifting along aimlessly, though Aidan and Mally had their eyes peeled for any potential threats. They passed under a train trestle, its massive dark timbers looking more like the shoulders of a giant against the grey of the sky. It would have looked at home with a two centuries old steam engine crossing its broad back.

A grapefruit-sized stone smashed into the middle of the bonnet!

They jumped. Mally cursed. And Jeanette screamed right on cue. But from its rather minor size it seemed that the culprits who threw it didn't want to kill them — at least not until after they had some fun with them — or they would have used a larger boulder. Fortunately the rock didn't blast its way through the windscreen and Aidan was able to maintain control of the vehicle. Aidan hit the gas and they sped forward putting distance between them and the evil swarm until forced to slow down by abandoned vehicles confounding the roadway. But they got enough distance to get them out of the immediate danger anyway.

"Good job, mate," said Mally.

"Thanks, but I don't know much further this thing will take us."

"It will take us as far as it takes us," Mally said philosophically, though somewhat less stoically. "Then, we always have our feet."

Aidan said, "I worry about Jeanette if we have to start walking again.

"I'll take care of me Jeanette, I will." Mally crossed his arms stretching the seams of his shirt across his thick torso, bristling at the notion that Aidan might think he'd do otherwise, and ended the discussion with an exclamation point. "Just as I always have!"

Back to their slow turn, it not by choice, they eased slowly out of town.

Jeanette fell asleep in the backseat, head tilted back over the lowered headrest, mouth open. Softly snoring. It appeared that the stress of all might finally be getting to her. Indeed the world was coming to an end and the small car uncomfortable. She wasn't made for these sorts of medieval torture. The warmth of the car's heater was misleading. It was still icy cold at mid-morning.

According to his mathematician's estimate, which most people would call an upper brain calculation, if the car would keep running they'd have plenty of petrol to get to Stonehenge. But if they found an opportunity to get some along the way they would take advantage of it, since they would still need more to make the return trip to Edinburgh. If Edinburgh were even still alive. It was somewhat less than doubtful that anybody was at the university, and thus, unnecessary for them to be prudent. But it was still home.

And besides, where else was one to go?

Fortunately for them, unfazed by the damage from the surprise attack, the tiny roadster kept running and they continued for hours before, already dimming, the sky faded dark as the evenfall began its revolutionary arrival. The small car's modern lights came on by themselves.

"I guess we need to start our usual routine. Find a place to sleep. And with luck we'll get to the Henge tomorrow by dark."

"Isn't it always dark?" said Mally, sadly.

"I knew you were going to say that," said Aidan.

Mally, thinking about the previous night's accommodations, said, "I'm not sure I can return to a wee house after getting accustomed to the castle. A landed man expects a certain lifestyle."

Aidan turned his head so Mally wouldn't see his stifled laugh and misinterpret it as animus.

Jeanette, still groggy from sleeping, said, "Whatever you men decide will be brilliant, but when you find a place, can you just carry me in, dear?

"Ye ken Ah will, mah loove," Mally said, as he lit a cigarette and angled his head toward the top of the window to exhale smoke through the wee crack.

She smiled and responded contentedly, "Mmmm."

It wasn't long before they came upon the first of a handful of small bungalows, all similar in look and feel, all part of the immediate post World War II era. The only noticeable difference being that a couple looked like they had been built recently, a couple looked like they were abandoned before Armageddon even began, and the others one would expect of nearly seventy-five year old houses, looked a wee bit lived-in.

"Let's try the first one first," said Aidan. Fortunately it was one of the ones that wasn't the worst but wasn't the best either. In all truth, it was probably an unfair assessment. The people who lived there were obviously owners and not renters; taking pride in their castle. Surrounded by trees as tall as a two-story house that due to their size and age didn't look cultivated, but like they'd been left alone by the builder rather than cut down like would be done now.

Aidan nosed the car into the cracked and broken-with-age concrete drive passing the mineral-colored postbox that read *The Smyths* in cursive script. Aidan thought the font was Edwardian and pulled to a stop in front of a one-car garage with a peaked roof. A rooster weathervane crowned it. A raven, black as evil, perched on top of the rooster vane. The garage's single door was open, a late model graffitied Vauxhall saloon was parked inside, looking forlorn with its place in the universe. After getting out of the car, afraid to take any unnecessary chances, they followed the muzzles of their rifles to the front porch where a smaller peaked roof sheltered it, proud of its welcome. They gently forced the slack door and walked into the small parlor.

Jeanette said, "This is just as cute as it can be. Although, I'd love to see those lacy yellow curtains in the sunshine." A well-used recliner, probably the throne for the man of the house, faced a newish but not latest and greatest flatscreen TV, the only thing decorating one wall.

"And look how cute this little kitchen is," she said walking through the living room toward the small eating area in the back.

After a quick turn around the two-bedroom cottage they found no bodies. A bedroom held a crib with a stuffed monkey looking through the wood spindles like iron bars on a cage. It depressed them to think about a happy baby once living in the home.

The one bathroom was dirty and smelled of shit and moldy piss from someone, maybe more than one someone, continuing to use it after the employees at the waterworks died. They shut the door without venturing in. They returned to the kitchen where they laid the rifles on the kitchen counter. Mally stormed the cabinets in search of food stuffs. A moment later, good fortune blessed them with an assortment of snacks, bottles of ale, and sodas.

"Blimey," said Mally. "Not a drop of whisky to be had in the place."

"But these bottles of Strongbow don't hurt my feelings," said Aidan, setting on the counter a six-pack of one of the U.K.'s most popular brews.

Mally tilted his head as if to acknowledge that was better than nothing. Outside, the grey of all-day dusk was turning to night just as Jeanette appeared from the hallway to the bedrooms with two candles to brighten the gloom. Mally and Aidan each popped the tops on bottles of ale and Jeanette opened an Irn-Bru, considering herself lucky to find a bottle of the most popular soda in Scotland. She even started to hum a somewhat cheerful tune.

They sat down at the small round table in the straight back wood chairs addressing it. Aidan tilted his bottle of ale toward the center of the table as he said "Cheers!" The others met his with their own, each politely taking an acknowledging swallow before setting them back on the wood grained table.

"I think we'll make Stonehenge before evenfall tomorrow," Aidan said, welcoming something he wasn't sure would ever happen.

"Speaking of that," said Jeanette. "What can you tell me about Stonehenge? I know less than little of its history."

"I certainly can't do it justice, but I'll try my best," he said. He took another substantial pull from the dark colored bottle of Strongbow to lubricate his vocal chords, cleared his throat, and began in a courtly voice and manner much like when conducting one of his tutorials.

"Bottom line is no one knows exactly," he started. The puzzled look Jeanette gave him told him that that wasn't how she expected him to start. "Yes," he said, "for the longest time people believed the Druids, high priests of the Celts, built it for sacrificial ceremonies, postulated as it was, by John Aubrey and Dr. William Stukeley, both British antiquaries, philosophers and historians."

"Believed?" Mally said.

"Yes, because through radiocarbon dating it has been proven that it was built at least a thousand years before the Celts inhabited the area."

Jeanette yawned and was beginning to regret asking. But Aidan was just getting started. He reached across the table to fetch another bottle of Strongbow from the six-pack, twisted the top, and took a healthy swallow.

"So, the most well thought-out theory among academics is that construction was done by three tribes over thousands of years, starting about 3,000 B.C., by Neolithic agrarians. Peoples who were a blend of local people and Neolithic tribe members from eastern England. They were nomadic and a strong apotheosis for circles and symmetry. They raised all manner of animals and crops."

Aidan paused and took a large gulp of the strong ale, then finished it.

"The second tribe was the Beaker folk who came from Europe around the end of the Neolithic period and invaded the Salisbury plain about 2,000 B.C. They buried their dead with beakers, pottery drinking cups, hence their name. They also buried them with weapons, battle axes and daggers. Scientist believed them to be sun worshipers and aligned Stonehenge with important sun events such as the solstices."

Aidan opened a third bottle of beer, took a soothing taste and hiked his eyebrows at Jeanette and Mally as if to ask "Any questions?"

Mally looked like he was falling asleep. Jeanette feigned enthused interest thinking it only polite since it had been her interrogative that started the disquisition. It was quickly turning tedious and beginning to sound like one of his lectures. Like many professors, Aidan was unable to discern when his audience was losing interest. Or mayhap he was enjoying the little lesson so much himself, he just didn't care.

The room around the table was growing dimmer, even though the sliding glass doors leading to a small cracked patio with a spindly tree-scattered countryside beyond, were undraped. Even indoors, the gloom drenched them.

Aidan ruminated with a pained look on his face; three horizontal creases appeared on his still-tanned forehead. "The third, and thought to be final group, was the Wessex Peoples who arrived around 1,500 B.C., at the height of the Bronze Age." His words slightly slurred. "They were one of the most highly advanced cultures outside the realm of the Mediterranean Sea. They were wealthy. Astute. Gifted traders. And used these talents and skills to complete Stonehenge into what we know it as today."

Caught up in his subject, Aidan did not notice Mally oafishly lifting both arms in a stretch and stifling a yawn while scratching his more than stubbled chin, clearly bored.

He continued. "And it's those cultures and their beliefs that are part of the reason I think it possible that if we call on them, respectfully, it's possible we could convince them to use their power to end The Plague."

"That's quite a story, professor, and I feel like I have received a thorough history lesson. And I hope your belief rings true."

"Splendid. But I usually get paid for teaching," Aidan said with a smartass smirk.

Mally said, "I do believe there's a little more than a wee sip of the whisky left if anybody cares to join me."

"I have time for one more, "said Aidan. "I'm just going to write a little before I turn in."

"And what about you, my luv?"

"No, thanks. I think I'll turn in.

"Looks like it's just you and me, mate," said Mally. Aidan tilted his empty glass toward him. "Let me take care of that," said Mally, and he took the glass to the counter where he'd set the bottle of Irish whiskey they got from the castle. He put both of their glasses in the sink a little too hard, then searched the cabinets until he came up with two more for the whiskey.

They both would have drunk it neat even if there had been ice. Mally returned to his chair, it squeaking achingly when he sat, then slid one of the glasses of smoky whiskey toward Aidan before taking a sip himself. He wondered if he should just keep drinking. It'd probably be better to face the end of the world bevvied up than sober. What did he need to be sober for, anyway?

Aidan took a thoughtful taste and wondered if maybe his creativity for writing would be even better if he were a wee bit under the influence. A minute later Jeanette passed through to go out the French doors to take care of her bedtime ritual. None of them would want to enter the bathroom. Even though it was cold in the unheated house it was much colder when she opened the door to the now full dark.

"Don't stray too far," Mally said, getting up and getting one of the rifles, just to keep an eye on her and to be on the safe side.

"I shan't," she said.

The memory of the cannibals was too fresh in each of their minds for them to relax completely and Jeanette barely ventured off the patio. Aidan looked out the glass doors to make sure Jeanette was okay but saw only his reflection in the glass. He was surprised at his appearance. He was old, tired, missing a tooth. He tried to remember how he was supposed to look. He couldn't.

A minute later, Jeanette returned and after kissing Mally goodnight, padded off down the hall to the bedroom that he and she had claimed. There was no difference between it and Aidan's, except for another idle TV bound to an otherwise unadorned wall.

Mally finished his glass of Irish whiskey and said "I think I'll join me wife." He left Aidan alone to open his journal and resume his writing. Aidan went to his bag still sitting on the kitchen counter where he'd first dropped it. He withdrew the old leather daybook which smelled not of old leather, but of Penhaglion's Blenheim Bouquet. He didn't particularly care for the scent since it had been a gift from a former paramour, but he was not one to waste an expensive cologne, or anything else, even if he could afford the extravagance. Somehow, it just didn't sit right with him.

He removed his Mont Blanc from his inside jacket pocket. Taking pen to paper to work on his end-of-world tome, he began but thought the scent of the cologne on the paper was distracting. He'd already discovered the excuse common to many writers: To write, everything must be perfect, no distractions.

After a short time he gave up, and after going outside to tend to his nighttime ablutions, decided that bed was a better idea. The Henge was calling him. So he quaffed his drink.

« Chapter One Hundred Thirty-Two

Cumming, Georgia:
The Good Guys 'HQ

The Time Draws Nigh

"Dude, it's almost time," Duncan thalked to his cousin.

"Almost time for what?" Patrick thought back.

"Tomorrow. The battle between the two Dwellers is tomorrow."

"You're shittin' me."

"I shit you not."

"What time?"

"The deadly hour. Midnight."

Patrick remembered from long ago with his beloved wife. *"That's so outré, but typical of Trudy. She always did have a flare for the dramatic."*

"They have a generator, so they still have lights."

"Well, I'll have to tell the others. Be ready to go."

"Okay, thalk to you later."

Z Chapter One Hundred Thirty-Three
Stonehenge, England:
Arrived

Arrival

The same routine as the weeks before, but on this day — hopefully the final day of their journey to save the world — their energy was palpable even at the end of their trip, and possibly of the world. Like all the others before, the day's drive was slow going, but uneventful. The omnipresent grey and cold unchanging. Still a few hundred meters away, the roughly twenty-five remaining standing stones, some pairs supporting capstones, rose from the ground. Similar in color to the unhealthy, unliving color of the shadowy grey sky of early evenfall, the stones were difficult to discern and appeared suddenly.

"Oh! They're magnificent," Jeanette said to Aidan.

"They are, indeed, and much larger and more impressive than the Callanish Stones," Mally said. On holiday early in their marriage, he and Jeanette had been to see the Callanish Stones in western Scotland, site of the formation known as the second Stonehenge. Mally took his wife's hand in a loving gesture of togetherness at the solemnity of the life altering event. Under severe circumstances they had made it here, and if they were to die, at least they would die together.

And glad that they would die doing something worthy.

Aidan got as close as he could with the car before pulling up on snow-covered worn grass. Setting the brake aggressively, he said, "Well, let's do this."

He and Mally grabbed the rifles and put extra thirty-round magazines in their pockets. Still one hundred-fifty meters to walk, across snow-covered ground, they didn't want to take unnecessary risks in the aloneness of the dead bleak landscape.

An evil landscape at that.

Recalling his Latin studies, Aidan said, "Semper Vigilo."

Mally, deducing that Aidan meant keep aware, said simply, "Aye."

So they set out on the last leg of their journey. Relentless in their quest and bent into the maw of a bitter wind. It had been exhausting, and still they hurried in the snow toward their weeks-long goal, cold and tired but enthusiastic. Their tread left a ragged three-person-wide path through the crusty snow. Lassitude driving them relentlessly to their end and the hoped for repose that would follow. Thunder rumbled in from the sea. Lightning lit angry gibbous clouds.

"A sign?" Asked, Mally.

"Mayhap it is," said Aidan.

Jeanette said, "let's just hurry and get this done, and be on our way."

Indeed, already cold, the temperature dropped precipitously in but seconds. They came first to the earthen embankment, the shallow ditch surrounding the entirety of the Henge. Careful of their footing, they descended the exterior bank and slowly ascended the interior one. The outer ring of sarsen stones, capped with lintels, was next. No one knows for sure, but originally there had probably been thirty of the upright sarsens. Most had fallen and most of the lintels were missing.

Aidan wanted to go to the center of the Henge, his belief being that their chance of pleading their case with the gods would have the best chance for success at that holiest of places. The next circle was bluestones, now turning grey with age.

Chilled from the cold and bleak, Mally said, "I hope I shall be able to shake this ague."

Aidan sweated from exertion and exhaled heavy breaths of excitement. They passed the nearest stone of the outer ring pointing toward, it was as if if their imaginations ran wild—for from what appeared to be from the dark side of the moon, a lightening bolt flashed jagged, and popped electrically from the clouds striking the capstone it joined in supporting.

The Powers of Darkness protecting the beating heart of Stonehenge?

Mally turned his back on the monument to say something to Jeanette. He was probably going to tell her he loved her unknowing they would be the last earthly words he would ever speak. But had he known it would have made him happy. And Jeanette would liked to have heard them. She knew the words would have been authentic and genuine, even if not particularly deep. Mally would've spoke from his heart and his soul.

A useless gesture for she would never know for certain what would be his words, because all he was able to get out was, "Jeanette —"

The first loud thud was the sound of an ancient granite slamming into the earth. A second, smaller, but more gruesome thud was the sound of Mally's head being crushed under the weight. The last image he saw on earth was his precious Jeanette. It would be burned into his consciousness for eternity. One arm stuck out from the eternal tomb and twitched once, nothing more than an involuntary neurological reaction to the fatal trauma. He never saw his black-hooded, curved axe-bearing executioner—the falling ten-ton stone, killing him under its weight and excavating his tomb in a single malevolent act.

Just as he never saw the cold dark earth coming up to welcome him into its pernicious hold. Was the lightning or the boulder the evildoer? Or were they accomplices in the execrable act?

If Mally could have planned his end, he wouldn't have had it any other way.

The sparkling white snow around the granite gravestone becoming a penumbra of red from the strong man's life-giving force. It would stay that way until the next snow or the next rain, whichever came first, to cover it or wash it away. All trace of Mally would disappear.

"Mally, my luv, noooo!" Jeanette shrieked.

She collapsed to her knees, a sickly pallor overcoming her face. Her hands clutched at her newly gaunt, near skeletal countenance, fighting to stifle the flux rising from deep in her throat as she watched her life's love barbarously killed before her eyes.

Aidan saw for the first time how old she'd looked. She appeared to have lost a third of her weight and aged a lifetime in only a few weeks. Of course, it hadn't helped that she'd been unable to color her hair its usual mature brown that was now turning greyer by the minute. He suspected he probably looked aged too, but he couldn't see his own face.

Jeanette rocked on her knees sobbing. "Pie Jesu Domine, dona eis requiem."— *Our Lord Jesus, let them rest.* her plaintive plea from the Catholic mass.

At least she wouldn't have to lament the day for long. Her purgatory would be as short-lived as the earth's future. She was sure she'd happily join him soon for eternity. And then a voice, this one not of their imaginations, and most assuredly not of Heaven, but nevertheless just as imperious as the voice of the God of Man, roared over the thunder it admonished —

"It Is Done!"

Aidan wished the planet could be put into retrograde, spinning it backward to any time before the tragedy and reverse its actions. Although he came to the Henge to pray to the minor deities of the Druids and other heathen Pagans, he now beseeched the firmament, "Oh Lord, God of all that is holy, save him, as he is the best of us." Not a requiescat of his forgotten youth, but a heartfelt prayer, nonetheless.

Yet, a prayer for naught. Mally had already seen The Light beckoning him upward. Jeanette began the grieving process that for her might not end before her own passage.

She began screaming, "he wouldn't want to go like this; in the mud and the snow. He would have wanted a shower before meeting our Lord."

Aidan knew she was in shock. He put his arm comfortingly around her, even though he knew it wouldn't help. Nothing would.

Then with a hint of reality appearing to seep back in. "Oh, he so loves Christmas. Christmas won't be the same without him. He always goes out in the woods and chops down a tree for a Yule log. He's so manly. How will I ever get a Yule log? Alas, there's no guarantee any one of us will live to see Christmas even though it's but a mere weeks away. If only we'd known life would be so ephemeral."

Aidan realized it was over, and already he hoped he'd see Mally again, though not too soon. And others, people whose faces he couldn't even recall at that moment, for they'd been gone too long. And people he hadn't yet met. Alas, that's the way it is for everyone. Faces succumbing to the darkness in our brains. Forgetting the sounds of voices. It's the mind's way of protecting us.

And sometimes it even works.

» « Chapter One Hundred Thirty-Four
Sawnee Mountain, Georgia

War

The day dawned like all the others for the past several weeks, gray and cold. They sat in the study where Jeff was hefting a flare gun, not because he was nervous, but confirming that both he and it were ready. Bill was checking a dozen magazines, making sure they were full of thirty rounds each of deadly .223 ammo, and preparing the rocket launchers. Warriors preparing for battle on a mountain top. Classic.

"I just heard from Duncan. Plans have changed. It's time to ride," said Patrick, entering the small room.

Jeff jumped to his feet. "What? You're shittin' us?"

"Wish I were. The fight in the arena has been moved up twelve hours. To noon."

"I wish we were still attacking at night." As a former Forsyth County Deputy Sheriff, Jeff had participated in a number of nighttime drug raids.

Colonel Crain said. "Too risky. At night we would set off their lights alerting them to our arrival. Our element of surprise will be better during the day."

"Makes sense. Guess that's why you're a colonel," he said with somewhat more than a small hint of smartassery, "and I'm just a lowly deputy."

They carried weapons and ammo to Patrick's huge SUV. Rear shocks groaned as they filled the truck's bed, but the SUV's heavy duty shocks were up to the task and held up under the load. Unsure of what they would encounter when they had to fight the Dwellers en masse, they'd each hoped the drive would take longer. But it was a short, less than fifteen minute ride up Sawnee Mountain. On the way, Colonel Crain went over his battle plan with them one last time. But like all such plans, they knew it was fluid until they reached the setting and found out exactly what they were up against. Crain had barely finished when they arrived. After passing through deserted downtown Cumming, they drove slowly up the winding, narrow, two-lane road to where it dead-ended and the estate's scenic drive began. They backed into the woods to hide their stash of weapons. Since each of them were carrying a heavy load of two rifles, rockets for the launchers, and a flare gun and full complement of flares, they got as close as they could without giving away their presence.

It was time to stage their assault.

A roughly two-hundred yard walk up the asphalt drive, they could see the newly-constructed wooden arena through the dense trees still lining the drive. At a small clearing, the granite-based mountain provided huge boulders for cover and from which they could rain down hell on the unsuspecting targets in the rough-hewn bleachers of the small coliseum. Dwellers numbering in the hundreds were already seated, well, those that actually could sit. Various other hooved and winged creatures that couldn't sit, perched or stood on all fours to watch the spectacle.

Two entered the arena to silence since most couldn't or weren't so moved to cheer. No one cheered the angry, snarling, upright, larger-than-life gray wolf or the young man wielding an ugly medieval weapon of iron chain with a deadly spiked steel ball the size of an overripe cantaloupe. Now, it was fifteen minutes before the appointed hour. The assault team waited for Queen Gertrude to arrive so she could experience firsthand what was about to happen to her kingdom. A few moments later the queen arrived in pomp and grandeur.

Duncan thalked to Patrick. *"Dude, are you guys ready?"*

"We're firing three rocket launchers simultaneously into the stands for mass destruction and mass confusion."

"Sounds like a good plan."

"Thanks to the colonel. It was his idea. Better let me go. The fireworks need to start on time."

"See you soon."

"Wish you were with us now."

"Me, too; I hate I'm going to miss it, but, it will be over before you know it."

Patrick turned his attention to the task at hand. Each targeted a different section of the stands to cause as much destruction and disorientation as possible.

Colonel Bill Crain commanded, "Ready. Aim. Fire!"

Three whooshes sounded and resulting in a trio of almost simultaneous explosions of fire, burning timber and making smoke. And terror. Surviving Dwellers gawked at their fully dead — instead of just undead — or dying comrades before starting to stampede in all directions.

The three attackers quickly reloaded and fired three more of the devastating rockets. More of the same results followed. They switched to .223 caliber rounds in fully-automatic mode, spraying the retreating and attacking Dwellers all of whom were in different stages of metanoia. Although probably none were thrilled about being undead, most likely none were ready to be fully dead and meet their maker either.

Flanked by Drummond, Queen Gertrude ran in the opposite direction to the protection of her aerie. Breathless from seeing his wife, the love of his life, Patrick ran after her, a rifle slung over his shoulder, a flare gun tucked in his belt, and a nine millimeter semi-auto Glock in his right hand.

Jeff Byrd and Bill Crain continued to rain down hell on the Dwellers with the rifles. Bill thought it was worse than any massacre he'd ever seen or read about, even at the military academy. To Jeff, it was more fun than the University of Virginia's Thanksgiving weekend annual rivalry game against Virginia Tech. And come to think of it, it was almost Thanksgiving.

Patrick followed Trudy and an upper middle-aged man he assumed was a bodyguard. He couldn't see a gun, but he was carrying a walking stick and didn't appear to need it. They disappeared through the mansion's double cathedral doors.

Patrick entered the mansion just as Trudy and the stranger disappeared around a turn in the stairs. Patrick tailed them as quickly as able, with his own limp improving from his years earlier stroke. On an interior wall, a medieval sword was displayed. Deciding it couldn't hurt to add it to his arsenal, he holstered the Glock and tugged it from where it was affixed to the wall.

It was an appropriate choice, for on the next landing, the bodyguard waited for him with a long blade. It must have been concealed in the walking stick he carried. Patrick had seen those in movies. With its first pass, he sliced open the skin of Patrick's left forearm. The blade had been so finely honed that he barely felt it. The pain however, was exquisite. The blood brilliant in its crimson.

The fight was on...

Patrick used his years of karate training, which although different, was still an advantage in using the sword to parry the man's next thrust. His sword's heavier blade deflected and fractured the much thinner stiletto's blade. No less invigorated by the broken blade, the opponent thrust forward in an attempt to expose Patrick's entrails to the cold air. The move so smooth it appeared he had done it many times before. Patrick threw himself back, decided he'd had enough of this bullshit, and withdrew his Glock. He fired until the ten round magazine clicked empty and the other man was not ever going to move again. Pissed off about the deep cut on his arm gushing blood, he shoved the Glock back into its worn leather holster and staunched the flow.

Winded from the encounter, Patrick continued his breathless sprint upstairs to find even in a dying world, Queen Gertrude's elegant quarters. Doors open, he spied her on the small terrace, her nest where she'd plotted the doom of the world. She glanced demurely in his direction. Recognition in her eyes?

"Trudy, its me. Patrick."

She tilted her head in acknowledgment. Recognition and sadness? Or antipathy?

Either way, the wan smile he thought he saw turned into an angry snarl. Knowing this unknown interloper had been behind the destruction of her kingdom, she lunged for a petite but deadly pink revolver on an antique dresser. But he was faster with the weapon in his waist band. The thought flashed in his mind that her choice of weapon was interesting, for when she had been a park ranger, she carried a much larger caliber — and nothing in pink.

He fired a large-barreled single-shot flare gun at her. Out on the small terrace, under a pewter sky, the Queen of the Dweller's day went from bad to worse as she exploded less in flesh and blood than a more ghoulish disembowelment in shades of black and gray bone, embers, smoke, and the acrid smell of dust and ash. Ironically, to be scattered on the somewhat less than slightly capricious wind that she'd controlled as the most recent handpicked scion in the vast, millennia-long succession of Dwellers leaders. Hers one of the briefest reigns.

No more than the latest manifestation of the ones that came before her. Each believing they were the true chosen one.

She, the first female — of any species — and by far the youngest, in at least a century.

Patrick watched in quiet acquiescence, finally coming to terms with the realization that the Queen of the Dwellers had stopped being his wife long before.

And then the clouds parted discordantly, allowing a brilliant sun's golden rays to shine for the first time in months.